MW01135289

PRAISE FOR RECKLESS

"Hotter than hell and way more fun.
Skye Jordan's writing sizzles!"

-- *Elisabeth Naughton*
New York Times Bestselling Author

"Skye Jordan has written a captivating, erotic,
contemporary romance."

-- *Cocktails and Books*

"I was blown away. Blown away by the story telling
and the depth of the book."

-- *Magical Musings*

"Be careful with this one, it's sure to melt your e-reader...not
to mention your heart."

-- *Miss Construed's Reviews*

"I started reading and didn't stop until my body finally
gave up on me at 3 AM!"

-- *The Smutty Kitty Reviews*

"Sexy and steamy, and heartwarming and romantic, all
wrapped up in a bundle of sexy as all get out."

-- *A Tasty Read Book Reviews*

ONE

Jax Chamberlin wanted to kick this backstabbing bitch's perfect ass all the way to Malibu.

He really, *really* did.

Even though his patience was worn as thin as air, Jax clasped his hands behind his head and kicked his booted feet up on his scarred desk. Renegades' on-site work trailer was a piece of shit, and he and every one of his stuntmen preferred it that way. Then it didn't matter if they came in muddy and bloody, wearing biker boots or spurs, dragging along rigging or a saddle. They knew they had a place to relax between takes.

Jax was not relaxed now. And Veronica was so obviously out of place in all her classic Hollywood perfection.

"We don't have anything to talk about," Jax kept his voice even, "and I'm on my way out."

He didn't want to know why she was still on set at midnight during the week. Didn't want to know how she'd been since they'd stopped seeing each other—or, more accurately, fucking each other. Didn't want to have anything to do with this woman.

Jax lifted one arm and tilted his head back to look at his watch. Typical of Wes to drag his ass when Jax really needed him.

"Have a date?" Veronica crossed her arms. "Who are you seeing now?"

He wasn't seeing anyone—for the first time in about a decade. Since she'd betrayed his confidence, Jax couldn't seem to drum up any interest in cultivating another fuck buddy.

He replaced his hand behind his head and massaged the knot in his neck with his thumb. His body still ached from a sixteen-hour day of riding motorcycles in the desert. He'd stood under the hot shower for a full thirty minutes, stretching, but his muscles and head still throbbed.

He'd like nothing better than a beautiful woman with a

gorgeous body to distract him from his discomfort. Nothing. The lack of sex after being so sexually active for so long felt a little like what Jax imagined an alcoholic might experience going dry. So the fact that he felt no draw to Veronica standing in front of him in shorts so short the frayed edge barely covered her ass cheeks said something about the state of his psyche.

"I've got a hot date with an airline pilot," he said. "I'm on a red-eye to New York."

"Oh." That mouth, Botoxed every three months whether she needed it or not, pouted. She straightened, and her tits stretched the fabric of her hot-pink T-shirt to its limits. "What film?"

"*Robin Hood* remake." Then, just because he knew it would make her turn green, he added, "I'm doubling Brad Pitt in the fights, opposite Tyler Manning."

Her little gasp, the way her lips formed an O, followed by a look of deep disappointment gave Jax a sliver of satisfaction. He'd definitely go to hell now, but he'd been headed that way before this.

"How long will you be gone?"

"At least a week, maybe two." Probably less, but she didn't need to know that.

"Why?"

"*Why?*" Jax laughed, trying to keep this light, but frustration burned beneath his skin. She didn't deserve the satisfaction of knowing her betrayal had pulled the rug out from under him, or that he was struggling to get back on his feet. "Because a man has to make a living, V. If you hadn't jumped into Roloff's bed and spilled our pillow talk, I could have been working right in downtown LA for the next year. Now I've gotta go where I've gotta go to keep Renegades running. We all do what we gotta do, right?"

Her deep brown eyes flashed with petulance. "You don't need the money, Jax."

Snap.

The sound of his patience cracking had to have been a figment of Jax's imagination. But the tightness in his chest was not. He dropped his feet to the linoleum floor. The thud echoed through the hollow walls of the trailer, and Veronica startled. Her arms uncrossed, spine straightened, nipples tightened beneath the cotton tee. Jax's balls didn't even heat.

He sat forward, anger storming through his gut, but he kept his voice low. "I have five guys working for me. *Five.* They have responsibilities. They depend on the jobs Renegades attracts to get paid. Whether or not I need the money personally is immaterial. If you stepped outside your shell once in a while, you might realize there are other human beings living in this smog pit."

He didn't bother going into what had been eating at him on a personal level—how badly he'd wanted that job for the *work*, not the money, because she'd known. He'd lain in bed after giving her every damn thing she'd wanted, as many times as she'd wanted it, in exactly the way she'd wanted it, and told her how the stunts that movie called for were ones he'd dreamed of performing.

Then she'd sold him out for a new playmate.

Veronica dropped her hands, fisting them alongside her thighs. Fantasy-inducing thighs. Tanned and toned and mouthwatering in Daisy Duke cutoffs. A month ago, Jax would have been drooling at the sight. Tonight, he glanced at his watch again and cursed Wes's late ass.

Veronica leaned forward, jaw tight, eyes hot. "You weren't going to let me drive. All I wanted was a tiny part. Just one chance to drive a stunt car."

Crackle.

Warning flares darted into the darkness closing in on his mind as fumes of anger gathered, just waiting for a spark to ignite.

"You. Aren't. *Qualified.*" He stood, shoulders back, hands at his hips. Her size—half of his—became instantly obvious. "And *nobody* dies on my set."

She kept her stubborn chin up, but those dark eyes darted away from his.

3

A horn sounded outside. Jax's gaze darted to the trailer's single, dirty window and the headlights of Wes's truck. Relief swept through him like a breeze off Belmont Shores.

He raised a hand to let Wes know he'd seen him and returned his gaze to Veronica. She pouted like a spoiled child. All Jax felt was residual bitterness at himself for being stupid enough to trust her in the first place. And deep disappointment she'd turned out to be like every other woman he'd been with for the last…

He didn't need to go there.

"You wanted to drive," he said. "Congratulations, V. You fucked your way into the driver's seat. I hope you live to enjoy the experience." He picked up the duffle beside his chair and strode past her. "Lock the door on your way out."

"Jax." She grabbed the back of his T-shirt and jerked him to a stop.

Pop.

He stared at the door, just three feet away, and ground his teeth. Rage steamed from his ears. *Hold it together.*

"I didn't come to fight."

She turned on the I-want-to-slide-around-in-the-sheets-with-you voice, and it pinched low in his gut. But not because he wanted to slide around in the sheets with her. He just wanted to slide around in the sheets with…someone. Some gorgeous, fun, sexy, no-strings woman.

Yep. That would happen. That would happen about the same time humans started inhabiting Mars.

"I came because…" Veronica continued, oblivious to his distress. Her hand slid up and down his arm. Instead of turning him on, it made his skin crawl. "I miss you. I was hoping we could—"

"Nope." He pulled from her grasp and pushed out the door. "Not interested. At all. Ever again. Lock the door, V, and don't come back."

Jax's hand tightened so hard on the duffle's handles, his palm stung. He clenched his teeth until his jaw ached. At the truck, he yanked the passenger's door open and tossed his duffle on the floorboard, then hoisted himself toward the seat with the help of a ceiling-mounted handle.

"What if I can get you the contract back?" Veronica asked.

Jax froze halfway into the cab. His gaze met Wes's. His coworker and friend hated Veronica. Had wanted that Bond movie as badly as Jax. No, he'd wanted it worse. For Wes, the movie was both a stuntman's dream gig *and* a gold mine. And Wes, like all the other guys, needed the money.

Wes's gray eyes narrowed, an impending storm ready to break. He laid a muscled forearm over the steering wheel, his tanned face tightening with tension.

"Murder'll get you ten in California's pen. Hit men always talk," he said in a very low, very serious voice, but his brows rose marginally when he said, "But snuffing someone could come in handy on the résumé." That stony gaze settled on Veronica again. If Jax didn't know the man inside and out, he'd be nervous. "If she says what I think she's going to say, I'm gonna—"

"They're not happy with the group they contracted with," she called across the space separating them.

"Fucking A." Wes's eyes positively glowed with hatred in the shadow of his ball cap brim as they darted toward Jax. "You're not buying this—"

"Shut up, Wes," Veronica said. "Jax, if you'll consider hooking up with me again, I'll talk to the director. I know I can get this turned around."

Jax still stood on the running board, halfway into the cab. He was still staring at Wes, but his gaze blurred over his friend's taut face.

She was using his dream like a carrot.

But his mind turned to his guys. Of how much work this would bring them. Of the boost it would give Renegades, a boost they would all benefit from for years to come.

He should swallow his pride.

"No, man," Wes said. "I can see what you're thinking. And, just…no."

His gaze sharpened on Wes. "You guys need the work. I won't go back to her. I'll just string her along until we get the contract—"

"She fucked you once; she'll do it again. And I guaran-goddamn-tee, if you do this, you won't have a crew to staff the contract, because the rest of us will bail on your pussy ass."

A whisper of relief eased Jax's tension. He turned to face Veronica and all her bogus beauty—inside and out. "I'm not interested. Don't come around again."

He climbed into the truck, slammed the door, and closed his eyes until he could tell by feel that Wes was on the 405 Highway. Jax stared straight ahead at the taillights of the other cars, his gut tight with a combination of pent-up anger and self-disgust.

"We don't need work *that* bad." Wes pounded a fist against Jax's shoulder with a grin. "Have some fucking pride, dude."

Jax sat forward and shoved his arms into his jacket. "I'm so sick of this bullshit."

"You could try fucking someone with a few morals for a change." When Jax turned a frown on Wes, he held up a hand. "Just sayin' the insanity angle doesn't seem to be working for you. You're not seeing it yourself, and it's killing me to watch you, dude."

"The what?"

"Insanity—you know, doing the same thing over and over but expecting a different result? You keep going for the same type of superficial woman and you keep finding the same damn trouble."

"Morals don't seem to be in high demand in our industry. Those women are a little hard to find."

"You're not really going to use that cop-out on me, right? I mean, I live it too, and you don't see me banging my head against the wall till it explodes. But, hey, it's your life, your head. Bang away. I'd prefer you didn't take Renegades down with you, because this is the best job I've had in five years. But, whatever.

"And the last thing I'm gonna say on this, because it's really your problem, if morals don't interest you, how about hooking up with a chick who's at least nice to you for a change? I'm starting to think you've got some masochistic fetish."

Jax had just worked sixteen hours. Now, he would jump on a plane, arrive in another city, and work another sixteen hours. Then he'd drop into a hotel bed—alone—only to wake up the next morning and do it all over again.

Rinse. Repeat.

Masochistic? Not in a sexual sense, but when it came to work and women... Hell. Maybe.

He closed his eyes and leaned his head back against the seat, his mind drifting over the plentitude of sweet girls Wes seemed to have in his life. Girls who not only gave him great sex—or so he said—but did all those thoughtful things. Jax had seen women bring him lunch and coffee to the set. Had seen them rub his shoulders when he sat down at a shoot.

Just the thought of a woman treating him that well made Jax's muscles loosen.

"What's your girl's name?" Jax asked. "The one you're with now? Kelly?"

"Kayla."

Kayla, that's right. Jax immediately pictured the woman. Midtwenties, cute, sweeter than sugar. A waitress or something. "How'd you meet her?"

"She waited on my table at the restaurant where she works."

Jax propped his elbow on the window ledge and rubbed his forehead. "I've got time to hit the bar before the flight, right?"

"She's got girlfriends who aren't in the business. Granted, Kayla's not Veronica, but I'm sure not kicking her out of bed for eating crackers either."

"She's cute," Jax said. "I've seen her come to see you on the set."

"Her friends are too. We could hook you up."

Oh, *hell no*. The thought made him break out in a cold sweat. "No way. I've got girls I could call—"

"Girls like who? Like Veronica?"

"No," he snapped. "There's Kim—"

"Who fucked you for an introduction to Scorsese."

Oh, right. "Okay, then Candy—"

"Who got you to pay for three months of acting classes in exchange for fucking you."

"Or Jolie," he shot out, scouring his mental list for the least offensive women in his dating data bank.

"Who was secretly fucking you *and* Holt at the same time? *While* Holt was *married*?"

"I'm not telling you another goddamned thing." Jax rubbed his face with both hands. Christ he was tired. "You fight dirty."

"This is why your life never changes." Wes smacked the steering wheel as he took the ramp toward LAX. "You're not willing to get out of your rut. If you want different results, you've got to use different tactics. You've got to decide where your priorities lie—exterior or interior. You've done the hell out of exterior, and it's not working for you."

Jax closed his eyes and pressed his fingers against the lids. "Okay, I'll consider it. Not saying yes. Just that I'll consider and I'm not doing it blind. I want a picture or something. And information." He uncovered his eyes and glared at Wes. "And if you get me in more trouble than I can get myself into, you're so dead."

Wes laughed and pulled in front of the Virgin America terminal. "It'll work out great. When your head's on straight, good shit always happens."

Jax wasn't so sure.

TWO

The Ferrari banked hard left and revved out of the turn. The rear tires fishtailed and squealed on Los Angeles's famed Sunset Boulevard, skidding as the sports car gunned forward.

In the passenger's seat, Lexi LaCroix reached for the handle along the doorframe and smiled at her best friend. "I should have called a taxi."

From the driver's seat, Rubi Russo shot Lexi her evil you-love-it-and-you-know-it grin. "But this is so much more *fun*."

Lexi couldn't hold back her nervous laughter, and Rubi joined in with a wild-child scream to the warm Los Angeles night through the T-top.

Every last cell in Lexi's body bubbled with adrenaline as Rubi gunned the sports car down Sunset, weaving through the sparse traffic at midnight in the middle of the week. "It won't be fun if you get another ticket, lose your insurance, and can't drive at all."

Rubi flashed those wide, clear blue-green eyes, so sharp and striking against her light cocoa skin. Added the glimmer of perfect teeth in her silent I'm-going-to-take-that-as-a-dare look. "I can always move to New Hampshire."

And she jammed the gas pedal to the floor.

Squeal. Smoke. Streak. G-forces.

"Shit, Rubi." Lexi laughed the words as her body slammed back against the seat and adrenaline surged up her chest. "You know you can't leave me, and you know I can't live in New Hampshire. And I'd like us to get to the airport *alive*."

The plea drowned in Rubi's triumphant scream as she sped toward the freeway on-ramp. Lexi tightened her fingers on the handle again and let the warm air whip her long hair into a witch's nest through the open windows. The Ferrari's powerful engine roared in her ears and shivered through the small car. Rubi's sweet, effervescent giggle floated through the car, and Lexi drank it all in. Reveled in the rush. The relaxation. The abandon. The freedom.

If only even for a few delicious minutes.

Rubi shot onto the Los Angeles freeway, screaming the Ferrari past existing traffic, weaving among cars until she settled into the fast lane at a sane speed. At least sane for Rubi.

Heart ticking quick and hard against her ribs, hand frozen around the handle, Lexi glanced at her friend. This was one of those moments when Lexi wondered how they could be so close when they were so different in so many ways.

But one look at her too beautiful profile made Lexi remember how they'd met modeling here in Los Angeles many years ago, and how much they also had in common. They shared a physical beauty at opposite ends of the color scale—where Rubi was a mix of African-American, Japanese, and Caucasian, Lexi was an all-American blonde. In that way, they'd pulled a full house from the deck. As far as family, though, they'd both crapped out big-time.

In the end, that fact had enabled the two of them to build an even stronger bond, and for nearly a decade, they'd taken care of each other like family. They shared a far tighter relationship than most blood-related sisters she'd met.

Rubi's elbow rested on the ledge of her open window, her hair sexily tousled, lids heavy and knowing. "You could have gotten there *really* alive if you'd fucked Jake in the back room at Stilettos."

Lexi's belly burned with embarrassment, but she'd known this was coming. "Don't even start. I never will, and you know it."

"But you wanted to. *Admit it.* He was *so* hot, and he was drooling over you. Did you see that package he was sporting in those jeans? You wanted to take him into the back room, push him down on one of the settees, and—"

"Rubi!"

"—rock him to some ear-shattering Nickelback."

Lexi's body throbbed at the image Rubi created. But not because of Jake's hotness or willingness to screw her in public. It was because Lexi had gone too long without a decent man in her life. She'd been working too long and too hard without a break and was under way too much pressure. "He was like…what? *Twelve?*"

"You know damn well he was twenty-one. The older woman–younger man thing is totally the rage. Besides, you're only twenty-eight and you look twenty-two."

Lexi shot her a get-real look.

"Without your makeup," Rubi amended. "Twenty-four with."

"I still can't believe you took me to a sex club. That's over the top, Rubi, even for you. See if you ever get another thank-you drink out of me."

"Maybe I won't recover your crashed program next time."

Lexi quirked an irritated smile. "Why are you being so pissy with me?"

"Desperate measures, I admit. When's the last time you created a really fresh design?"

Lexi closed her eyes in dread. "I can't believe you're bringing this up now."

"Three, four months?" Rubi asked, knowing damn well how long it had been, because Lexi showed Rubi every one. Often consulted with her on each. "And before that, how often between fresh designs? Really ground-breaking designs, Lexi? Another three, four months?"

Lexi slumped in her seat. "Nice, Rubi. Point out what a loser I am the night before I fly across the country to meet Martina Galliano to discuss the proposition of my career."

A life-changing opportunity Lexi couldn't think about too long or she'd hyperventilate. One of the most successful female designers still active in the fashion world, Galliano wanted to talk to Lexi about a partnership for a new line. The woman had the money and reputation to shoot Lexi's company of couture wedding gowns into a stratosphere she could never reach on her own.

"There's never a good time," Rubi said. "You're always too busy. You never want to talk about it. But it's becoming a problem, and as your friend who loves you and wants to see you succeed, I'm telling you what we both already know—you can't go into a partnership with someone like Galliano operating at half capacity."

Lexi's frustration mellowed. Rubi was right. Lexi was quick to anger lately. Easily frustrated. Creatively bound.

Stagnated.

Her great designs came far too infrequently for a designer looking to break out. And Lexi had to twist her mind into a pretzel on crack to find them. Her creative side felt more like a desert than the lush tropical jungle it had once been.

The lack of sex in her life—for pleasure, stress relief, intimate human connection—only seemed to bunch the issues, like fabric gathered too tight. And the emotional snags keeping her from seeking a lover pulled the string taut.

Yes, she admitted, feeling like she should stand up and profess, *My name is Lexi and I'm a sexual train wreck.*

She'd never expected the weight of potential success to be heavier or more stressful than potential failure.

Rubi took the ramp to LAX like a normal Los Angeles, California driver.

"I know why you're careful." Rubi's soft, serious voice drew Lexi's gaze back. Her friend's compassionate old soul had eclipsed the wild child. "You have real obstacles to cultivating a relationship. But your OCD has leaked out of your designs and overtaken your life, Lexi. And I'm not talking about picking up a guy like Jake. He is too young for you. And I don't expect you to go to a sex club. Those were props to make my point."

"A point that could have really hurt me," Lexi said as they slowly passed the different airline terminals. "All it would have taken was one of those stupid photographers following us from the studio."

Rubi waved a hand carelessly. "I made sure they didn't."

She slid up to the Virgin America terminal, and Lexi smoothed the knots from her hair as her mind turned toward her flight, her meeting, her future. All the stress her few hours with Rubi had released now coiled tight in her chest again.

She didn't like this feeling. Didn't want this sickness. And suddenly felt trapped—trapped by success. How had that happened?

"Now there are a couple of fine examples of men who could get your creativity flowing."

Rubi's voice pulled Lexi's attention from the glass doors leading into the terminal. She followed Rubi's gaze to the truck stopped in front of the Ferrari—big, dark gray, and dirty. Lexi's blood stirred without even looking at the men. She knew exactly what kind of guys drove those trucks.

Then her gaze traveled over the two fine male specimens on opposite sides of the truck, talking over the bed. Both built as rugged and sexy as that vehicle. The one on the driver's side was in his midtwenties. Golden, sloppy hair sticking out from under a baseball cap. Unshaven. Tank top and cargo shorts showing off tanned muscles. Just about six foot.

It was the other man who set Lexi's body all out of balance. The one on the passenger's side, who looked about Lexi's age. His hair almost black and too long. His face dirtied with a couple of days' worth of scruff. His tattered duffle sat in the truck bed near his hand, and his long legs filled out torn black jeans ending in scuffed black boots. The finishing touch—lighter fluid on a struck match—his muscled torso was covered in the sexiest black leather motorcycle racing jacket she'd ever seen.

"That's a Brutale jacket," Rubi murmured, referencing the Italian motorcycle company. She grinned at Lexi. "There's a conversation starter for you."

"Talk about a fashion statement." She and Lexi had modeled in Venice for a short time, which was where Lexi had been introduced to the fine leather sport jacket. Sleek. Fitted. Sexy as hell. Expensive. Kinda out of place with the ratty duffle and torn jeans…

"Maybe he won it," Rubi said as if her thoughts were along the same lines. "You know, in a race. Or maybe he's a model for the company. Maybe—"

"Maybe you should stop guessing." The boots were for motorcycle riding too. She knew all about the habits and hobbies of boys from the dark side. Lexi lifted her brows and released a long, slow sigh without taking her eyes off Biker Boy. "He's just…" She couldn't find words in the lust heating her blood, the desire zapping new connections between cells all over her body. "*Jeez.*"

Rubi's laugh drew the men's gazes. Their heads turned lazily, mirroring each other's movement in a way that reminded Lexi of the way she and Rubi sometimes mirrored each other. But they were completely opposite, again like Lexi and Rubi. Golden Boy all light and smiles. Biker Boy all shadows and intensity.

Golden Boy grinned at Rubi. "Looks like someone's got too much money to play with."

"I'll share," Rubi called back, raising her voice to be heard over the traffic and noise around them. "As soon as she gets out, I'll have a spare seat. Wanna ride?"

He laughed, the sound low and husky. "Sorry, sweetheart, I'm taken."

"All the good ones are."

Lexi only heard the exchange but saw none of it. Biker Boy had locked on to her with an awareness that made all the hustle of the airport fade. He didn't smile. Didn't blink. Didn't…anything. He just gazed at her with the kind of stare that heated her insides until she wanted to start shedding clothing and made her envision the crazy, sexual things she'd witnessed earlier at Stilettos.

She couldn't see the color of his eyes, only that they were lined in lashes as dark as his hair. His face was just…gorgeous, with hard lines and perfect angles. But he wasn't pretty. Definitely rugged.

Her gaze roamed and roamed, trying to memorize him. Words like intense, deep, and complicated came to mind—not descriptive at all—but all ways she would have described him.

"Looks like someone's zeroed in on you," Rubi said quietly beside her. "Get your ass out of this car, girl. He's hotter than nuclear fusion. What's wrong with you?"

"I...can't breathe," she said without breaking eye contact with Biker Boy.

Rubi laughed again, making Lexi smile. The man's lids grew heavy. His tongue slid over his bottom lip, and Lexi's lungs seized to hold back a moan.

Oh, yeah. It had definitely been too long.

"Dude," Golden Boy called across the truck to his friend. "Hel-lo, dude. Did I just waste my breath?"

Biker Boy's long lashes fluttered like he'd come out of a trance. He turned away from Lexi, focusing on the other man, who said something else Lexi couldn't hear and shook his head.

"I'm Rubi Russo." Rubi called, drawing Golden Boy's gaze again. "In case, you know, you become available."

Biker Boy swung that horrible duffle over his shoulder, turned away from both the truck and the Ferrari, and walked into the terminal without looking back. His jacket had a white strip of leather high across the back and the letters of the motorcycle company, Brutale, in red block letters from shoulder to shoulder.

That was the most gorgeous jacket...

On the most gorgeous man...

And he was walking away.

Disappointment pinched Lexi's chest, but oh, the way he moved...fluid, smooth, confident... Then he was gone, leaving an unfamiliar hunger deep in Lexi's gut.

"Is he the lead singer of Hysteria?" Rubi asked Golden Boy as he opened the driver's door of the truck.

The man glanced toward her and laughed. "Him? He can't

carry a tune to save his life."

"He looks familiar," Rubi said.

Golden Boy shrugged.

"Is he taken too?"

"Rubi," Lexi whispered.

Golden Boy grinned. "Trolling, beautiful?"

"I'm not asking for me. I've only got eyes for you." She tilted her head toward Lexi.

Golden Boy's gaze jumped to Lexi and held. She didn't experience any of the same sensations one look at Biker Boy had slammed through her body. Golden Boy glanced at the door his friend had disappeared through, then back at Rubi. "He's...got a lot on his plate right now. It's not a good time for him."

The man reached for the driver's door handle.

"Hey, handsome," Rubi said.

He opened the door and paused again.

Rubi sighed dramatically. "Nothing. I just wanted one more good look. Thank you. My dreams will be sweet tonight."

He gave her a killer smile, a two-finger salute, and slid into his truck. Rubi sighed as he drove away, and the two waved to each other out their windows as he disappeared.

Lexi collected her hair into a ponytail, coiled it into a bun and slid on her hat, thinking how quickly two people could make a connection through a smile and a few words. Or a look. And grew all tingly again at the memory of that hot, deep gaze in Biker Boy's eyes when they'd connected with Lexi's.

"You know he's going to think about me when he does his girl tonight," Rubi said, her voice dreamy, watching Golden Boy's truck disappear onto the 405. "It'll be the best sex he's had in months. And he'll remember me."

Lexi closed her eyes and dropped her forehead into her hand. Then pushed her door open and stood.

"Biker Boy is flying your airline," Rubi said, using the same temporary name Lexi had applied to the man in her mind. She and

Rubi did that a lot. Rubi glanced back at Lexi, took in her hat, and smirked. "But he'll never know you were the hottie he wanted to devour if you're wearing that."

"But it will keep other guys from trying to tell me their life story or asking for my phone number."

Rubi tossed her hands in the air. "That guy looked at you like he'd do you in the nearest bathroom. Go find him. The extent of your conversation can consist of 'yes.' You certainly won't be worrying about any other guys talking to you."

Lexi set her carry-on down and shut the Ferrari's door, shaking her head. "Screwing in an airport bathroom. That would be paparazzi heaven, wouldn't it?"

"No paparazzi here, Lex. No reporters on your trip who know what you do or who your clients are. None of your customers will ever know. That is the beauty of a business trip. I'm not talking forever, girl. And you know I'm not serious about the bathroom. I'm just talking about letting go a little."

God, that sounded good. Lexi would love to let go—a lot. It felt like forever since she'd been able to.

"But since I know you," Rubi said, her voice filled with resignation, "and I know you won't be doing anything more enjoyable while waiting for your plane, take a few minutes to play with my app and give me some feedback. I loaded the prototype onto your phone. I'm going to build the final app off that model and want to have it spit shined when I meet with those guys next week."

Those guys were top men at the National Security Agency. That was a very different group of people than Rubi was used to working for or dealing with, but she seemed as confident as always.

"If they lowball me," she said, "I'll make a few quick changes and offer it to Apple and Google for a whole different purpose. There's an instruction screen when you open the app." She grinned. "But read it fast, it self-destructs in five minutes."

Lexi laughed. "You kill me, you and your fascinating world. Can't wait to see what top-secret stuff you've hidden on my phone." Lexi met her friend's gaze. "Rubi, drive like me—for me."

"If you'll go find Biker Boy, I'll drive like you."

She grinned, had no intention of doing any such thing, but said, "Deal."

"An easy hookup with an anonymous hottie, Lex," Rubi said, revving the engine, poised to pull away from the curb. "It will improve your mood and your designs."

THREE

After clearing security, Lexi wandered along the rows of stores and restaurants in the airport corridors, stopping into Hudson News for a bottle of water and a magazine. But with nothing interesting to look at and no more Biker Boy sightings, she planted her pathetic ass in a quiet corner at her gate.

Instead of pulling out her sketch pad, as she usually did whenever she had a free moment, Lexi stared down at the magazine she'd picked up. And smiled. This wasn't the first cover one of her designs had graced, but this was the cover and the design that had prompted Martina Galliano to come calling. And Lexi had been thrilled to find it on the newsstand. She hadn't thought it would see mainstream distribution for another three or four days.

Two men came into the area's open seating area chatting, and their deep voices carried to Lexi. Recognizing the use of reporting terminology, Lexi glanced at them from beneath the brim of her cap. She recognized one man as a writer for the Style section of the *LA Independent*, but not the other, and relaxed when they sat in another row of seats facing away from her.

She opened the magazine to the spread showing the cover gown and several of Lexi's upcoming pieces from her fall line. The dresses were haute couture—one of a kind—the simplest design priced at twelve thousand dollars and going up to twenty-five thousand. They'd each been put together completely by hand, every fabric panel, every gather, every individual bead hand sewn. The fabrics were the highest quality and often European, the designs complicated and utterly unique.

Seeing layouts like this always reminded Lexi of just how far she'd come—all the way from the ghettos of Kentucky. Emotion swelled inside her, tightening her chest. She was proud of what she'd accomplished. Excited about her future. But she had to admit, she was also lonely. Too often painfully so. She knew mindless sex wasn't the answer, but it wouldn't be a bad start either.

To keep her mind off the fact that more bankers than studs had frequented her life for far too long, Lexi pulled out her phone and slipped her Bluetooth headset onto her ear, then tapped into the speech-to-text program.

She opened Rubi's Secret Squirrel app without ever touching her screen. Even after she'd read both the introduction and the instructions,

Lexi was more confused than ever.

By voice, she directed her phone to dial Rubi's cell, then switched back over to the app.

"Lexi," Rubi answered, "you know I love you, but I'm a little busy, if you know what I mean. Are you okay?"

"Sure, fine. Tell me about this app."

"Did you just hear—?"

"He'll wait," Lexi said, referring to whatever hot guy she'd picked up between the time she dropped Lexi at the airport and now. "They all do. What is this app all about?"

"It's an information-gathering app. A highly secured and encrypted tool. Did you read the—?"

"Yes. You might be a brilliant designer, Rubi, but you're not the best technical writer."

"Couldn't possibly be the reader, could it?"

Rubi whispered something to whomever she was with. Fabric rustled.

"Okay," she said, "it's not a complicated application. It uses technology hundreds of other apps out there already use, called augmented reality. You know the ones where you use your phone's camera to view the surrounding area and the app overlays information on top of the picture—like neighborhood restaurants and the type of food they serve or gas stations with their prices."

"Sure."

"This app is exactly the same, only I'm gathering different information from the targets."

"Targets?" Lexi frowned at the screen. "I don't think I like the sound of that. How is the NSA going to use this?"

"I can't say. That's why it's called Secret Squirrel."

Lexi heaved a sigh as fatigue settled in. This day had been almost twenty hours long. "Fine."

"For testing purposes, the prototype simply collects cell phone numbers. So just start the app and scan the area. Where there is a cell phone, the number will register on your screen.

"Then, just call the numbers by tapping on them to make sure the person possessing the phone on your screen is the person who answers that phone in reality. That's it."

"But, what am I going to say? I can't just hang up on them. They'll have my number, they'll call me back—"

"Your number is both blocked and encrypted. Their numbers have no identifying information attached, so unless you were to go to crazy lengths to get it, their privacy is retained. I don't need any lawsuits. If you get confused about who you've contacted, you can assign tags to their numbers. That way you're not contacting one person multiple times by accident."

"Still…that's kind of uncomfortable."

"You never made crank calls as a kid, did you?"

"We didn't have a phone when I was a kid."

Or a car. Or air-conditioning. Or, often, food. Heat and water had been sketchy too. Medical and dental had been covered through welfare. Lexi had told Rubi she'd grown up poor but no more. That was another one of their opposite traits—Rubi's father was a multibillionaire, and Rubi was a millionaire in her own right. She'd made her share of the money modeling, but far more from her IT consulting as a programmer and these crazy apps she created. Lexi had funneled all her modeling income into LaCroix Designs—her real passion and the only reason she'd modeled to begin with.

"Can I text them instead?" she asked.

"As long as you can be sure the number you see on the screen corresponds to the person holding the phone, that's fine. The data is transmitted to me through the app, and I'll analyze it on my end to make sure the program is pulling in what I need, the way I need it from the radio signals being used. All I want to do right now is test the app under different circumstances and make sure it's targeting accurately."

Lexi glanced around the terminal at the unsuspecting travelers whose privacy she was about to breach. With the app open, she lifted the phone toward the lobby. Several people sitting nearby appeared on the screen. Within half a second, phone numbers popped into view above their heads like thought bubbles.

"This is kinda creepy," Lexi said.

"This is our national security at work."

"That makes it even creepier. I like your other apps better. The ones that do frivolous everyday tasks or create games to reach a goal or—"

Biker Boy strolled around the corner, an open magazine in one hand, a large coffee cup from one of the restaurants nearby in the other. He had his duffle slung over one wide shoulder.

Lexi's breath caught.

"Look at it this way, Lex," Rubi said. "If NSA buys this, you will have aided our national security. If they don't, we'll do something frivolous and fun with it. Deal?"

When Lexi looked down at her screen, Biker Boy appeared in the viewfinder. And, *pop, pop,* so did *two* little white bubbles above his head, both with local phone numbers.

Holy shit.

Lexi laughed, the sound rolling out of her so unexpectedly she covered her mouth. "Sure," she said. "Sounds good. Hey, Rubi? If I get two phone numbers for one person, does that mean they're carrying two phones?"

"Yes. Any last questions? I've got a very hot boy waiting for me."

So do I. He just doesn't know it yet.

"You're absolutely sure none of these people can get my phone number or my name or any other information about me, right? 'Cause that could be incredibly…awkward, not to mention difficult to explain."

"Positive, Lex."

Lexi disconnected, watching Biker Boy from the corner of her eye. She kept her head down and maintained rapt interest in her phone. He glanced around the lobby, and she could swear his gaze paused on her, but surely he couldn't recognize her from the car. Not with her hair up, the hat hiding her face.

When his gaze drifted past her, Lexi let out a breath—of both relief and disappointment.

Damn those reporters. If they weren't here, she might just be desperate enough to do something impulsive—like be the one to initiate a conversation.

But not with Justin James from the *Independent* sitting a couple of rows away. The reporter had been at Lexi's studio just two weeks before for a joint interview with Lexi and her client Bailey Simmons, daughter of Hollywood director Charles Simmons. James had been fascinated with Bailey's thirty-thousand-dollar haute couture gown, which included one-of-a-kind fabric from France, pearls, and Swarovski crystals sewn over the entire bodice, and a thirty-foot train with embroidered cutouts.

Those were the kind of clients who ran background checks on Lexi before they dropped big money on a dress for one day in their life—or their daughter's life. The kind of clients who brought bodyguards to their fittings. The kind of clients who made Lexi sign confidentiality agreements.

And those clients made up the bulk of Lexi's income. Over the last two years, she'd become the most expensive, most in-demand couture wedding dress designer in Southern California. Any significant smear on her image or reputation would cost her big business—the kind of business that paid her rent and put food in her mouth.

The rich and famous in LA were well connected and knew all the other rich and famous in LA. That was how her client list had grown so quickly. And it was also how her client list could tank just as fast.

Biker Boy chose a seat on the opposite side of the waiting area, where he leaned forward, forearms on thighs, gaze on his open magazine. His duffle and coffee sat on the floor at his feet.

Just seeing him, that thick, dark hair, the wide shoulders stretching that hot leather jacket, the biker boots, rekindled the yearning he'd created with that one long look into her eyes earlier.

This was the kind of man she craved—a rough-around-the-edges, blue-collar, hard-loving man. A few tattoos, a dark background, confidence in the bedroom...or the bed of a truck...or on the back of a motorcycle...

The very kind of man she'd spent too much time with in her youth. A place she would absolutely not revisit. And she'd learned far too well a few years ago just how quickly the wrong man could trash all her decades of achievement.

But that had been a relationship, wide-open and public, which had been a huge element in his leverage against her. Lexi hadn't made that mistake since. Couldn't imagine ever making it again. Besides, she didn't have the room or the desire for that level of commitment to a man in her life.

What she could easily imagine right now was Biker Boy pulling her up against his hard body, tasting her with his hot mouth, dragging off her clothes, pushing deep inside her...

The thrill of it pulsed in her blood. Pumped heat between her legs. Shot need low into her belly, where it gnawed into an unbearable ache.

Lexi bit her lip, her mind racing. She could use Rubi's app to text him. A little harmless anonymous flirting would allow her to get to know him better. Then if he played along, and if she liked him, she could look for a more opportune moment—sans reporters—to introduce herself.

Lexi tested the texting feature out on a couple of other innocent bystanders first. When it worked perfectly—each target picking up their phone and looking at the display immediately after she'd texted them—she sent Rubi a one-word text: *smooth*, and reevaluated her own "target."

She zeroed in on him with her phone, and those two numbers popped up in the bubble alongside his dark head again. Two phones. That piqued her curiosity. She'd known businessmen to carry two phones—one for personal use, one for company use. But this guy was the furthest thing she could picture from a businessman. Which made him the perfect sexual fantasy.

Now...she just needed some clever way to open the conversation.

As she watched him on her phone's screen, something flew into the picture and bounced on the floor near Biker Boy. Lexi glanced up without lifting her head, keeping her face in the shadow of her cap's brim. A little kid, maybe five, argued with his mom several chairs down from her target. The kid, his face scrunched in a scowl, threw one of his toy trucks at his mother and stomped off in search of the other projectile.

"Kevin, get back here." The mother's scolding kick-started the boy into a run. "Kevin, don't run."

Biker Boy ignored the argument, lazily turning the page of his magazine.

The mom slapped down whatever she'd been reading and huffed, clearly short on patience. "Kevin, watch where you're go—"

The kid looked back over his shoulder toward his mother and slammed right into Biker Boy. The coffee flew onto its side. The lid spit off and liquid shot out, splashing the duffle sitting alongside him.

Lexi gasped and covered her mouth.

Biker Boy dropped his magazine and caught the kid by both arms just before he took a nosedive into the carpet.

"Holy shit," Lexi murmured. Biker Boy had some quick

moves.

Kevin stared up at the man. The boy's eyes were wide, his face lax in shock. Biker Boy said something to the kid. Kevin nodded. The man's mouth turned up on one side in a grin, and Lexi's stomach released a gymnastics team of butterflies.

That grin turned him from fun-to-fantasize-about-sexy to positively magnetic.

He pulled something from his pocket and held it out to Kevin. When the boy reached for it, Biker Boy pulled it back and said something else. The boy nodded again and received what looked like a toy.

Kevin dropped to his knees and pushed a small car back toward his mom. After the woman had offered apologies, Biker Boy evaluated the spill damage. Judging by the look on his face and the frustrated way he shoved clothes around, the result hadn't been good.

Lexi remembered the words of his friend at the truck: *"It's not a good time for him."* Then of their long flight ahead and how Biker Boy would have to suffer with that smell, then find a place to wash his clothes. Lexi felt bad for the guy. And he'd been nice to the kid.

When he sat back, staring at his bag with a mixture of irritation and resignation, Lexi chose one of his numbers and texted him using her speech-to-text app.

"If you're on the flight to New York," she said into her microphone, the words appearing on her phone's screen as she spoke, "you're in luck. I just read a survey that women in that city are most turned on by the scent of coffee." It was actually true, so she added, "No joke."

She grinned, hoping the note would at least cheer him up a little.

That was her excuse, and she was sticking to it.

Lexi said, "Send."

Then pulled out her sketch pad.

FOUR

Jax's day was going downhill fast—and it wasn't even one a.m.

Now he'd have to arrange getting his clothes and bag cleaned when he got to the hotel before he went out to the set. He stared down at his coffee-soaked bag with thoughts of Veronica, the Bond contract, each one of his five stunt guys, his nonstop schedule for the last month…and sighed.

He definitely needed to change something in his life. But when he felt like this, it was hard. All he wanted to do was fall into his old habits. Especially when the woman he'd spotted in Hudson News was sitting nearby.

He'd smelled her first. He'd been reaching for a motocross magazine when her scent—light, floral, sensuous—stirred the air…

Jax's groin tightened in memory. He wanted to go sit next to her, just to breathe her in. But he knew himself. It wouldn't stop there. And he was choosing her based solely on his assessment of how she'd filled out her jeans. She was slim, tall, perfectly proportioned. And that ass… If he'd thought Veronica's backside was perfect, this woman lifted perfection to a new level. Her hips had flared from an ultraslim waist, her ass cheeks high and round beneath sparkling pockets sporting big, jeweled buttons. That was all he'd seen of her, with her back turned toward him, her hair and face hidden by one of those military-style caps with the wide brim that were in style. But it was all he'd had to see to know.

She was showy. She wanted that ass noticed. Which figured. She was the type of woman he'd always gone for—flashy, gorgeous. Just like the passenger in that Ferrari. His heart hammered one extra hard beat. Damn, she had been a serious knockout. Those eyes, so blue. And the way they'd held his, never once leaving his face for Wes's…as so many women's did.

27

His phone chimed with a text message. Jax pulled out of his head and dragged his phone from his jacket pocket while using the few napkins that had survived the spill to wipe at the coffee residue on his boots.

When he sat back and glanced at the message, he frowned.

UNKNOWN: You're in luck. I just read a survey that women in New York are most turned on by the scent of coffee. No joke.

Jax stared at the message, confused. Then at the identification, showing 'blocked number', even more confused. It was really late—or early, depending on how he looked at it—and he'd desperately needed that coffee. His mind spun but couldn't find traction. His cell number was unlisted. Only his family, his Renegades, his friends, and the women he'd dated had it. Everything related to work went through a separate cell or the office phone. No one who had his phone number had a blocked identity, but those bastards he worked with could hack, rig, and wing anything they got their grimy hands on.

Had to be one of them fucking with him. So typical.

Jax returned a text to unknown.

He couldn't think of any reason his guys would be flying in or out of town. Renegades didn't have any jobs scheduled outside LA this week other than the one Jax was handling in New York. Wes wouldn't be coming out for another few days.

UNKNOWN: I do hear the women at Kiss N Fly go both ways, but I don't, so I'm sure you'd be far more popular at the bar than I would.

"Sir?"

Jax lifted his frown from the phone. A young woman stood in front of him holding a coffee cup. She wore a green apron from the restaurant where he'd gotten his coffee earlier, the coffee that now resided in his clothes.

"I was asked to deliver this to you."

The text and the coffee clicked at the same time. Not one of his guys. *Ooops.* "Who asked you to deliver it?"

"I don't know, sir. It was called in." She glanced at his soaked duffle and smiled. "I guess you had an accident here and someone wanted to replace it."

Jax glanced over at Kevin and his mother. The boy was still sliding the car around on the carpet at her feet. His mother read Jax's silent question and shook her head. He took the offered coffee and thanked the girl from the restaurant, reaching for his wallet.

"Oh no, sir. It's been taken care of."

He paused with his wallet in his hand. "Let me at least give you something for bringing it over."

She grinned. "That's been covered too, but thank you."

And she walked away. His phone chimed again.

> UNKNOWN: And while I do love coffee—both the scent...and the taste—I have no doubt I'd prefer the scent...and the taste...of something...more personal.

Jax stared down at the message. Heat gathered low in his gut. "Whoa."

He glanced up and around the terminal, where the space was filling with more passengers. But no one particularly interested in him, which was good. He took red-eyes as often as possible to avoid what little recognition he occasionally still received. But now he didn't want to get caught up with one of his exes. Didn't want to start something inappropriate with one of his friends.

> JAX: I'm guessing I should thank you for the coffee?

> UNKNOWN: No need. We all can use a little pick-me-up now and then. It was nice for me to be able to do it. Hope this turns your day around.

Jax took a sip. The fresh, hot brew filled his mouth, and his shoulders relaxed. He finally asked:

JAX: Who is this? Your number is showing up blocked.

The tension returned as he waited for the answer.

UNKNOWN: We don't know each other.

Jax frowned. His mind darted.

JAX: How'd you get my number?

UNKNOWN: Just a little harmless hacking. Don't worry, I won't bother you or share it. I just wanted to tell you how great you were with the kid and how I'm drooling over your jacket.

He laughed. The hacking part didn't bother him overly much. Any of his guys could have surely done the same. And he appreciated ingenuity. If she became a problem, he'd just block her.

At the moment, he could use a frivolous diversion. And since he had no idea who he was talking to, this could be considered focusing on the inside of a woman, right?

And...she *had* bought him coffee.

JAX: Wait. My...jacket?

UNKNOWN: You know that jacket is totally hot.

JAX: But you're missing the fact that what's *inside* the jacket makes it hot.

UNKNOWN: Mmm, no. I can assure you I haven't missed any of that goodness. You do a lot for fine leather. Did you get it in Italy? Do you favor Brutale bikes?

Jax's eyebrows rose.

JAX: You know your bikes. Yes, I picked it up in Italy and I'm impressed with Brutales. Why don't you come over and chat with me until the plane loads?

UNKNOWN: No, but thanks for asking. Tell me, do you always

carry toys in your pockets? What else have you got in there?

He laughed at her toy innuendo, but puzzled over her refusal to meet him. Curious. Without moving his head, he simply lifted his eyes to watch the lobby for busy fingers and noticed several women using their phones, but it was nearly impossible to figure out who was doing what. Unfortunately—or not—the woman from Hudson News had a sketchbook out and a pencil in her hand moving lightly over the page. On the upside, all the women in the area appeared relatively attractive. A couple of them were quite pretty. And whoever it was had to be close enough to have witnessed the incident with Kevin.

He refocused on his phone.

> JAX: You'll have to come over to find out.

> UNKNOWN: Are you flying to New York on business or pleasure?

Dammit. She didn't take the bait.

> JAX: Business. You?

> UNKNOWN: Business. What do you do?

> JAX: What's your guess?

> UNKNOWN: Construction.

> JAX: Good guess, but no.

> UNKNOWN: Model.

> JAX: Excuse me while I choke on my coffee.

> UNKNOWN: Give me a break. Totally possible. Escort?

Jax chuckled.

> JAX: Now that has potential. Are you looking?

> UNKNOWN: That is a complex question.

JAX: We'll come back to it. What do you do?

UNKNOWN: Dress designer.

Jax muttered a curse. She couldn't have done something he could talk intelligently about, for Christ's sake?

JAX: And how does a dress designer know about hacking phones?

UNKNOWN: I didn't say *I* hacked your phone.

JAX: Sneaky. Okay, I'll let it go for now. But I don't think I'll be able to speak on the topic of dress design.

UNKNOWN: Good. It's the last thing I want to talk about. You haven't told me what you do.

A woman who didn't want to talk about herself? Now that was definitely different for Jax. And a welcome change.

JAX: I was working the escort angle. But I'd like to know a little more about you before I say yes.

UNKNOWN: You must be a salesman.

JAX: Another good guess. I have been known to sell an Otter Pop or ten to Eskimos. But back to us, my problem is that I could be chatting up an eighty-year-old transvestite. We should probably get a few things straight if we're going to continue this flirtation.

UNKNOWN: There is no us...yet. And we're just chatting.

The "yet" gave Jax a little zing in his gut. Yet while part of him found this exciting, another part found it incredibly...pathetic...somehow.

JAX: Discussion of toys in one's pockets, drooling over one's hot...er...jacket, insinuating the pleasure of tasting one's personal places...that would have to fall into the flirting category.

UNKNOWN: Oh my. I did do all that, didn't I? I've passed more comfort zones than I'd realized. I suppose I have to admit to flirting.

JAX: Great, now that we've got that straight...you are female, correct?

UNKNOWN: Correct. You are straight, correct?

That made Jax laugh out loud. From his peripheral vision, he noticed a few people look over at him. But, again, in the next moment, he puzzled, wondering if the woman truly didn't recognize him or if she was pretending not to recognize him. He'd had women play the strangest games and do the strangest things over the years, all because in their own twisted minds, they thought it would make them more attractive to him.

But Jax was a firm believer that he couldn't win if he wasn't in the game. He was also fully prepared to strike out, and he had a bevy of let-down lines cued in the event that this went wrong.

JAX: Correct. You are not involved with a significant other, correct?

UNKNOWN: Nice question, and correct. You're scoring quite a few points, Biker Boy. And you?

Jax quirked a grin.

JAX: Biker Boy?

UNKNOWN: Sorry, a nickname, since I don't know your name.

JAX: Uninvolved. What's your name? Do you live here?

UNKNOWN: Lexi. I do. How about you?

JAX: You hacked me...why don't you already know that information?

UNKNOWN: I told you I didn't hack you. Okay, not really. I'm testing an app for my friend who's a programming wizard. She put in privacy guards, so I can't see any of your personal information.

This was wild. Just a peek at what Jax already knew went on every day in the cyber world. If he thought about how many different ways his privacy was breached by legal and illegal entities, he'd be a paranoid lunatic. And he had enough problems.

UNKNOWN: You don't have to tell me your name. I'll still talk to you as Biker Boy.

Jax laughed and took a second to reassign her ID with her name. This was a good time to give her his and see how she reacted.

JAX: Lexi's nice. Sexy and smooth. Beautiful and playful. Maybe even a little naughty. I'm Jax.

He watched his phone in anticipation. This would be the test. If she'd been lying about knowing who he was, feigning ignorance, she'd be disappointed by his name. Jax was his middle name. During his acting years, he'd gone by Bentley, his given name. When he'd left acting to start Renegades, he'd gone back to Jax, the name he'd used growing up.

LEXI: You've got to be kidding me.

Damn. His stomach tensed with disappointment. She'd had such promise. Well, this wasn't the first time he'd been wrong. Especially about a woman.

JAX: Nope. Jaxon. People call me Jax. Why?

He braced for anger at the discovery that she'd wasted her time flirting with someone who wasn't who she'd thought.

LEXI: Because the name is as hot as you are. Fits you nicely. So what do you do, Jax?

Since she hadn't reacted as he'd suspected to the name, he moved forward.

JAX: I'm a stuntman.

The first hesitation in their conversation had Jax staring at his phone for an extended moment, sensing the information had tripped some invisible wire.

FIVE

"No…" Lexi whispered the word in dread and pulled off her Bluetooth.

She let her stare blur over the page in her sketchbook where she'd been doodling. *Dammit.* All the bubbling excitement slowly cooled to a simmer. Then went flat.

A stuntman.

He would know her clients. She'd already told him her first name. Already told him she was a dress designer. Already told him she lived in LA. Those three pieces of information entered into Google would tell him all there was to know about her if he cared to search deep enough.

"Shit." She should have known better than to try to play this game.

Stupid.

Her cell vibrated in her hand, and Lexi started.

JAX: Lexi? Did I lose you at stuntman?

Lexi swallowed and slipped on the Bluetooth again.

LEXI: Sorry. So you're in the movie industry. Do you act too?

She closed her eyes, and disappointment came down heavy on her shoulders. He was funny, easygoing, quick, and clever. It might be pathetic, but she was having more fun in these twenty minutes of texting with Jax than on too many of her real dates.

JAX: No acting. I do the hard, dirty, crazy work while the actors lounge in their trailers. Best possible job—but don't tell anyone. It's a secret. Do you have issues with the industry?

Lexi bit her lip and answered honestly.

LEXI: I know as much about the movie industry as you do about dress design. I don't even own a television. I like movies, but I don't have time to go. I haven't been to one in forever.

JAX: You're shitting me.

LEXI: Last movie I saw in theaters was...hold on, have to think...oh, Into the Blue.

JAX: Into the Blue. The scuba movie?

LEXI: Yes. With Paul Walker and Jessica Alba. My friend, the one who wrote this program, has it bad for Paul Walker.

JAX: Lexi...that movie was released in 2005!

She laughed softly. She liked this side of him. He'd lightened up since they'd started texting. At least she'd helped with his tension, not added to it.

LEXI: Exactly. I have to say your end of the business sounds the most fascinating. I imagine it's challenging? Fun as hell? Let me guess—you're an adrenaline junkie.

JAX: Yes. Yes. And definitely. Why don't you come sit with me? I'd love to hear more about your plans while you're in New York.

Lexi closed her eyes and gritted her teeth. Regret and anger surged beneath her ribs. This offer felt as important to her personal life as the offer of her designs on the May cover of every bridal magazine would to her business. And she felt trapped against taking it. She knew what Rubi would say if she were here, but Lexi also knew she wasn't Rubi. She didn't have a trust fund to fall back on. She couldn't live her life however she pleased without any repercussions on her business.

LEXI: Another time, another place, I might take you up on that. But right now, you're a little too tempting for my blood. The offer is…difficult to turn down.

JAX: Too tempting? Is there such a thing?

LEXI: You're proof. I'm not up for any involvement at this stage of my life and I can see…even from a distance…it would be plenty difficult not to want to get up close and personal with you.

JAX: I'll admit, that was my hope—you wanting to get up close and personal, not being too tempting.

"Ah, hell," she muttered. "Don't tell me that."

LEXI: You don't even know what I look like. How can you make that kind of statement?

JAX: 1) Deductive reasoning. You have to be close to know what you know and every woman I can see is fairly attractive. 2) I like your personality, so your physical appearance isn't a deal breaker.

Lexi bit her lip. Seriously, could she let this guy go? Maybe he was full of shit, but there was only one way to find out. She glanced over her shoulder toward Justin James and the other reporter, still sitting there, chatting. Lexi wondered if they were both on the flight. Wondered where they would sit. Wondered what in the hell she was thinking.

Her phone vibrated.

JAX: Would you feel better if you told me what you looked like? Why don't you give me a little visual, you know, something to fantasize with. Blonde, brunette, redhead?

She didn't answer right away, but it couldn't hurt to see how he reacted to someone less than perfect.

LEXI: Blonde.

JAX: Refreshing. Hair long, medium, or short?

LEXI: Long.

JAX: Nice. Natural or bottle?

Lexi grinned.

LEXI: If I had a ruler, I'd smack your hand for asking.

JAX: I'd probably like that. Under or over 21?

LEXI: Over.

JAX: Under or over 30?

LEXI: Under, you?

JAX: Under...just. Over or under 5'5"?

LEXI: Over.

JAX: Over or under 5'9"?

LEXI: Under.

JAX: Perfect. Measurements?

LEXI: Not unless you're interested in sharing yours.

JAX: 46 regular, 32x34 Levis, 12 shoe. Your turn.

LEXI: Not as perfect as yours.

JAX: Perfect is a matter of opinion. Though I'm glad I fall in your favorable category.

Lexi hesitated, sighed. Nothing was going to come of this. Another reason to lie.

LEXI: 34-28-34

JAX: Hot. Cup size?

Lexi strangled a laugh.

LEXI: Penis size?

JAX: I'm assuming you mean erect. 9" length, 2¾" diameter, which corresponds to 8½" girth. Cup size?

Lexi made a sound in her throat. She was good with measurements—centimeters, inches, yards… But she still had to form the sizes with her hands to get the full effect. And, boy, did her body get the full effect. Her sex clenched around a shot of fire.

LEXI: LOL. You wish. How did you come up with those measurements anyway?

Across the space, Jax's laughter reached her ears, and Lexi's mouth curved in a frustrated smile. She liked making him laugh. Loved the sound of it.

JAX: I don't wish. I know. Got them during a stupid drunk challenge when I was much younger. I'd love the opportunity to tell you the story, and…let you verify through experience.

"Oh God." Her mouth was watering.

LEXI: Whoa. This flirtation just jumped to a whole new level. I think I'm running a fever.

More of Jax's laughter drifted through the lobby and over Lexi's body. The sound twined with the sensations his words created in the strangest and most unique sensual experience.

JAX: Whatever you've got is spreading to me, baby. I've got to take this jacket off. If you come over, I'll give it to you—to keep.

LEXI: You're such a tease. That is a wicked ploy.

JAX: I'm a lot of things, but a tease is definitely not one of them. If you come talk to me until we board, it's yours. Scout's honor.

Lexi's heart pounded. Her chest felt tight. Her sex felt tight.

Her skin felt tight. She wanted Jax to stretch everything out. She licked her dry lips.

LEXI: You were never a scout.

JAX: I was. For a week. Until my father realized he couldn't just take me and drop me off, that he had to participate.

Lexi winced. Her heart tugged.

LEXI: Ouch.

JAX: I'm over it. Really. Come try on your new jacket. I bet you'll look good enough to eat alive.

LEXI: Moan.

JAX: Oh baby, I'd like to hear that in person.

Lexi shook her head.

LEXI: Jax, this is crazy. You don't even know me.

JAX: And I already like you.

Lexi couldn't remember the last time a guy had gotten her so hot. This was beyond bizarre. She shifted in her seat, rubbing her thighs together to ease the ache that had been growing since she'd seen him at the truck.

LEXI: Right now? Right off your back? All warm from your body, smelling of leather and...you?

JAX: Yep. No strings.

LEXI: I'd sleep in it naked. Roll around under the covers with it held to my nose, breathing you in.

JAX: Holy shit. Serious heat wave. Sweetheart, don't make me embarrass myself in public. Do you even realize how sexy you are?

No, she didn't. Not until she was saying these naughty things to a hot stranger.

LEXI: You make me feel all kinds of sexy.

JAX: There's so much more where that came from, that I can promise you. And it starts here.

In her peripheral vision, she saw Jax push to his feet. Fear launched a rocket up Lexi's chest. She'd been discovered.

But Jax didn't come toward her. He didn't even look at her. He set his phone down on the chair. And started taking off his jacket. But his movements were slow and exaggerated. He was giving her a show of what she could have if she'd only reach out and grab him.

He shrugged the jacket off wide shoulders, and the leather slid down buffed arms. He wore a plain gray T-shirt underneath, the same dark color as the truck he'd been standing beside earlier. The muscles of his shoulders and back played underneath, rolling and stretching and making Lexi's throat go dry. Thick, tanned biceps and forearms stretched beneath the sleeve hem, a black tattoo snaking over his skin.

Lexi wet her lips and clenched her hands on the arms of her chair. His wide shoulders tapered to a muscular waist and hips. She'd already seen his long legs, but now, with his upper body exposed, she could see just how perfectly he was put together.

Lexi's desire overtook her entire body. The majority of red-hot coals sat low in her pelvis but radiated heat between her legs, down her thighs, up her torso. The want throbbed through her sex with every beat of her heart.

With the jacket held out to his side, hanging on his index finger, Jax turned a slow circle, giving her a full view of just what she'd get if she gave in. By the time he laid it over the arm of the chair next to his and sat back down, Lexi was sweating and weak.

He sat forward, pressed his elbows to his knees, and tapped on his phone's screen.

Lexi took a moment to catch her breath, wet her throat, and still her dizzy head.

JAX: It won't stay warm forever.

LEXI: I want to lick every inch of your body.

Jax rubbed a hand over his mouth and scanned the lobby with a wickedly hot gaze. Then returned his eyes and his fingers to his phone.

JAX: I'm so down with that. But only if I can return the pleasure.

Lexi squeezed her eyes shut. She was so out of control. For whatever reason, she felt comfortable enough with this guy, in this anonymous setting, to express this uninhibited side of herself—one that had been under lock and key for too long.

LEXI: What kind of sex do you like?

She closed her eyes and pressed her fingers to her eyelids, unable to believe she'd actually texted that to him. If she were somewhere private, she would probably scream at herself in the mirror, laugh hysterically, talk herself out of this. Because she was trapped, it felt as if she had only one exit, and it ran straight through the sexiest man she'd ever met.

Her phone vibrated, and she released her eyelids.

JAX: Honestly?

"Shit," she whispered. She half hoped whatever he was going to say was so far out in left field she wouldn't even consider meeting up with him. She half hoped this guy would save her from herself.

LEXI: Absolutely. Always.

Lexi held the inside of her lip between her teeth as she waited.

JAX: I like the fiery, fast sex so passionate your vision blurs.

JAX: I like wild, frantic, have-to-have-you sex that burns you alive.

JAX: I like deep, driving sex where sweat drips off my chin, rolls down your spine, and tickles the dip between your ass cheeks.

Lexi let out the air backed up in her lungs, trying to hold back the moan that needed to come with it, but failed miserably. She had to lean forward and cover her mouth to keep from giving herself away.

JAX: I like secret sex in naughty places, and naughty places to have secret sex.

JAX: I like the kind of sex that includes sliding my tongue into all your very tight spaces.

JAX: I like any kind of sex that drives animalistic sounds from your throat.

Lexi's fingers were shaking when she managed to text again.

LEXI: Got it. Stop. Please stop.

A moment passed.

JAX: Sorry. You have me a little...frenzied. The gist of that is I'm all about pleasure. I'm not into anything bizarre or dark. No fetishes or crazy piercings. I don't know if this will be a benefit or a drawback to you, but I just really love wickedly hot sex with a woman who loves wickedly hot sex.

"Good morning, ladies and gentlemen..." The Virgin America desk attendant's voice pierced the airport din, and Lexi startled. Talk about coming out of a trance. She blinked and squinted as if the lights had just turned on.

The attendant announced imminent boarding, and renewed

panic settled in Lexi's chest. Let the first guy with potential in years slip through her fingers? Or risk everything she'd spent years building by taking a chance on him?

"Why can't anything ever be easy?" she muttered.

> JAX: If you tell me where you're sitting, I'll trade your neighbor my seat and hang with you for the flight.

> LEXI: Are you working tomorrow...or...I guess it would be today.

> JAX: Due on set as soon as I can get there. Last call for the jacket. I want you to have it. You appreciate it a hell of a lot more than I do.

> LEXI: That's sweet. Thank you, but I'm going to pass. You need your sleep. Doing what you do when you're tired isn't safe. And I need to untangle some things in my head. This is complicated for me.

> JAX: I understand. Just so you know, I'm cool with something temporary and light—no expectations. I'd like to get to know you better, Lexi, but it's your call. Get some sleep, baby. Dream of me.

SIX

The grating beat of Nickelback's "S.E.X." blasted through Jax's hotel suite and pounded through his blood. The room was dark, hot, fragrant. Steam floated from the open bathroom door, casting the only light into the small living room in ethereal, glowing clouds.

Jax stood behind Lexi, her naked body held tight against his, one arm wrapped at her hips, his hand between her legs, his fingers stroking her soft, wet, swollen pussy. The other across her breasts, his palm massaging and plumping while his fingertips pinched the nipple. He walked her forward, biting his way down her neck and across her shoulder, her silky hair caressing his face.

Lexi's murmured sounds of pleasure—sighs, moans, pleas—inched his body temperature up. When the front of her thighs bumped the sofa back, his cock—as hard and hot as a rocket—indented the supple, soft flesh of her ass. With her body slick from the oil he'd used on her in the shower, his cock slid easily, smoothly along the crease of her perfect, full cheeks. Lexi pushed into him and rocked her hips, doubling the motion and making him moan.

He slid both hands to her breasts, squeezed hard. Pushed one foot between her feet, edged hers wide as he caressed the length of her arms and circled her.

Her chest heaved as she tilted her head back, mouth open and begging for his. He covered hers and took everything her generous tongue offered. Drank in her musky-sweet taste as he spread her arms wide and used his chest to press her forward until her belly lay flat against the sofa, her luscious breasts hanging free over the cushions, her ass high in the air.

He covered her hands with his and dug her fingers into the cushions, whispering in her ear, "Stay put, hold tight, and enjoy the ride, beautiful."

Jax skimmed his teeth over her shoulder, licked his way down her spine, bit a trail along her ass until she was squirming.

He lowered to his knees, pressed his hands high on her thighs, and spread her legs even farther.

"Jax…"

The rasp in her voice, the need, the pleasure, the lust… They shot fire straight to his cock. Tightened his balls.

"Shh…" he ordered, holding both supple cheeks in his hands, brushing his thumbs along the sensitive skin bordering her opening until she mewled into the cushions.

In the shadows, she looked like a work of art, perfectly smooth, glistening. Ripe for his mouth. And he was starving. There would be very little teasing once he tasted her. Once he tasted her, he'd feast.

He pursed his lips and blew gently on the oversensitized flesh. Lexi lifted her ass and rocked toward his mouth. He slid his hands up her calves, her thighs, caressed her ass. Pulled her open, massaged her closed.

"Jax." More frustration sounded in her voice. Pushing him.

He pulled her open, bathed the erotic flesh with a hot breath, followed by a hard sweep of his tongue from clit to perineum.

Lexi cried out. Clenched. Arched.

Jax massaged her slick opening with his thumb as she shivered. "You taste like heaven."

He pulled his hand back and licked again. A deep groan vibrated in Lexi's throat. The sexiest sound Jax had ever heard. He continued to slide his mouth over her, moving his tongue higher, across the smaller, tighter opening of her ass. Lexi gasped.

Intrigued, Jax licked her there again and again, eliciting almost frantic reactions—wire-tight muscles, hands fisted in the sofa, high-pitched sounds in her throat.

She was epically tight. This spot naughty to the nth with the potential for something wickedly extreme. And the thought of getting wicked with Lexi, of experiencing that ultimate thrill, shot his blood temperature off the charts.

He removed tantalization to other areas to isolate her response to that specific spot and caressed his thumb across the sweet pucker.

"Oh fuck," she whispered as if she were on the edge of impending explosion.

"Do you like that?" He did it again.

She gasped, her fingers knotting the sofa cushions. He wet his fingers in her pussy and dragged them the short distance to caress again, adding slight pressure.

"Oh yes."

The creases around the small opening relaxed, contracted, relaxed, contracted. Imagining that happening around his cock almost pushed him over the edge.

He used his mouth to wet her, caressed the tight muscle with his tongue. Pushed inside, retreated, pushed in.

"Jesus...Jax...don't stop."

Bing. Bing. Bing.

Bing. Bing. Bing.

Lights flashed behind his closed lids.

"Good morning, ladies and gentlemen. The captain would like to let you know we will be landing in approximately twenty minutes."

"Fucking A," Jax muttered. His chest heaved as he fought to adjust to reality. He ached from the roots of his hair to the balls of his feet. The area between his thighs throbbed, every inch engorged with too much blood. He pulled a bottle of water from the seat pocket and downed half. In his peripheral vision, he saw his neighbor awake and working on a laptop.

Jax capped his water and took another minute to get himself together. Glanced at his watch. Lexi filled his mind. Along with a shitload of angst, a million questions, and a sinking sensation of loss and disappointment. Of having just missed out on a golden opportunity, a lot like that time when his lousy agent hadn't been on the ball and he'd missed out on the lead role in the *Mission Impossible* remake.

After that, he'd fired his agent and hired Cruise's. He'd never missed out on a role again.

The flight attendant stopped at his row. She was in her midfifties with short, stylish red hair, light blue eyes, and a friendly smile. She held out a piece of paper. "A passenger asked me to give this to you."

Jax's heart surged. When he went to take the paper, he grabbed the woman's entire hand and held tight. Her expression shut down in shock.

"Which passenger?" he asked, way too much desperation in his voice.

"She asked me not to say." A stubborn anger darkened her eyes and deepened the minimal lines around her mouth. She pulled her hand from his, straightened, and gazed down at him with the kind of disapproval he'd seen far too often in his mother's eyes. "I'm simply a messenger. If you have a problem, let me know. Otherwise, we'll be on the ground in twenty minutes. Work it out then."

He swallowed, not quite prepared to open the message and get the big brush-off. He glanced at his neighbor, who was eyeing him like a bird in a cage might eye a cat lazing nearby.

Jax glanced out the window. Countryside passed on the distant ground. He was making way too much out of this. He just wanted the unknown. He just wanted what he'd gone too long without. He wanted her because that dream had pumped him to the edge of orgasm.

A deep breath cleared his head. Banished the desperation. There were plenty of women he could call on if he really needed to get off. But that wasn't what this was about. He was trying to get to know her because, from what he'd discovered, he liked her. But he really didn't have time for anything more than sex in his life anyway. So, ultimately, a brush-off would be a good thing.

Jesus, he could rationalize anything.

At least the brain twist had given him some control back. He even finished the water bottle before he opened the note.

Her handwriting was feminine, with thin lines, a slight slant, and trailing ends on her letters, almost a cross between cursive and print. The sight of it made him want to touch her. Made him want to look into her eyes.

He was starting to think she was driving him a little insane.

That was when he actually read the words she'd written:

Yahoo Instant Messenger:

VirginAmericaLexi

VirginAmericaJax

Log on when you wake up if you want to talk.

A spark of hope filled his lungs with air. That was a good sign, right?

Another flight attendant passed, and Jax flagged her down. "Ma'am." He showed her the note. "How would I do this?"

She explained that he needed to log in to the Internet with his phone, download the application, and sign in to the chat software.

Within minutes, he'd logged in, and Lexi's message came up in the chat window.

> LEXI: Sleep well?

> JAX: Aside from wet dreams about you, yes. Did you get some rest?

> LEXI: Some. What did I look like in that dream?

> JAX: Long blonde hair, between 5'5" and 5'9", 34-28-34, but the cup size is...fuzzy.

> LEXI: C

Jax smiled, and the muscles of his chest released. He felt like he'd found solid ground again.

> JAX: What are your plans today?

> LEXI: Most important meeting of my career at noon. I imagine that will last at least two hours. Then I'm going to hit the fabric mart, spend too much money on satin and lace...and maybe even a little leather. Doesn't that sound fascinating?

Most important meeting of her future? And she hadn't even mentioned it? The women Jax dated couldn't stop talking about themselves.

JAX: Satin, lace, and leather? Yes. Absolutely fascinating. Tell me about this meeting.

LEXI: Popular designer is interested in partnering on a new line. It would give my designs mainstream distribution to major stores. Something I haven't been able to manage on my own even after moderate success and fifteen years in the business.

Jax frowned at his phone. That was big. He was curious and wished he'd talked to her more about it earlier instead of focusing on sex.

Wait. No. Yes. No.

Shit. He just wanted to do it all. Talk business, have sex, get to know her. Have more sex. Then a thought occurred to him and his doubt meter shot up.

JAX: Impressive. Congratulations. How could you have been in the industry for that long if you're under 30?

LEXI: Thanks, but it's not a done deal yet. And I've been designing clothes since I was three. Tearing things apart, taping or stapling or tying or hand sewing them back together in a different way. Started selling my work in my teens. What are your plans for the day?

He stared at the message, surprised when she didn't continue talking about that big meeting even when he'd left the door open. She didn't drop the name of the popular designer, didn't mention the names of the major stores, didn't try to impress him by telling him how much money she'd be spending at the fabric mart this afternoon. He didn't realize how much he liked that subtlety, that quiet confidence, until he'd experienced it.

JAX: Just working. Can I take you to dinner tonight?

LEXI: Where are you filming?

He sighed, frustrated with her pattern of selectively not

answering questions.

> JAX: Pelham Bay Park. How about drinks? Somewhere neutral, safe, like your hotel restaurant?

> LEXI: And what kind of stunts are you doing?

"Shit." In his peripheral vision, Jax saw his neighbor glance at him.

> JAX: It's a medieval. We're filming the fight scenes. I'll be on horseback, wielding a sword all day.

> LEXI: That sounds fun. I'm jealous. Want to trade for the day? You'd be a hit at the fabric mart.

That comment hit Jax with an unexpected pinch of irritation beneath his ribs. His mind flashed back to Veronica's seduction for the single-minded stunt-driving opportunity. He shook himself just as his phone dinged. She wasn't seducing him. She was resisting his seduction—even though she'd started it.

> LEXI: Wait. Scratch that. I haven't been to the gym in months. I doubt I could lift a ten-pound weight let alone a sword. And I haven't been on a horse since I was about eight. Ouch. That's not sounding so fun anymore. But it's definitely solidly in the fascinating category. And imagine, I thought you were interesting before.

> JAX: Fascinating enough to reconsider dinner with me?

> LEXI: Will you even be able to lift a fork after all that today?

> JAX: I'll be able to do a lot more than lift a fork.

> LEXI: Where are you staying?

His heart kicked. His mouth turned in a smile.

> JAX: Four Seasons. You?

LEXI: Spencer's.

Jax's smile faded. A lot of thoughts collided at once. More questions arose. A lot of questions she probably wouldn't answer. He chose his words carefully.

JAX: A woman who values security and privacy.

LEXI: You know the hotel?

JAX: I do.

LEXI: Then you must value the same.

A tingle of mixed emotions rose in his torso. Excitement, dread, anticipation…

JAX: I do.

A moment passed, and Jax knew they were both wondering the same thing: the true identity of the other.

Spencer's was a small, exclusive, high-end hotel run by Spencer himself, a retired Army Ranger who managed the hotel with a highly skilled security team. Spencer ran backgrounds on everyone who stayed there, refused entrance to anyone with any questionable history, didn't accept entourages, and had a zero-shit tolerance policy. Spencer didn't house criminals, adulterers, or users regardless of the fee they were willing to pay. And he expertly kept paparazzi at bay. His rates were high, but lower than the Four Seasons where Jax was registered.

Spencer spoke of no guest to any other guest. Every guest had some kind of personal connection through Spencer, so he knew every person staying at the hotel by name and reputation. Every employee and every guest signed a confidentiality agreement upon entering the premises, and Spencer enforced the agreements through the courts.

Spencer's had a long history of integrity, quality, discretion, public security, and personal safety.

JAX: Lexi, would you see me tonight if I could get a room at Spencer's?

Jax felt like his belly contents had been carbonated as he waited for her answer.

LEXI: Yes.

Jax's face burst into a grin. His chest with relief and excitement. He sent a text to Spencer, then wondered if she'd said yes because she doubted his ability to get a room on such short notice or because Spencer's endorsement by giving him a room made her feel safe enough to take a risk with him.

JAX: Fair enough. Good to know I'm not an axe murderer, right? A woman in today's world...

LEXI: Yes. But I have to be honest, Jax. I'm also a businesswoman in a competitive industry where image drives reputation and reputation drives business. And I'm on the brink of merging with an established designer whose reputation has been decades in the making.

His smile vanished. His gut tightened. But he forced himself not to jump to conclusions. He was admittedly sensitive—overly so—on this subject and had been known to snap at innocent comments.

JAX: You used some big words there, Lexi, but it sounds like you're saying your image may suffer if your interest in a...biker boy...were somehow known publicly?

LEXI: Unfortunately, yes.

Jax dropped his hands to his lap, where his phone stared up at him. A flash of cold raced over his arms underneath his jacket. Spread through his chest. Anger quickly formed a shield around the hurt, but it took Jax a few long moments to get through the seething transition.

He picked up his phone, his fingers hovering over the letters of his keyboard, but he couldn't find anything to say. His head was filled with years of his mother's disapproving comments on how he dressed, how he wore his hair, whether or not he shaved, how he presented himself in public. Images of his father and older brother in their favored five-thousand-dollar Brioni suits, his middle brother in Upper East Side chic—whatever the hell that was—flashed alongside his own tattered, tattooed, *biker boy* look.

> JAX: Well, shit, honey. I didn't see that coming.

> LEXI: I didn't foresee having to explain. It's a problem that wasn't much of an issue until I saw you. Until I fell in lust with you. It's not my personal view. It's something I deal with for financial survival.

Kind of the way he'd been willing to go back to that bitch, Veronica, to get the stunt contract back for his company? Until Wes had slapped him upside the head.

Jax dropped his forehead into his hand and massaged at a growing headache. His phone vibrated, and he opened his eyes. But it wasn't another message from Lexi; it was one from Spencer.

> SPENCER: Might have a cancellation on a suite tonight. Will know in next twenty minutes. If it doesn't pan out, you can always bunk with me, bro. Later. Spence

Jax grinned, but an ache had developed low in his gut. Not a good one. This one stemmed from the revival of an old wound. Of feeling...like one big disappointment.

> LEXI: Being in the movie industry, I was hoping you'd understand the whole image dilemma. It's refreshing to see someone who's been able to retain his identity and live authentically. I'm sorry if I've upset or disappointed you. I've always believed in honesty—even if that's being honest about the need to be...less than transparent.

> JAX: I understand more than you know. How long are you in

New York?

What the hell did he care if his style was an issue for her? What the hell did he care if she didn't want to be seen with him? This wasn't the change he'd been hoping for, but it was a start.

> LEXI: Just today. I fly back tomorrow. Early.

> JAX: Then reconsider dinner. I couldn't get a room at Spencer's, but I did get a suite.

> LEXI: Shut. Up.

Jax burst out laughing just as the pilot announced their imminent landing and requested everyone turn off their electronic devices. Yeah. He'd take one night with her. He loved the way she made him laugh. And he really liked a lot of other things about her. Even admired a few. All before ever seeing her.

This was a big move forward for Jax. He felt the shift inside him. The hint of belief that there might be hope for him yet. And he owed it to an anonymous text from little Lexi.

Another text came through from Spencer.

> SPENCER: Cancellation confirmed. You're set up in room 714. Lots of good luck coming your way, bro.

Jax hoped he was right. As he sent Spencer a thank-you text, the flight attendant reminded him it was time to put his phone away. He texted Lexi first.

> JAX: I have to shut down. When I get to the hotel, I'm going to take a shower. If you join me, we can fulfill one of the incredibly nasty dreams I had about you.

> LEXI: I thought you had to be at work right away.

> JAX: I haven't done what I was told since I was two. And I can guaran-goddamn-tee I'll set you right for that big meeting of yours this afternoon, sugar. But if I don't hear from you by the time I'm showered and dressed, I'll be back at the hotel by

seven. I'm in room 714. That's got to mean something positive, right?

He was going to shut down, but quickly added,

JAX: I'm yours, but you have to choose to take me.

And he turned off his phone.

SEVEN

Lexi's heart ticked quick and hard against her ribs. In her hotel room, she pulled out everything in her luggage and stood there naked, just out of the shower, staring at her clothes spread across the four-poster bed.

"I have nothing to wear," she said around the fingernail she kept clenched between her teeth. "That means I can't go, right?"

Her gaze darted to the clock on the nightstand. The glowing red numbers created a countdown pressure in her chest. Her rational mind kept telling her to just wait to see him until after he got back from work. Just take the day to think about it.

Her body kept telling her she should already be in his bed.

She glanced at her underwear again. Black and white, satin and lace, nothing special. Nothing pretty.

"Well, shit." She dropped her hand to her hip. "I didn't expect to meet dream man."

And dream man was probably used to the sexiest women in the sexiest underwear.

"He's a guy. He probably won't even notice. They all just rip it off anyway."

Lexi's mind flashed with that image—Jax's mouth attacking hers, his hands frantically searching her body, fingers wrapping in the hip of her panties and yanking until they tore. Her whole body tightened in gooseflesh. Her nipples peaked. Sex tingled.

"Fuck it." She grabbed the skimpiest pair of bikini underwear she'd brought—lace with satin edges, strings and bows at the hips, and the matching bra—and pulled them on.

"Now what?"

God, like it mattered? Still...

She had cute casual clothes, business clothes, and one nightclub outfit. But nothing sexy for a Jax encounter. Nothing perfect for her first visit to Jax's room. Correction—suite.

The fact that he'd gotten a suite so fast made discomfort pinch deep in her belly. He was someone. He had to be. Even Rubi's billionaire father couldn't get that kind of service with Spencer. But Jax wasn't famous. People hadn't been approaching him at the airport, asking for his autograph. Yet there was no doubt he wielded a certain amount of power. That he possessed a certain level of wealth. Everyone who stayed with Spencer did. Lexi considered herself his charity case and had been introduced to Spencer by Rubi and her father.

She'd thought Jax's ability to get a room here would make her feel more secure. And in some ways it had. But in others, she'd grown uneasy. Power and wealth made Lexi leery. Power and wealth could turn people ugly when something—or someone—they wanted slipped out of reach.

Her stomach prickled with hundreds of cold pins and needles as her memory turned to other men in her past who'd had power and wealth and had tried to use them to control her.

While she'd always known her looks played a big part in men's initial interest, her relationship with one successful real estate developer, Steven Connelly, had taught her it was far more complex than that. Lexi had learned that for many men, having her on their arm made a statement about them as a man—from the obvious *I'm a stud to catch such a hot babe*, to the far more subtle assumption of a man's overall power in business.

She'd also realized that losing her said just as much.

Steven hadn't been willing to accept whatever negative self-assessments he'd associated with Lexi breaking off the relationship and threatened her studio lease after she'd upgraded the space with her entire savings. He'd had the money to hire attorneys if she fought. He'd had the power to create a media frenzy if she went public.

He would have crushed her life, her dreams, all so he could wear her on his arm.

Rubi's father had been Lexi's ultimate savior. For all his

faults—and he had many—he'd come through for Lexi at Rubi's pleading requests. As grateful as she would always be to Rudolpho Russo for his help, Lexi never wanted to be in a position to need him again.

Her nerves kicked up. She'd felt so capable when she was flirting with Jax. So sexy. So in control. Now, she just felt inept. And incompetent. And…reckless.

Reckless. God, she needed more of that in her life. Spontaneity. Passion. Freedom. The kind she felt when Rubi gunned her Ferrari.

That thought was the impulse she'd needed to pull on the frilly short skirt from her cute set, the sexy halter from her business collection, and the sparkling four-inch heels from her club outfit.

She ran her fingers through her hair, shook it out, and glanced in the mirror. Yes, she looked like a woman ready for steamy hot sex with a stranger.

Lexi grabbed her room key and her phone and left the room before she couldn't. Purposely keeping her mind clear and her gaze averted from the obvious interest of other guests at the way she was dressed at nine a.m. on a weekday morning, Lexi rode the elevator, praying Jax hadn't left the hotel yet.

She found herself at the door of 714 suffering an anxiety attack. Her heart ticked way too fast. Her head floated. Her lungs struggled.

She pressed a hand to her stomach and wandered a few feet from his door, trying to drag in enough air to calm her brain. The hallway remained empty, so she leaned her back against the wall and texted him.

LEXI: Are you still in the hotel?

JAX: Just barely.

She winced, hating herself for the sliver of relief sliding through her belly.

61

LEXI: No time to meet, then?

JAX: I'm willing to make it work. When?

God, he was so sweet. She could do this. She could *do* this. She had to do this, because she couldn't go through these nerves again tonight. And if she went home without meeting him, she would always regret it.

LEXI: Now?

JAX: Yes. Absolutely. Now.

She laughed, breathless, giddy.

Her phone vibrated again.

JAX: Shit, that sounded just a little desperate, right? Sorry.

JAX: Do you want to come to my room or do you want me to come to you?

Lexi bit her lip. She was really going to do this. Sex with a stranger. A cold sensation slid from her forehead to her chin, as if she could feel the blood leaving her face.

Her mind seemed to crack, her thoughts skipping each time they hit an uneven surface. What if she was wrong about him? What if he wanted to see her when they got back to LA? What if she lost everything because of this one impulsive action?

She put a hand to her head. "This isn't a big deal," she whispered. "Rubi does it all the time."

She swallowed. Closed her eyes. *Push through it.* Opened her eyes and texted him.

LEXI: I'm at your room—STOP—don't open the door. I'm...nervous. I need a few...indulgences.

Lexi took a breath and sent the message. It couldn't hurt to shoot for just one more safeguard. He could always say no...right? Christ, she really wasn't thinking right.

JAX: Woman, you test me. What?

LEXI: Please know you can say no.

JAX: No.

Her throat shrank.

LEXI: Really?

JAX: Kidding. I'm nervous too. Tell me.

He was nervous? That was cute.

LEXI: Let me open the door. Just leave it cracked. Give me some room to get adjusted. I love brain-numbing passion, but I need to feel comfortable first.

JAX: You got it.

The metallic click of a door opening startled Lexi. She pushed from the wall. Her heart jumped. She peered at the door to room 714 and found it open two inches.

"Oh Jesus," she whispered, a hand to her chest. That made this all so real.

JAX: What else can I do?

LEXI: Dark. No lights, curtains closed?

A pause. Lexi held her breath.

JAX: Baby. Seriously? I've been dying to see you. Is this a fetish?

LEXI: Sorry, yes, I'm serious. But, no, it's not a fetish.

He didn't respond. Lexi closed her eyes as regret welled in the pit of her stomach. If she had more time, she might be able to get logic to overpower fear.

JAX: Sweetheart, I'm a man. I'm visual.

LEXI: I'll let your hands and your mouth and your body see every part of me.

JAX: Jesus Christ.

She waited. Hoped.

JAX: How about leaving on the bathroom light? I don't want to be tripping over myself. That would be embarrassing.

True. He was probably right about that. Bathroom light? How much could he see with the bathroom light?

LEXI: Bathroom light, door open two inches.

JAX: Door open halfway.

She grinned. His playfulness eased a couple of nerves.

LEXI: Three inches.

JAX: Four.

For God's sake.

LEXI: Done.

JAX: Hold on.

Lexi glanced at the door just as the space darkened. Her stomach fluttered. Heart picked up speed.

JAX: Okay—your demands have been met. Now I need a few things.

Oh shit.

LEXI: Yes?

JAX: Clarification: You are NOT married or involved.

LEXI: Correct.

JAX: We did not know each other before talking at the airport.

LEXI: Correct.

JAX: You are not a hired killer.

She laughed out loud.

JAX: God, you've got a great laugh. Get your ass in here.

Her stomach twisted with excitement.

Walk, Lex. One foot in front of the other.

EIGHT

Lexi's mind blurred between the moment she took the first step and the moment she stood in front of Jax's door. She focused on the numbers—seven-one-four—pulled air through her lips, and pressed her hand to the cool, painted metal.

As the door opened, light from the hall cast a wedge of soft yellow on the deep blue carpet in the entry.

Lexi swept her gaze over the dim interior setting and found Jax's shadowed form where he sat on the arm of the sofa deeper in the suite's living room. Hands lazily clasped in front of him. Jeans, bare feet, white T-shirt…maybe. Too many shadows to tell for sure. Which was good. If she thought she was nervous in the hall, her heart was about to jump from her chest now. The darkness helped.

She stepped into the room, closed the door, and pressed her back against it, letting her eyes adjust to the darkness. Silence seemed to swamp the space, the quiet so complete Lexi swore it compressed her lungs.

"You lied, sugar." His first words startled her, like a touch from the dark, but the distant bathroom light showed he hadn't moved. His voice, low and languid, created a sultry, sensual sensation all through her body, as delicious as the thought of melted chocolate on salty, warm skin.

"Lied?" She sounded like she'd run the stairs to his room. "About what?"

She glanced to her left, through a doorway that must have led to the bedroom. Another door that could only be for a bathroom stood open a few inches, just as he'd promised.

"You've got a sweet voice."

She jerked her attention back to him as he stood from the sofa. Taller than she'd expected. Broader than she'd expected.

A different kind of nervousness squirmed through her chest. Her hands clenched, the palm of one hand digging into the edges of her phone. "W…what did I lie about?"

"Your body."

He stepped closer, and the first cut of unease shot crackling heat through her chest. Had she misread him? Was she misreading herself? If this was passion, it was more intense than anything she'd ever felt. Overwhelming. Obsessive. Dark.

She found the door handle at her back with her free hand. Curled her fingers around it. "Is…is that a problem?"

"Why?" he asked.

Her brow pulled. Why what? She couldn't remember what they'd been talking about. This was so out of her scope. She should never have tried to play in Rubi's league.

"I'm not sure…" she started.

He closed in. His scent drifted to her—fresh, spicy.

Real. So in-her-face *real*.

This was no fantasy. Two hundred pounds of stranger stood less than two feet away. Her throat closed. She turned, pressed the lever, and pulled the door open. "I'm sorry, I don't think this…"

The door shut. Lexi gasped, her gaze darting up. The shadow of Jax's hand lay against the white door. Her mind froze. The sound of her own heartbeat filled her ears as his heat washed the length of her body.

Don't panic. Don't panic.

"Hold on, baby. Hold on." His voice, soft and apologetic, took some of the sting out of the fear.

She kept one hand gripping the door handle, the other flat on the door, and tried to slow her breathing.

"You're okay. We're okay." His hand disappeared from the door. "I'm sorry. I didn't mean to scare you. You can leave, Lexi, honey, anytime you want. I just… Talk to me, Lex. Then if you still want to go, open the door and go."

The regret in his voice felt like a rock in her gut.

Mortification made her stomach ball into a fist. "I'm sorry too. I don't know what I was thinking coming here…"

One of his hands lay gently on the top of her head, then slid all the way down her hair where it ended past the middle of her back. The touch felt good. Sweet. A few nerves released their tension.

"Wow," he murmured, "I should have added extra long to the possibilities. I love it."

A smile turned her mouth. His fingers slid past the ends of her hair, brushed the bare skin of her back in the open halter, featherlight, tentative.

"Can I touch you?" he asked, his voice softer than a whisper but so much deeper.

She nodded, unable to speak. His hand slipped beneath her hair and pressed against her back, between her shoulder blades. His hand was big, his skin rough. Heat sank into her body in the shape of his handprint, loosening her muscles. Lexi sighed and closed her eyes.

"I think," he murmured, "you were thinking the same thing I've been thinking for the last ten hours. How badly we want the other to ease this need that's grown between us."

"*God, yes*," she whispered. Once the words were out there, the fire that had been smothered by fear burned through and engulfed her body. "I'm just not used to…I mean, I've never done this."

He moved closer but didn't press against her. His heat and scent grew stronger. His hand made another pass over her hair, this time pushing his fingers in and combing it. Her scalp tingled. The sensation traveled down her neck and spine. Tightened the skin of her chest and puckered her nipples. She'd never known such a simple touch could feel so sexual.

His head lowered, and his smooth, freshly shaven chin rubbed her temple as he murmured, "I'm just figuring that out. I'm sorry I didn't catch on sooner. I was focused on the identity thing when I should have been focused on—"

"It's not you," she said. "You're perfect."

He laughed softly, the sound filled with yeah-right attitude, and trickled over her skin, prickling like warm water on cold flesh. His breath was warm and minty, making her want to taste him.

His hand paused in her hair, and she tilted her head back, her temple touching his. "Don't stop. That feels amazing."

His hand immediately started moving again, and Lexi moaned soft and low. "Thank you."

"Oh, little Lexi," he said on a long exhale and turned his face toward hers, nuzzling her hair away from the side of her face. "I think I know why you're so skittish."

She stiffened. Forced her eyes open. "What?"

"You're…sweet." He said it like it was a tender surprise, like she was precious.

"Sweet? I should be offended, shouldn't I? But I…kind of can't think when you're…touching me."

He brushed his closed lips along a path from the spot behind her ear to the strap of her halter on her neck and back again. No kissing. No tongue. Just rubbing. And heating her skin. And making her sex grow damp and swollen and hot.

"Why would that offend you?" On the last word, his open mouth pressed against the curve of her shoulder.

"Because sweet isn't exactly…" Wasn't exactly what? God, she really couldn't think. She released the door handle and reached up, hooking her hand behind his head. His hair was soft. His skin smelled spicy and sexy. "Jax."

He groaned. The sound lit a match between her legs. He fisted the hand in her hair and moved his mouth to her neck, suckling. She echoed his moan.

"You taste even better than I imagined. Can I feel you, Lexi? Can I feel you everywhere so I can create you in my mind?"

"Yes."

His hands closed on her waist. Heat shot both directions, into her sex and her breasts. His hands slid up her sides, creeping under her halter, and the rough skin on his fingertips scraped gently. Gooseflesh rose beneath his hands. His hands slid around front, covering her entire belly, long fingers stretching low between her hipbones.

"Mmmm," he hummed in approval.

Lexi started to turn, ravenous for his mouth. For his body to be pressed fully up against hers. But Jax had a firm hold on her. "I'm still checking you out, sweetheart. It takes longer without light."

His hands moved over her hipbones and down the front of her thighs, avoiding her throbbing sex but bringing his chest low and against her back. She turned her head, kissed his cheek. His temple.

"Jax..." Then he found the hem of her skirt; his hands slid over the skin of her thighs. "Yes..."

But, again, his hands traveled around to her hips, then back to her thighs, and higher, grasping the cheeks of her ass firmly enough to make Lexi gasp.

"Goddamn, Lexi," he growled as his forehead pressed against her temple. "It's a good thing I didn't see you in the airport. We might have missed the plane."

She laughed, hardly more than a soft puff of air. Then he leaned in until his body pressed the length of hers. One long, lean wall of muscle and heat. Finally.

Her fingers curled into her palms, and she groaned, the pleasure rocketing through every part of her body. "Oh, so perfect."

But it got better. He added pressure with his hips and a thick, hard rod of heat sank into the low curve of her spine. Lexi groaned. He bent his knees until he'd wedged the line of his erection snugly between the cheeks of her ass and released a long, deep growl Lexi felt all the way to her core.

"Now *that* is perfection," he said, his voice husky. "I've got one more measurement to check..."

His hands slipped up her sides, around her ribs and, with the confidence of a man who'd handled a lot of women in his life, took her breasts in his palms. Her skin tightened as Jax cupped and squeezed and molded. His hips matched the nearly unconscious movements Lexi made to rub her ass against his cock. And when his fingers closed on her nipples, Lexi whimpered.

Her hand fisted his hair. Her head dropped forward, eyes closed, lips parted. A noise came from her throat, but she couldn't describe it. She was too dizzy with lust. She was glad the lights were off. She didn't have to blush with mortification at her intense need.

He lowered his mouth to her ear. "Not one of your measurements was true."

She tightened the hand around her phone. "You sure didn't fudge on yours." God, she needed him inside her so badly she was trembling. "But I still feel the need to…verify."

"You'll get your chance, baby, no worries there. But I don't have time to fuck you properly right now, and there is no way in the fiery pits of hell I'm going to rush a goddamned thing with a catch like you."

He had to be joking. His cock was a damn rod of burning steel. "Jax—"

"Tell me why you lied, Lexi."

He released one of her breasts, his hand sliding down her abdomen. The touch of his fingers on her skin was electric. They slipped beneath the band of her skirt, and Lexi's breath caught. Muscles tightened with nerves and need. But he didn't touch her where she wanted him to touch her. He took the edge of her panties between two fingers and just slid the satin back and forth. Back and forth. Until she thought she'd go mad…waiting, wanting.

She turned her head, her lips brushing the rough stubble on his jaw, and whispered, "Touch me."

"I wouldn't want to distract you from your answer. Truth, Lexi."

She groaned. "The truth is that men are attracted to me for

72

my…body."

She almost said looks, but amended at the last minute. She wasn't ready to turn on the lights and give up everything. Wasn't ready to look this stranger in the eye and confront her reckless behavior.

"You're a handsome man, Jax…" She couldn't get a full sentence out without panting. "And in your business, you can't tell me…you don't know what it's like to be seen only for what's on the outside. Maybe, as a guy, it's no big deal…but as a woman, it's frustrating. And sometimes even scary.

"We had such a good thing going with the texts…I didn't want that to change. It was nice to feel attractive before you knew my body."

"Sweet," he murmured. His hips pressed against her backside. His erection, so wickedly erotic, so deliciously hot and thick, made her body crave in a way she'd forgotten she could. Her sex softened. Opened. Ached.

Lexi arched into one of his slow rocks forward, pressing the indention between the cheeks of her ass against his jeans-covered cock. Jax dropped his chin to her shoulder and breathed out hard, growling through his teeth. His other hand released the band of her panties and slid across her stomach, a hot, solid weight.

"I'm going to ease your ache, Lexi." He bit her earlobe gently. Soothed the spot with his lips. "But I don't have a lot of time, so tell me what kind of release you want. Hard and fast? Fast and deep?"

She didn't want to think. Didn't want to talk. Sure as hell didn't want to tell him what to do. Besides, she couldn't think straight. She was floating. Drifting in an electric storm cloud.

"What's the difference?"

Jax's hand stopped moving along her belly.

Lexi rose from her heavenly void, wondering if she'd done something wrong. "What?"

"Does that mean you don't care? Or were you asking?"

73

Growing frustrated, she leaned her head back, stretched to press her mouth to his neck. His skin was hot, and, oh, he tasted good. Clean. Male. "Aren't they all the same? I'm dying here."

A low, rough laugh rumbled in his throat and shivered beneath Lexi's lips. He pressed a hand to her jaw and lifted her face to cover her mouth with his. And, oh, his lips were full and warm. He used them to savor hers, sucking and sliding. His tongue eased into her mouth in slow circles. By the time it met hers in long, erotic, sexual strokes, Lexi was breathless.

"Hold still," he whispered, tightening an arm around her waist. "I'm going to give you hard and fast to relieve you. We've got all night to explore the many different kinds of orgasms that exist. And no, baby, they're not all the same."

He lowered his mouth to the base of her neck and pulled her into his body until she felt every beat of his heart against her shoulder blade. The hand at her stomach slid beneath the waistband of her panties, and Lexi tried to wiggle into his touch but couldn't. Then he eased the need by pushing his hand low. She gasped in surprise and excitement. At the feel of having a man's hand between her legs. A real man. The kind of man who made her hot and wet and needy. The kind of man who wasn't afraid to take charge or give real pleasure.

The kind of man who could bring her entire business down around her knees.

She covered his hand with hers. His wrist was thick, his forearm muscled. His intense strength suddenly, overwhelmingly evident. A shot of excited lust burned through her body.

"You like it?" he asked, voice rough. "Or you want me to stop?"

"Love it." Lexi's eyes closed. Head fell forward. She swallowed. The only thing keeping her from pushing his hand between her legs and using it to cut this wild need was her own mortification of doing so. "More. Please."

Instead of giving her more, Jax turned his hand over, took hers, and guided it back to the door handle. "Hold on, baby.

You're gonna need it."

One of his feet pushed between her high heels and eased one of her feet to the side. His hand slid into the heat between her legs, and Lexi's whole body exploded with the electric excitement of his touch. Her hips pushed forward. A moan rolled out of her throat.

"Easy, baby," Jax whispered, his touch too light for Lexi's needs. She pushed harder against his hand, and he pulled back. "You'll get what you need. I promise."

She whimpered in disappointment.

Jax nudged her other foot to the side and pushed his big hand deeper between her legs.

"Yeeees." She pressed both hands against the door and pushed back against him, but his body was a wall of rock. He didn't move.

"Hold still, beautiful." His tone was a blend of dark and naughty. "This one's on me. You can help next time."

With his hot palm heavy over her sex, he stroked her outer lips with those big, strong fingers. Hot, heavy strokes.

"Perfect. So wet." With a growl, his teeth sank into the curve between her neck and shoulder.

One thick, hot finger pressed past her folds and dipped inside. The touch of a stranger. A sexy, unknown man who was going to do nothing but fuck her. The reality thrilled Lexi to ridiculous levels. If she had time to think about it, all her fear would have washed back in. But Jax didn't give her time to think. His chest pressed against her shoulders as he pushed deeper, his mouth on the side of her neck, a growl of pleasure vibrating in his throat.

He did something inside her when he pulled out that created a delicious pressure. Lexi arched, wrapped one arm up and around his neck again, holding him tight. "Jax, not enough," she whispered, panting. "Fuck me."

"No way." He scraped his teeth across her shoulder, and when he moved inside her again, it was with two fingers, sizzling friction along her walls and a new sensation of delicious fullness. "When I fuck you, baby, it's going to be for *hours*."

She'd heard that before. But it had never happened. Given the men she'd been with, she was glad. This time…this time she both believed he'd follow through and that she'd be glad he did. But she wasn't thrilled she'd have to wait.

He pulled out of her, dragging two fingers back and forth until his thick fingertips were seated deep within her folds on either side of her clit. His touch was confident, featherlight, and shot zings of excitement to her core.

"This is what I want," he murmured, his voice low and hungry.

A streak of unease flared. Lexi wasn't into pain. And the combination of her need and his very specific attentions on her most vulnerable nerve center made her tense.

"Jax—"

Her concerns never made it out of her mouth. His fingers tightened at the base of her clit, and Lexi's throat convulsed. Her brain whited out in a neon snowstorm. Liquid fire burned through her pelvis, melted down her legs. Lexi struggled for air. Her fingers had fused to the door handle.

When Jax's touch eased, the extreme pleasure faded into something deeper and more widespread, something that made Lexi want to ride his hand. But she was afraid to move, not prepared for another electric shock of ecstasy. Her muscles went soft, and she let her head fall against the door.

"Holy. Fuck." She breathed the words on a whisper.

"Mmm," was all Jax had to say as he wet his fingers inside her again, making slow, luscious circles at her opening before turning back to the very delicate art of blowing her mind with nothing more than the pinpoint-fine movements of two fingers.

"This is where the ride starts, Lex," he whispered in her ear, a dark thrill in his voice. "In this little bundle of nerves. Don't pump into my hand, baby, or this won't feel as good as it could."

The arm at her waist tightened again, drawing her back snug against him, trapping her. Making sure she didn't have a choice to move or not. Lexi fought the thread of her personality that automatically needed to take back that sliver of control, because the rest of her reveled in letting him have it.

Then he made her forget all about control with the slightest movement of his fingers—gentle slides, tender tugs, slight pulses tantalizing this place hidden deep in her sex. Something that had always been there, but no other man, not even long-time lovers, had ever found. Something even Lexi had never explored. Yet, something a sexy stranger used to drive her to the moon within fifteen minutes of touching her.

He chuckled in her ear, dragging her down from the stratosphere and shooting tingles along her skin.

"God, I love the sounds you make," he murmured, adjusting the angle of his arm and pushing deeper between her legs. His fingers squeezed just a tiny bit more, and Lexi lost herself on the very edge of orgasm. But Jax immediately eased his touch. "No, not yet. Hearing you ache for it turns me on."

She hadn't realized she'd been making sounds. Lexi was so out of her mind with the sensations tightening her body, she was oblivious. Orgasm was close. It loomed bright, sparkling, and phantasmic. And she wanted it. *Bad.*

"Jax." She dropped her head back on his shoulder. "Can't do this… Need more…"

"I know." He dotted a trail of kisses over her cheek, her eyelid, her temple. "But you feel so good."

Her mind wasn't working. She couldn't understand what he was trying to say. And he was moving again, his fingers searching until Lexi gritted her teeth and groaned. But the moment he'd found his mark, fireworks of pleasure shot through Lexi's body. She dropped the hand around his neck to his forearm, digging her nails into his thick muscles.

He released his hold on her waist, added a magic amount of pressure to her clit, and murmured, "Rock yourself to heaven, baby."

Lexi couldn't have held still even if she'd tried. Her hips lunged and rolled automatically, easily syncing with Jax's slight movement. She braced herself with one hand flat on the door, the other on Jax's arm.

The orgasm built from her center out, rolling through her pelvis, filling her belly. Rose through her chest and swelled in her throat until it tingled on the back of her tongue. "Oh, fuck…"

"Hard and fast, Lex." His voice was dark in her ear. His body wrapped around her. His hand drove her. And one of the last sensations that floated through Lexi's mind was one of being completely taken over. Yet safe. Cared for.

The slightest change in his touch released a lightning-bolt orgasm, and the shaft of pleasure ripped through Lexi. She lost control of her body. Her muscles contracted, released, flexed. Sensation flooded her brain, wiping out all thought.

"That's it." Jax's murmur slipped in and mixed with all the excitement, his voice thick, darkly sexual. "Yeah. Soak it up, Lexi."

Her hand slipped off Jax's arm, and she fell forward. But she didn't go anywhere. Jax held her too tight to allow her to fall. But she groped for the door handle, the strength in her legs gone. Uncontrollable shivers racked her body. Cries and moans of delirium drifted from her throat.

Her mouth moved. Formed words. But nothing made sense. The words didn't even sound like much to her own ears. She wanted to tell him how good she felt. How amazing he was. But it all came out as jumbled murmurs and whimpers of pleasure.

The orgasm's intensity dimmed, but delicious aftershocks still occasionally shuddered through her body.

"I don't have to see you," he said, his own breaths fast now, "to know how fucking beautiful you are."

That sharpened her mind. A little. But Jax kept his hand between her legs, still and steady, almost as if he was holding the delicious feelings in. And they seemed to obey. Floating deep inside, easing her down from the peak gently, in decadent increments.

His head lay on her shoulder, his breath hot on her neck. "You're amazing."

Oh, God no. He had that backward. But Lexi basked in his praise. No one had said that to her—regarding sex—in…what felt like forever. She had the urge to reach up and rake her fingers through his hair. Turn her head and kiss every inch of his face. But she couldn't move.

"God damn, Jax," Lexi finally whispered. "I don't think I've ever come that hard."

A beat of silence hung before his serious, smooth voice slid in with, "I'm going to do it all again tonight" —another beat— "with my mouth." He pressed his lips to the space just below her ear, then whispered, "But when I'm inside you, you're going to come so hard you scream."

NINE

Jax's brain kept trying to slip out from under his control. And if that happened, he'd never get to work. Which, at this nearly perfect moment, wasn't a hell of a lot of incentive to keep his mind corralled from the thought of throwing Lexi down on the couch, spreading her legs, and showing her just how much harder he could make her come. It would be easier now. The first orgasm was the hardest to get. Everything after that—cake.

And he would get downright pissed off if he thought too long about all he was missing by walking out on her now.

"Fucking jobs," he muttered. "Mess up everything."

Lexi was tight. Hot. Dripping wet. So responsive to his every touch he'd be able to shoot the woman to the moon.

Tonight she wouldn't be begging him to make her come.

Tonight she would be begging him to stop because she couldn't take it anymore.

That was if he could last. He'd never had a problem before, but… He wasn't sure if it was the darkness, the whole stranger thing, or the little surprises she kept throwing at him, but he was having a hell of a time holding back.

"Aren't they all the same?"

Jax smiled, pretty sure Lexi was convinced not all orgasms were the same now.

She was so goddamned sweet she made him ache. And he had a whole new appreciation for Wes. Jax might even have a basic understanding about the elusive formula Wes swore by: cute plus sweet equaled great sex and happiness.

God, he wanted to take her to bed and spend the day there with her. But it would cost the production company tens of thousands in wasted filming costs, Renegades thousands in income, and a ping to Jax's stellar reputation as the most dependable stunt guy in the business.

That was a pretty damned expensive day of sex.

He had to use every muscle in his body to control the pressure of his fingers as he eased his hand from the soft heat of Lexi's nearly bare pussy. His cock was still a shaft of lead cradled against her ass. The woman had an amazing body. He could imagine why men would hit on her at the sight of it, because the feel of it made him want to throw thousands of dollars and a reputation he'd taken years to build to the wind.

But even with his mind hazed, her excuse for hiding her identity didn't completely ring true. He was more apt to believe her comment on the plane about his ability to damage her reputation. His own family had shied away from claiming him at numerous Hollywood events when he'd shown up in anything less than Armani, including the Taurus World Stunt Awards. His first movie where his company ran every stunt, nominated in four categories, and only his father and oldest brother had shown. Then they hadn't sat in the seats he'd had reserved for them—next to him up front.

A familiar hollow shadowed his excitement. He'd like to believe that painful memory had come out of the ether, but the thought of her comment on the plane had been the prompt.

Not something he wanted to think about or face right now.

Jax winced as Lexi pulled her nails from his forearm. That would leave a mark. Five of them, actually.

"I'm sorry," she murmured. "I didn't realize…"

"I'm fine." Though he was still dizzy from the adrenaline and testosterone pumping through his blood.

She turned in his arms, pressed the front of her body against his, and Jax lost every thread of control he'd gained. All that softness, all those curves. Good God in heaven…

"Lexi," he groaned, his hands at her waist.

She combed her fingers through his hair, let them slide over his forehead, his closed eyelids, his cheeks. "What color are your eyes?"

"I don't know," he muttered.

He felt stupid assigning his eyes a color. No one had ever asked him that before. The women he dated knew everything about him. At least everything they'd memorized from the Internet or what friends told them.

She laughed, the sound light, happy, and Jax found himself smiling. "You don't know the color of your own eyes?"

"They're...brown-green-something-boring."

"Hazel?" she asked, a smile lifting her voice. "Are you too hot to say hazel?"

"No, I'm too stupid. Are yours blue?"

"Mmm-hmm." She cupped his face, found his lips with her thumbs, and pulled his head down. Her mouth was soft, hot. Delicious. The way she slid her tongue between his lips made him moan and tighten his hands on her waist. He pulled away. "Lex, honey, you're not making a day on horseback look any easier." God, he didn't want to leave. "Baby, I gotta go."

"I know." Something in her voice changed, deepened. She pressed her hands against his chest and walked him backward, toward the sofa. "But I'm not sending you out to ride horses all day with a hard-on like that."

His thighs hit the arm of the sofa, and she grabbed his belt. His adrenaline kicked up again. Heat burst low in his belly. He covered her hands with his, but that didn't keep her from getting his pants undone quicker than he could.

"Lexi, I'm sorry, baby, I don't have time to fuck you—" Her hand slid into his underwear, and Jax sucked air. The flesh-on-flesh contact shot electricity to the base of his spine. He gripped her arms, more to steady himself than to pull them away. "Ah, shit."

"You're not going to fuck me. *I'm* going to fuck *you*." She pushed his jeans and underwear low enough to pull his cock into her hands. "With my mouth."

She dropped to her knees. Excitement surged through Jax.

He didn't always enjoy the sight. For him, it depended on the woman. Depended on the reason she was on her knees. The real reason. Because sucking him was ultimately just a means to an end—a nonsexual end.

But even in the dark, even only able to see Lexi's silhouette, his chest hitched at the sight. His gut clenched in anticipation.

She slid one hand up his belly, scratched her nails back down to the base of his cock. His shaft twitched. His balls swelled. She caressed his length in her hands. Jax fisted his hands in the sofa's plush fabric at his hips. She licked his tip, and heat shot down his cock, exploded in his pelvis. Jax gritted his teeth.

"And since you're short on time," she said, "I'll just follow your lead and make this hard and fast. I'll have all night to suck you off slowly and enjoy every second of it. No rushing. Right?"

She held his cock with one hand; the other gripped his thigh through his jeans. Her words were still sinking in, the meaning not fully registering in his clouded brain when her mouth closed over the head of his cock.

"Oh *fuck*," he groaned. "Lexi—"

She slid his entire length into her mouth. His head pushed into her tight throat, and a blast of ecstasy exploded through his shaft, pounded his balls, and ricocheted through his ass. The muscles of Jax's back clenched. His head dropped back. She prolonged the thrill by circling her tongue around his length and sucking him all the way out. His entire body shuddered.

"*Fuck*, that's good," he moaned, head light, legs shaking.

She laughed, low and sexy. "Hold on, handsome. The ride starts here."

This time when she took him in, her mouth was strong—lips hungry, tongue insistent, suction that made Jax dig his fingers into the sofa. He couldn't control the sounds that came out of his throat, more animal than human.

When she'd sucked him from her mouth and circled his head with her tongue, Jax forced a hand from the sofa and combed a hand into her hair. It was so soft. So silky. It felt good between his fingers. Lexi slid her tongue down the underside of his cock, and need expanded in Jax's belly. Rose along his spine.

"Baby…" he growled. And couldn't get anything else out when her tongue stroked his sack.

He fisted the hand in her hair, and Lexi moaned in pleasure.The sound shivered over his balls and into the base of his cock like a vibrator.

"Lexi, shit…"

She smiled. He felt the curve of her mouth against his cock. As her tongue slid over his length again, both her hands roamed up and under his T-shirt. Hot fingers traced his muscles, found his nipples, brushed. His skin tightened. Body trembled.

"You're trying to make me late."

"Not exactly trying…" she murmured, pleasure softening her voice. "You're just so…delicious. And I am going to lick every inch of you tonight. But you're right. I need to stay focused."

She dragged her hands back down his chest, his belly, her palms leaving a hot trail. Then she took his hand still on the sofa and pulled it to her head so he held her with both. "Touch me."

He'd slipped to a slouched seat on the arm of the sofa. She shouldered his legs wider, pressed her arms to his thighs, and took his length in her hands. Jax spread his fingers and combed them through her hair, pulling it off her face.

The feel of her hot mouth sliding over him made Jax's mouth drop open, his eyes squeeze closed, a deep moan roll from his chest. There wasn't any such thing as a bad blowjob, but the really, really good ones weren't all that common either. To get a really mind-blowing mouth fuck, a woman had to love doing it. Had to get turned on by doing it. Had to want to suck a guy as much as the guy wanted to get sucked. And seeing as men would rather get sucked than eat, it was a rare quality in a woman.

Lexi clearly had that quality. She was relentless. Creative. Generous.

He had to admit, the lack of light heightened every other

sensation—her scent, her every touch, every sound she made. It was hot in a way Jax had never experienced. Intense in the way it created an extreme intimacy with a complete stranger. But this was one place he wanted lights. Blazing lights. He wanted to watch every move of her fingers, her tongue, her lips over him. He wanted to watch his cock slide between her lips. He wanted her looking into his eyes when she took him deep into her mouth. Like now.

The head of his cock bumped the back of her throat. The shocking pleasure froze the air in Jax's lungs. God it had been a long fucking time since he'd been given a thrill like this. Lexi picked up on his pleasure and exploited it. She opened her throat and took him in. The tight, rigid channel squeezed his head, and excitement shot into his shaft, spread deep into his balls.

"Fuck, yeah." Jax groaned the words, sensation building deep at his core. "Baby, that's so incredible."

His hands fisted in her hair. He tried to be gentle, but he was nearly out of his mind. He couldn't keep himself from pulling her in, pushing his hips forward. Just to feel that perfect stricture pump him. Just once. Or twice.

Stop. Stop. *Stop.*

He forced himself to pull back. He was going to choke the poor girl, and he'd never see her again. Jax was still trying to get himself back under control when Lexi's nails dug into his hips, pulling against his hold. He immediately let go, a zing of fear heating his chest.

"Sorry…sorry…" He panted. "Sorry, Lex. I didn't—"

Her fingers covered his mouth. "Let me suck you off." Her voice was soft but low, thick with desire. "I can and I want to."

His brain was spinning. His body shaking with the need to explode. He turned and sucked her fingers into his mouth. "Lexi," he murmured, "you don't have—"

She pulled her hand from his mouth, reached up, and took his head in both hands.

When her mouth closed over his, he froze in a second of

surprise. Her tongue swept in and demanded response. Jax's brain went right back into the clouds. She tasted musky from loving him, pleasing him. His chest tightened with a sensation completely different from what spilled through his body. One that was going to cause trouble for him. He knew.

She pulled back. "I love the feel of your cock in my throat. I love feeling you moving me the way you like it."

This was a fantasy. It couldn't be real. She was just too hot.

She kissed his lips, whispered, "I want to feel you come in my mouth."

His cock surged. A wicked need consumed him. "Lexi…"

"I want to taste you."

He grasped handfuls of her hair. Pulled her forehead to his. "You're a fantasy."

"Let's finish it off right, then." Her hands slid into his hair, down his neck, and she whispered, "Say yes."

He didn't have to think about it. "Yes."

She kissed him again. Long, slow, sweet. Lovingly. She kissed him like he hadn't been kissed in years.

Then she eased back on her heels and took him into her mouth again. Jax was already shaking when she opened her throat and took him in.

"Ah, God, Lex…"

She kept her mouth loose around his cock, and all the sensation focused on the squeeze and thrust of his head. Lexi varied the speed. The depth. Seemed to sense when she'd brought him to the edge of release, then backed off, sucking his length from her mouth. Until he thought he'd go insane.

He gritted his teeth and growled her name. "Lexi."

She licked his head, the feathery touch ridiculously tantalizing as a contrast to the abusive strength of her throat. "Maybe you should show me how you like it."

Dark innuendo lilted her voice. Jax's mind tilted. His hands fisted her hair. She gasped. Her hands slid around his hips, dug beneath the edge of his jeans, her nails scraping his skin.

She took him back into her mouth, and Jax pulled her close, driving his cock straight into her throat. A surprised sound bubbled from her chest. He held her steady, his head against her closed throat. Reflexive, he was sure. He hadn't given her a chance to adjust. Gently, he moved his hips, rocking his cock against the tightness of her throat.

"Open, baby," he said, his voice darker than he'd ever heard it. Realized he liked it. Liked the way she made him feel so...alive. So...dark. So...okay to be dark. "Take me in."

Her throat slowly released with each nudge of his cock until she was open and oh...so...perfect.

His grip loosened in pleasure, and Lexi moved with him, syncing with his thrusts until he was deeper than he'd ever been, the sensation like nothing he'd ever known, ever imagined. The sounds she made acted as both a vibrator to his cock and a stimulant to this new sexual shadow.

He was going to explode. He hadn't come in a woman's mouth in a long time. Damn fucking long time. He couldn't think about why this seemed so important to him. Could only feed the need to get closer to her.

He bent at the waist until he pressed his face to her head, held her head between his legs. Completely sexual, yet...somehow it felt like more.

"Lex," he scraped out, fisting her hair. He wanted to give her a chance to change her mind. This was intense. Was going to get more intense. "I'm gonna come."

The sound she made in her throat was so deep, so filled with lust it shattered over him. Before he could come on his own, Lexi swallowed. Her throat closed on his cock in a slow, rolling motion that shot him out of his skin.

"Jesus Christ..."

The orgasm blasted his body with fire and pressure. All Jax's muscles constricted, and he let go, gave himself over to it. Lexi's throat continued to close and compress and rock around his cock as she swallowed again and again. Continuing to suck and tongue him through the breaking waves of sensation.

The pleasure rode up his chest, out his limbs. Cleared his mind of everything. Jax's hands fell from her hair; he leaned sideways against the back of the sofa. Lexi gentled her mouth as the orgasm eased. But kept loving him, holding him in one hand, pressing gentle kisses to his length.

If that wasn't sweet, he didn't know what was.

As the last shivers skittered through his body, Jax groaned and dropped his head to the side, against the back of the sofa. His chest continued to heave with quick, heavy breaths, heart hammering. He coughed, and the resulting spasm knocked him backward off the arm of the sofa. He landed on the cushions on his back, knees hanging over the arm. His jeans tugged lower on his hips.

"Shit." Hell, that was smooth. Good thing the lights were out.

Lexi started laughing. The giggle turned into a full belly laugh as she gripped his knees from the other side of the furniture. "Are you okay?"

Jax's chest swelled with a sweet emotion he didn't recognize. He used the last of his strength to curl up, grab her arms, and drag her down on top of him. Her squeal only pushed his happiness deeper.

"Think that's funny, huh?" Her weight, her heat, her curves all felt delicious. He wrapped her in his arms, nuzzled her neck, and opened his mouth against her skin.

"Jax." She groaned his name. "You have to go to work, remember?"

He hummed against her skin, moved his mouth lower.

"I'm already hot from sucking you." Her hands fisted in his T-shirt. "Don't make me call your boss and tell him you can't come in because I fucked you blind."

Laughter rolled from his chest and exploded against her

neck.

She giggled and pushed away. "That tickles."

He grabbed her back, his hands seeking other ticklish spots.

She squirmed and squealed. "Jax, stop!"

"Hell." He wrapped her tight in his arms again, and she relaxed against him. "You're too damn much fun."

She sighed. Lay against him another decadent moment. Her hand stroked the bare skin of his abdomen where his shirt had ridden up. "I better let you go."

"See you tonight?" He brushed her hair off her forehead. "I didn't scare you off?"

A low, sexy laugh sounded in her throat. "You're kidding, right?"

"Don't laugh like that. I'm getting hard again."

Another moment passed.

Another sigh.

"I should let you go," she murmured again.

"Yeah."

Neither of them moved.

And Jax couldn't stop smiling.

She took a slow breath, held it a second. "Jax?"

Dread pierced his cloud nine. His smile dropped. His throat tightened. This was that moment. That fucking moment—after sex, after a woman had given him what he wanted, or what they thought he wanted and that too sweet *Jax?* came. Followed by a request.

"Can you introduce me to producer x, director y, casting director z?"

"Can you invest in my latest indie movie?"

"Can I be your date to the Oscars this year?"

Or the latest: "Can I drive a stunt car in this Bond movie?"

He lifted a hand from her body to rub his eyes and readied himself before asking, "Yeah?"

"Do you want me to get your clothes cleaned? That coffee will stain and smell terrible after sitting all day. I have time before my meeting."

He rested his hand on his forehead, stomach clenched, still waiting for the punch.

But nothing came.

Her head moved on his chest. The hand on his arm shook. "Hey, don't fall asleep. You've got to get your ass on a horse and wield a sword."

He laughed again. He hadn't laughed this much with a woman in forever.

She pushed up and rolled off him, getting to her feet. The absence of her weight left him craving it again. He groped for her in the dark. Caught her arm and tugged her close. Felt for her face and pulled her in for a kiss.

"Thanks," he murmured against her lips, "but I called the desk. They're going to take care of it."

"Okay." She kissed him again and straightened. "Have fun today. Don't cut off anyone's head. And...don't hurt yourself doing...whatever you do. I have plans for you."

He smiled. Held on to her hand, reluctant to let go. "God, you're cute."

"Cute. Sweet. Hmm..."

"And you've got the mouth of a goddess. That's the best I've ever had, Lex. Seriously."

"You've got the best cock I've ever sucked. Seriously." She squeezed his hand. "I'm leaving now."

He pulled her back in, put a hand to her face, and whispered, "Knock that big designer on her—or his—ass today."

"Thanks." She kissed him one more time before she straightened and adjusted her clothes. Then slipped out of his room.

Jax struggled to see more of her as she opened the door. But with the light coming from the hall, he couldn't catch sight of anything more than when she'd come in—a killer silhouette and the gleam of blonde hair.

And, hell, it couldn't have mattered less.

TEN

Lexi tried hard to focus on the women sitting around the table with her. They'd been doing the casual chatting thing while they'd waited outside for their table at Gotham Bar and Grill in Manhattan, but now that they were inside the ornate space, Lexi found herself craving simplicity and relaxation.

When she'd been told by one of Galliano's assistants that they would be having their lunch meeting here, Lexi had been relieved. Even pleased. With her caliber of clientele, she spent way too much time in these fancy settings and had really been looking forward to a different atmosphere for a business meeting for a change.

But, there was nothing "bar and grill" about this place. Dark wood, elegant fabrics, and pristine china. Extravagant floral arrangements that surely cost the monthly rent on her Sunset Boulevard studio. Starched waiters with impeccable manners. Patrons in Brooks Brothers suits and Dolce and Gabbana dresses.

The Gotham Bar and Grill was exactly what Lexi had originally dreaded. Though, she had to admit, Martina Galliano and her assistants, Beth and Casey, made it seem as if the restaurant was nothing more formal than a neighborhood café.

"I haven't gotten a chance to see your designs in *American Bride*," Casey said, drawing Lexi's attention from a gilded mirror across the restaurant the size of her loft. The dark-haired, dark-eyed woman cast a sidelong smirk at Beth. "Someone's been hogging the advanced copy you sent."

"I'm not hogging it," Beth said. "I told you I wasn't going to let you get Cheetoh dust on the pages."

Casey gasped, but grinned. "You lie."

"No, she doesn't," Martina said, grinning from directly across the table from Lexi. "Why do you think I haven't shared mine with you?"

"Fine, fine." Casey lifted her brows and folded her hands with an expression of mock insult. "I'll just have to wait for a week until it hits the shelves to get my own copy. But don't be surprised if I call in sick that day."

"I've told the girls all about how I've been watching you grow your business and develop a very sophisticated style for years," Martina said.

The older woman hadn't stopped complimenting Lexi since she'd hugged her on the sidewalk out in front of the restaurant like they were old friends. She was used to hearing customers, fashion reporters, and media rave about her work, but to hear Martina Galliano say these things to her would be the equivalent of Rubi being showered with praise by the likes of Steve Wozniak.

Martina was handsome—in that exotic Mediterranean way. Not beautiful, but attractive. And stylish, though Lexi could tell the woman lived a tug-of-war between her reputed natural tendency toward conservatism and the current, youthful trend of self-expression. The cut of her suit was too flippant and careless for her age, the extremely bright eggplant silk blouse a forced color spot beneath the cool silvery-blue suit jacket.

"I think the magazine might have been distributed to select locations early," Lexi told Casey, reaching down for her portfolio beside her chair. "It wasn't supposed to be circulated until next week, but I found it on stands in the airport. You can have this one."

Casey gasped. "Really?"

"Of course."

Casey squealed and clapped her hands. Lexi laughed.

"As you can tell," Martina told Lexi, "they're very excited about this new line."

Casey thanked Lexi, her dark eyes caressing the image on the cover lovingly. She pulled in a gasp. "Look at that detail." She pulled the magazine close and inspected the photograph. "Is that appliqué?"

"No," Lexi said. "It's all hand sewn."

Casey's eyes rounded. Her mouth curved in an O as she gazed at Lexi. "*Hand. Sewn.*"

Lexi grinned. "Thousands of Swarovski crystals in six different colors to create the ombré effect in the pattern."

Casey's eyes grew wider. Her mouth rounder. "*Thousands?*"

Lexi nodded. "They cover the entire bodice and blend into the top of the skirt."

"I think you should do that for your final project," Beth told Casey with a teasing look. "If you start now, you might finish by the due date."

Casey choked out a laugh. "Yeah, a year would be about right."

They must have been talking about some kind of final design project they had to complete before they graduated. Both women were juniors at Parsons the New School for Design in New York. The leading powerhouse in the fashion industry, Parsons had been Lexi's fantasy college once upon a time. She'd been five or six when she'd realized she had as much chance of getting to college as her mother had of holding any job longer than three weeks, sobriety longer than three months, or a husband longer than three years.

At this stage of her life, Lexi wasn't exactly jealous of the other women. She sure didn't want to go backward. Lexi had paid heavy dues from a very early age to get where she was now. Had swept floors, delivered coffee, organized offices, cleaned lunchrooms. She'd pinned patterns until she needed a freaking blood transfusion from all the finger pricks. Had cut fabric until her hands ached so bad she couldn't hold a toothbrush. Had sewn piecework until she thought her spine had fused into a permanent C. She'd also taught herself by reading and asking questions and researching. And designing, sewing, ripping out stitching, and doing it all over again.

But while she was at least ten years ahead of these women in experience, their degree from Parsons would always carry more weight with some people. Beth and Casey would always be considered better designers because they had that piece of paper from an institution. And Lexi would always be looked down upon because she didn't. Which was another reason this partnership was so important to her. Because with hundreds of students like Beth and Casey graduating from programs like Parsons every year, if Lexi didn't continue to move forward, achieve, and grow, others would trample her as they passed. And the longer she waited to do it, the more competition—educated competition—she'd have.

Lexi didn't know how to do anything but design and sew. She knew a little about bookkeeping, a little about marketing, a little about customer service. But she didn't know enough about anything to make a career out of it. And sewing for other people barely paid enough to eat, let alone rent an apartment in Los Angeles.

Besides, LaCroix Designs wasn't just Lexi's sole financial income. It was her identity. It was her happiness. It was her life. And sitting here with Martina Galliano, Beth, and Casey brought out every insecurity Lexi tried so hard to hide…and deny.

Casey turned narrowed eyes on Lexi. "How long did this take you?"

"The whole dress…four months."

"And you know how much it cost?" Beth asked but didn't wait for an answer. "Thirty thousand dollars."

The look on Casey's face made Lexi laugh. She looked at Martina. The woman was watching Beth and Casey with the affection of a mother.

Her gaze shifted to Lexi without moving her head. "Still not enough for all that work."

Lexi shrugged. But she knew Martina was right.

"This partnership will change that, Lexi."

Lord, finally. It had taken her long enough to get to the point.

A waiter appeared and set salads down in front of each of

the four women. Lexi took the time to break from her intent train of thought. She glanced around the restaurant again, fatigue settling in. She thought of Jax and hoped he wasn't tired. Hoped he wasn't distracted. Didn't like thinking about something happening to him because she'd kept his mind and body too busy with sex to get the rest he needed.

She reassured herself he was fine and smiled at the thought of stopping at the gorgeous lingerie shop she'd seen on her way here when she was done with this meeting. She wanted to pick up something special for tonight. After their amazing time together this morning, she just might be ready to turn on the lights.

He was so much more than she'd ever expected.

"Pepper, miss?"

Lexi looked up at the waiter standing beside her, an expectant look on his dark face. He was a slim man in his fifties and held a pepper cracker poised over her salad.

"Oh no," Lexi said, "thank you."

He moved on to Beth sitting on Lexi's right. The young woman, Lexi guessed to be in her early twenties, enthusiastically accepted.

"I can't wait to hear what you have planned," Lexi said, waiting to pick up her fork until the waiter had peppered Casey's salad and left the table.

Martina beamed. Her bronze skin glowed from within as her smile overtook her features. She set down her own fork and clapped her hands over her plate. "Oh, I just love talking about this. Poor Beth and Casey." She sent both young women an apologetic smile. "They've had to listen to me nonstop for months."

Lexi chewed a small bite of lettuce as Beth said, "We could listen to her talk forever."

"Well, good. You girls just go ahead with your salads and I'll do what I do best—talk." Martina picked up her wine, ignoring her salad, and settled her gaze on Lexi. "Now, Beth and Casey will tell you that I rarely think or speak in a linear manner and I often veer off on tangents. But I generally get everything said that needs to be said, and there's always time for questions."

"Then I'll understand everything," Lexi said with a smile.

"Beth gave you an overview of what we're trying to achieve," Martina said, "a line of wedding dresses for the luxury wedding market."

The phrase "luxury wedding market" had only recently been coined, and she didn't know by whom. But the term had been showing up in all types of media more often over the past year.

"That would be a wedding with a budget of $100,000 or more," Lexi confirmed.

"Exactly." Martina's eyes sparkled with excitement. "Our market research shows this is currently a nine-*billion*-dollar industry and that the number of these weddings has increased every year for the last decade. But the best part is that they're forecast to *double* over the next five years."

Lexi already knew this. In fact, she knew a lot more. She knew the market value of every type of wedding and what percentage of each type went toward the gown. She knew their forecasted growths for the next decade, knew their target customers, and had about two dozen other different breakdowns on the topics.

"We're talking about gowns between fifteen and twenty-five thousand," she confirmed. "Occasionally more." When Martina nodded, Lexi asked a question there had been some debate over in business journals. "Do you think those forecasts are realistic considering the economy?"

"According to our research, for that target market, when a bride and/or the family of the bride are deciding how much to invest in that once-in-a-lifetime special day, the economy doesn't come into play."

Lexi thought of her own business and nodded. "I have to admit, I haven't seen a decline in my business despite the ongoing economic crisis. I've attributed that to my high-end clientele. It seems that people with money always have money." Lexi grinned.

"That's fantastic news for us, isn't it?"

"Very." Martina laughed. "But we're looking at this market for more than just wedding dresses. The couples or the bride's or groom's parents often host events over a two- or three-day period. We're looking at this as a multipronged sale, where one wedding dress turns into one wedding dress, half a dozen cocktail dresses, and a few honeymoon clubbing outfits or classy sundresses.

"And that's just for the bride. There's always the mother of the bride, the bridesmaids, the flower girls." Martina motioned in a circle with her wineglass. "You know how these things blossom."

"I sure do," Lexi murmured before sipping her own wine. She toyed with another piece of salad, but she was only eating to be polite. Even though she was hungry, she was too excited, too nervous to eat.

"Which brings me to the details about the designs we're looking for in this line," Martina said.

"The brides in this target market are slightly older." Lexi set down her fork and spoke with authority and confidence. This was her area of expertise. This was her business. This was the reason Martina had come to her, and she was going to make sure her strong points shone. "Between twenty-eight and thirty-two. Whether they're paying for the wedding with their fiancé or their parents are paying, they are savvy, demanding, and know what they want—over-the-top, unique, sophisticated couture—possibly haute couture—designs with a traditional flair. The most popular colors would be ivory, champagne, and light metallics, but white is a must."

Martina's lips parted. Her dark eyes widened. "Yes. Exactly." She sent an excited glance at each of her assistants. "Didn't I tell you she would be perfect?"

Lexi picked up her wine for a sip, feeling a little more confident.

"Now, I know it's early," Martina said, "but we've got an amazing marketing and sales department, and after pitching the line, we've been assured a spot in Barney's, Bloomingdale's, Lord and Taylor, Saks Fifth Avenue, Neiman Marcus, Bergdorf Goodman, and Nordstrom."

Lexi choked on her wine and covered her mouth with her napkin. Beth and Casey laughed easily.

"Oh my," Lexi finally got out.

She'd known Galliano's would have reach, but this…

"You're a big part of why they were interested," Martina said. "Part of the pitch included showing your spread in *American Bride*."

Lexi moved her hand to her chest. A mix of humility and pride swelled beneath her breastbone and stole her breath. Martina grinned, her eyes warm, as if she understood what that meant to Lexi.

"And that's only the initial tier of distribution." Martina picked up her fork and nudged the rabbit food around on her plate. "We've already nailed down several hundred high-end, specialty boutiques we'll approach once the release date comes closer."

Lexi's mind was spinning. Once she had an in with these locations, she could approach them to talk about carrying her gowns independently of Galliano's.

For the first time in two decades, Lexi could envision a future where she wasn't working fourteen-hour days. Where she got to the gym, the grocery store. Where she went to a movie, out on a date.

Her mind darted back to Jax. Her whole body warmed at the thought of sharing her excitement. And she couldn't freaking wait to tell him.

The waiter came and replaced their salad plates with entrees. The conversation shifted between personal and professional topics and flowed easily. By the time the check arrived, the four of them were laughing and chatting like long-time friends, and Lexi was 500 percent invested in this project.

Martina slid her credit card into the check folder. "Beth,

Casey, would you ladies mind bringing the car around while I tie up a few things with Lexi?"

They each hugged her before bubbling all the way out the door.

"They're wonderful," Lexi said, watching them until they turned a corner and disappeared.

"They are," Martina agreed. "Everyone at the company is really fabulous. I'm so fortunate."

"Sounds like you're also a very smart businesswoman."

"As are you, Lexi." She clasped her hands in front of her on the table and met Lexi's eyes, a serious expression filling her own. "Which is just one more reason you are my first choice."

"First choice?" The warmth simmering in Lexi's body cooled. "Are you…considering alternate designers for this venture?"

Martina sat forward. "If it was up to me, my decision would be made. I've admired your ingenuity, craftsmanship, and business savvy for years. But…" She lifted her palms toward the ceiling. "A corporation this size is really run by a board of directors. Of course, they take my input, which carries significant weight, but with others involved, nothing is ever as cut and dried as when a company is smaller and run by a sole proprietor, like LaCroix Designs."

"I see." A sick feeling nudged aside all the excitement and hope Lexi had been enjoying just moments ago. "What are you basing your decision on?"

Martina nodded. "Yes, that's what I wanted to talk to you about. It's quite informal actually, and not a true competition at all."

Competition.

Lexi's stomach soured. The word conjured images of backbreaking hours at a sewing machine, bloody fingers, burning eyes, tears, years ticking off her life span.

She'd spent many years entering competitions. They'd been a

valuable way to get noticed when she'd been nobody. Even more valuable for Lexi because she lacked a formal design education. But she'd gladly given them up long ago.

"You and the other two designers the board chose to consider are all participating in the Luxe Couture Bridal Fashion Show this year," Martina said. "Several key members from the board will be there and will put in their vote for the designer they prefer at that time."

Shock speared Lexi's stomach. "*This* year? You mean the one in *three months?*"

"I know its short notice, but Lexi…" She reached out and covered Lexi's hand with hers. "Your designs are so extraordinary, whatever you already have planned for the show will outshine your competitors. All I would suggest is that you add a few gowns that reflect the luxury wedding market we're targeting."

Add a few gowns. At the luxury-wedding-market level. In three months.

Lexi's brain blurred as if she'd run headlong into a door.

Then the ten custom gowns she'd already promised clients crowded her mind, and the next three months flashed in her head like a slide show. Takeout food cluttering her desk, fabric filling her loft until she couldn't find anything. Sleepless nights, bleeding fingers, headaches. Days without showering, haircuts, the gym. A frustrated Rubi. Irritable employees.

Jax.

Her shoulders fell two inches. Her stomach burned.

She dragged her thoughts away from all she'd be sacrificing—after she'd already spent years sacrificing—and directed it back to what she'd have to do to win. She knew all the designers signed up for the Luxe Couture show, and every one was her equal—or well beyond. Martina was either full of shit or completely clueless. Lexi couldn't believe the woman was either.

"And my competition would be…?" Lexi asked.

Martina pulled her hand back and threaded her fingers

together. "The board has decided not to share that information."

Lexi laughed. The sound surprised her. She hadn't known it was coming. And she'd never heard the edge it held now. Something inside her was alerted, like one of those cars with a backup buzzer that goes off when the bumper gets too close to an object. The alarm in her head was screaming she was too close to the edge of a cliff.

"I don't even know who I'm up against?" Lexi asked.

"The board feels that because this is such a small industry, the competition could create ill will among designers."

That was just plain stupid. "We'll know afterward. If someone's going to get pissed off, not knowing ahead of time isn't going to change that. And honestly, that's a rather immature view. Everyone showing at Luxe is at the top of their game, Martina. Consummate professionals."

"I love that about you, Lexi. I love the way you stick up for others in the industry, even when you're going head-to-head with them. That is a consummate professional."

"Are you saying the others aren't?"

Martina laughed, the sound relaxed and easy, as if this was truly no big deal. Which, in light of what a damn big deal this was to Lexi, only pissed her off.

"No, that's not what I'm saying. I love that too, the way you're so up-front. Say it like it is."

Jesus fucking Christ. Lexi's whole future had just plummeted to hell. Her stomach ached like she had a rock lodged at the very bottom. She picked up her wine and took a long swallow to loosen her tight throat.

She'd been too invested. She'd wanted it too much. She hadn't held anything back and gotten blindsided. Martina continued to chatter about the competition as they stood and walked toward the front door.

"The board will be looking for all the same things they do in normal competitions—things like creativity, ingenuity, craftsmanship, fit to the target market." She grinned over her shoulder. "Everything at which you excel."

Lexi forced a smile, but her mood had taken a severe dive. A spear of anger sliced deep in her heart to ease the pain of fear and loss. Lexi fought to keep a tight cover on it.

She exited the restaurant, squinting into the sun. Dazed from her fall off cloud nine.

"I'll contact you with all the partnership information," Martina said. She stopped when she reached the sidewalk and said, "Oh, Lexi, there is one more thing I wanted to mention."

She took another hit to the gut. Martina's tone of voice and the way she'd left whatever this was until last was not a good sign.

"The board did a full background on all the candidates, just like we do on all our employees."

Lexi's jaw loosened, and she barely kept her mouth from falling open. An icy fist hit her chest, and the chill spread outward. All the shadows from her past pinged through her mind. Her white-trash roots, her dysfunctional family, her loser boyfriends…

"And it came to their attention that you frequent a few…racy…clubs in Los Angeles," Martina went on, stunning Lexi with an unexpected left cross, "with a friend, a Rubi Russo."

A protective instinct surged forward and made that spear of anger burn white-hot. Lexi crossed her arms and clenched her teeth. "That kind of intrusion into my life is completely unacceptable."

Yet even as she said it, fear burned across her chest. Fear of losing this opportunity. Even while she wondered if she still wanted it.

"Lexi." Martina softened her voice, but her gaze remained steady. "I know you are careful about your reputation. You have a very specific clientele, one that often puts you in the spotlight. That is exactly the same situation we're looking at creating here and one of the big reasons you're such a promising candidate for this line.

"We're talking about selling dresses to tycoon's daughters. People who can be choosy about who they do business with and why. Look at it from Galliano's point of view. It's taken us decades to build our reputation in the fashion industry. When we attach our name to yours and your name is somehow tainted, we could have millions of dollars' worth of dresses hanging on racks that no one will touch because of one visit to the wrong club, one meet-up with the wrong people. Our board is concerned for the future of the line as well as the reputation of Galliano's.

"Because the reality is, Lexi, billionaires don't want to buy their daughters' wedding dresses from a designer who frequents sex clubs."

Lexi's chest burned with humiliation. Fury. Insult.

Yet Lexi agreed with her theory. Lexi lived her theory. This wasn't an issue. It wasn't like she and Rubi frequented Stilettos. It had been a one-time visit. And Lexi wouldn't be doing anything but eating, drinking, sleeping, and breathing wedding dresses if she took this challenge on.

But then there was Jax.

Her heart clenched. And dropped.

Stupid. It wasn't like anything was going to come of their rendezvous anyway.

She'd just thought…maybe…

Lexi shook the idea from her head. Her mouth curved in a wry, lopsided smile, but she felt no humor. No happiness. Not even hope. That had to be a bad sign.

"Rubi is a billionaire's daughter," Lexi said. "But I get your point, Martina."

Her expression softened in sympathy. "I know this may seem extreme. I'm sorry. Please don't think I'm telling you how to live your life. Consider it advice, sweetheart. You've worked so hard, risen so far above the competition.

"Let me just say that I've been in this business a long time, and I've seen how jealous, vindictive, and cutthroat other designers can be to nudge someone out of a spot they want. I'd hate to see that happen to you." Martina wrapped her warm fingers around Lexi's forearm. "You're truly exceptional, Lexi. A diamond all buffed and ready for a pedestal and a spotlight. I want to see you grab this opportunity."

Beth and Casey pulled up at the curb in a shiny gold Jaguar.

Lexi took Martina's hand in both of hers. "Thank you for the opportunity, Martina, and for lunch, of course."

Martina gave Lexi's hand a squeeze, then leaned in to hug her, with a whispered, "Talk soon."

She slid into the front seat of the Jaguar, and all three women waved to Lexi as they pulled away.

She stood there for a long time, staring at traffic and fighting the insane urge to cry. How could she have been hoisted so high only to be dropped without a net?

She pulled her phone from her purse and found her hands shaking. A text from Jax waited.

JAX: How did it go?

"Shit," she muttered. How sweet was that?

Damn this development. If this meeting had gone as expected, she could have taken the next step with Jax. Turning on lights. Sharing names. Making plans for their return to LA.

Now, she not only had to worry about how his image could possibly affect her, but about whatever secrets he held in his past along with her own. She had to worry about him turning into a Steven if they started a relationship she discovered she needed to get out of.

Those little sparks of "maybe" flitting through her head since she'd left his room this morning had just been completely doused. And she couldn't tell which hurt worse—the loss of a potential relationship with Jax or the change in this opportunity.

Lexi dialed Rubi's number, found a seat on a concrete bench, becoming invisible among the crowds, and pulled on her sunglasses to hide the escaping tears.

ELEVEN

Jax grimaced as he pulled at the chain-mail headpiece with both hands. The Friesian stallion beneath him snorted and pranced sideways. "Who the hell," he muttered to no one—at least he hoped no one was watching him try to pry his face out of this getup, "last wore this thing?"

Hoofbeats approached. Jax's horse veered right. He added pressure with his calf to keep the horse in place as he twisted his head, his fingers prying beneath the edges of the contraption. Something caught on his chin.

"Little trouble there, dude?" There was restrained laughter in Tyler Manning's voice. Jax could imagine the look on the actor's face—the co-star of the film playing opposite Brad Pitt at only twenty-four.

"Fucking A." He laughed out the words, making a production of yanking at the helmet, complete with sound effects and facial expressions.

Ty started laughing and sounded like he might double himself over any minute. The only thing that kept Jax from laughing his own ass right off the horse was the way the damn helmet was starting to cut into his skin. This was one of those hilarious moments that could only happen in this job.

Jax slumped in the saddle and held his arms out. "Little help here, partner?" But Ty sounded like he could barely breathe let alone help. Jax was frying in his armor as he muttered, "You worthless piece of shit."

He grabbed the helmet again, twisted it while turning his head, contorting his face, and swearing up a storm. The stallion didn't like Jax's jerky movements or Ty's laughter or the laughter now coming from other sources, and the animal's frustrated prancing circles weren't helping Jax. But he finally freed his head.

"Christ." He glanced down at the helmet, turning it over, looking inside, trying to figure out why the hell it stuck. "It tried to eat me alive. Did you see that? I barely escaped with my eyeballs."

Ty's laughter had the kid wheezing. When he listed sideways in his saddle, Jax tossed the defective helmet to the ground and looked up, grinning. Ty was nearly perpendicular to the horse, a white Andalusian as calm as Jax's Friesian was strung out.

And he had his iPhone in his hand. Pointed at Jax.

"You little fucker," Jax said around a laugh. "You better not have recorded that."

"Are you kidding?" he said, panting for air, leaning on the saddle to keep himself up. "That's going in the funniest-moments archive. When I'm roasted in twenty years for some life-achievement award, you'll be there, buddy."

"Not if you don't live that long." Jax grabbed his reins. He only had to release the pressure of his legs to have his horse lunging forward. He flew past Ty and snapped the phone from his hand, then rode off. He whooped and laughed over his shoulder. "That's what happens when you snooze, pretty boy."

Ty yelled something Jax didn't hear and came after him. They were equally talented riders, both on horseback since they were kids.

"If you erase that," Ty yelled when he grew close, "I'm going to skewer you in the next scene."

"Try, kid," Jax called back. "It'll give me an excuse to knock your ass off that horse."

As Jax and Ty neared the bay at the north end of the park, they slowed, both more interested in riding than playing keep-away with the phone. Jax pulled his horse to a stop where the grass gave way to the sand.

"Dude," Ty said, pulling up beside him, "these are some amazing ponies." He leaned over and swiped the phone from Jax's hand. "Relax, I won't do anything with it. I just want it for me." He started laughing again, crossing an arm over his belly. "Shit, no ab workout for me today. That was so fucking funny."

Sweat dripped down Jax's face, stung his eyes. This would be a fun week. "God, what I'd give for a swim right now."

"What I'd give for a break. Or some lunch." He turned a scowl on Jax. "You owe me dinner and drinks some night this week, dude. Your plane didn't get in late this morning. Now I'm starving because you stalled everything and they're running us hard. Hope she was at least worth it."

"You checked my *plane*?" Shit. He hated getting caught in lies. "Who are you? My mother?" Though his mother would never have even cared, let alone thought to check on his plane.

"What the hell else did I have to do?" Ty started tapping the face of his phone with his thumb.

"What are you doing?" Jax asked, suspicious.

"Just putting it out on Facebook." Before Jax could react, Ty put up a hand and leaned away as if he were protecting himself from an attack. "Kidding. I'm texting it to you. You can forward it to your girl. She'll pee herself laughing. Then maybe you'll get that text you're waiting on."

"What girl? And what text?"

Ty slid Jax a knowing look and tucked his phone into a space between his armor and his chest. "The one you've been checking your phone for every fucking fifteen minutes, dude. I'm not blind…or stupid. There's very little short of death and one killer-hot chick that can make you late."

Jax smirked and returned his gaze straight ahead. "The stupid part's debatable."

"Just tell me it's not the bitch who fucked you out of the Bond film—literally," Ty said, "or I really am going to skewer you in the next scene."

Irritation crawled up Jax's spine and gripped his chest like twin fists. "I've been screwed over by so many women in so many different ways, why is everyone so damn set on remembering that particular occasion?" He turned narrowed eyes on Ty. "And how did you find out?"

"I worked with Pine on *Into Darkness*. Pine heard it from Hardy. Hardy heard it from Bale. Bale heard it from—"

"Never-fucking-mind." Jax turned away. One of his guys had worked with all of those actors recently. Word spread so damn fast about the stupidest shit in this industry. Who the fuck cared about Jax's sex life? Since he'd left acting and now made one percent of what he used to, who the hell cared what contract he gained or lost? Or why? "You all need to get a damn life. And no, it's not her."

It was one thirty p.m. Lexi was probably still in that important lunch. That was what he kept telling himself, because he was not going to get crazy over her not texting him back when he'd sent her a message asking how the meeting went. Though that didn't account for her not texting about the jacket. He'd left it at the desk on his way out with a request for them to send it to her room. Of course he only had her first name, but he knew Spencer's staff, and he knew it would have reached her before she'd gone to lunch.

But he wasn't going to let that little fear in the back of his mind take over—the one that whispered she wouldn't be at the hotel when he got back. Or that she didn't want to hook up tonight.

He was staying positive. He hoped the meeting was going so well she'd forgotten all about him. Okay, *almost* all about him. He was anxious to hear the details. Hoped he could keep himself from attacking her until they talked for a little while, because he wanted her more now than he had this morning.

When he and Ty got back to the set, the crew still wasn't ready to shoot, and they steered the horses into the shade of some pine trees to wait. Someone from costume brought Jax another helmet. Someone else brought them each two bottles of ice-cold water.

Jax leaned on the metal helmet propped on the pommel of his saddle and took another deep drink from his water bottle, then poured the rest over his head and face. The real relief came from the way it trickled down his neck and into the metal armor covering his body.

"So, who is she?" Ty asked.

"Why don't you ask Pine or Hardy or Bale or someone?"

"Very fucking funny."

"I don't need any more rumors floating around."

Ty slapped a hand to his chest. "I didn't start or spread the rumors, dude. Have you ever heard of me saying anything about anyone?" He paused only a millisecond before adding, "'Cause if you have, it's a lie."

His flicker of uncertainty made Jax laugh. Ty was one of those tight-lipped guys, but Jax knew people could put words in a person's mouth in this industry. "I don't really know. I just met her."

"Just?" Ty asked. "How *just?*"

"We started talking last night. But I just...you know, *met her* met her, in the flesh"—soft, warm, juicy flesh—"this morning."

When he put it into words, it sounded ridiculously cheap. Lewd. Meaningless. So why didn't it feel like any of those things? Jax couldn't figure out what made it different. Or if it was just him making shit up in his head.

"Okay, wait." The smile was back in Ty's voice, but it was laced with disbelief. "You're telling me that you just met this girl this morning and she's already got you pussy whipped?" His laugh was low and hot. "Dude, she's got to be one awesome fu—"

"Whoa, kid." Jax restrained the snap of anger, but clear irritation filled his voice. "You're over the line. Back the hell up."

Ty's grin turned speculative, cunning. He adjusted his seat, leaned forward, and pressed his palms to the pommel of the saddle. "You're awfully defensive about a girl you *just* met."

Jax didn't answer. He was replaying everything in his mind. He'd known in the light of day everything he'd thought had been intriguing and sensual at the time would seem odd when he looked back on it. Having Ty pushing his mind in that direction when he was already feeling insecure about the whole damn thing wasn't helping Jax's anxiety.

"All right. What's going on?" Ty straightened in the saddle and pulled one foot from a stirrup to fold his ankle over the Andalusian's withers.

"What do you mean?"

"Dude, I've known you six years. I've seen you go through…I don't even know how many women. You've never acted like this. You've never held back on me. It's like you're…I don't know…embarrassed of her…or something."

"I'm not embarrassed of her. That's stupid." He pushed up in his stirrups to relieve his ass and yelled to the lead cameraman, "Carl, are we doing this or not?"

"Hold your dick on," Carl muttered.

"Is she married?" Ty asked, his voice rising in disbelief. When Jax shot him a scowl, Ty lifted his hand in a helpless gesture as he guessed again. "One of your friends' girls?"

"Ty."

"I'm telling you, dude, you may as well just tell me, because you're stuck with me for the next five, six days, and you know how relentless I can be."

Unfortunately, Jax did. It was the reason the kid was so successful at such a young age.

Jax tilted his head back and doused himself with his other water bottle. He shook his head like a dog, spraying Ty, who muttered profanities at him.

"This is the thanks I get for teaching you everything you know," Jax said, wiping his face.

When he dropped his hand, Ty was waiting, elbow on the saddle, chin on his palm, dark blue eyes intensely focused on Jax's face, mouth a serious line. Silently sending the message that he would wait Jax out and make his week hell on earth if he didn't give Ty what he wanted.

The kid reminded Jax a lot of Wes with his dark blond good

looks, though Ty was taller, leaner, and prettier without the scars Wes had picked up over the years. But Ty had the same maturity as Wes, one they'd both grasped in their very early twenties and one that most young men didn't grab hold of until much later. One Jax certainly didn't get a grasp on until about three years ago himself.

"That video could hit Facebook at any time," Ty said.

"You bastard."

"You taught me everything I know."

Jax didn't take Ty's threat seriously, didn't even give a shit if the video was on the Internet. He felt like a far bigger idiot saying, "She's sweet, okay?"

His horse grew restless again, stepping forward, backward, forward. He called to a guy by the cooler, held up two fingers, and got two more ice-cold bottles of water tossed to him. He passed one on to Ty.

"I don't know who she is." Jax poured half the other bottle of water over the stallion's neck, rubbing it into his coat to keep himself busy while he talked. "She was on my flight here, texted me anonymously at the airport. We texted for like an hour. She was funny and sexy. The conversation got hot, suggestive, but she wouldn't come sit with me."

A wary, suspicious sound came from Ty's throat.

"I know, right?" Jax turned to pour the rest of the bottle on the horse's hindquarters. "Anyway, I decided to take a chance, invited her to my room. She accepted at the last minute, when I was on my way out."

"That takes some balls. Guess you lucked out. Who knows what you could have gotten walking into your room." Ty shivered dramatically. "But don't be surprised if *Entertainment Tonight* calls asking for an exclusive on your new YouTube sex video."

Jax's skin chilled as if he'd poured a bottle of water over his own head. He hadn't thought of that. "She didn't seem to know who I was. And I lucked out all right. God, she's…" His whole body lit up. "It's crazy how much I like her."

Ty said nothing.

Jax glanced at him. "What?"

"Did she drug your drink?"

Jax sighed. "What does that mean?"

"Do you *like* getting fucked over, Chamberlin? Do you seriously think this chick *doesn't* know who you are?"

"Yeah, I do. I'm not you, kid."

"No, asshole, you're way bigger than me."

"Was," Jax said. "You'll learn once you're out of the spotlight, they forget you fast."

Ty shook his head, his expression filled with disgust. He picked up his reins, twisted to sit right in his saddle, and cantered through the trees back toward the filming perimeter.

"Tyler!" Russ Matthers's yell never reached the kid. He was long gone. The director, who was also acting as stunt coordinator, called to Jax, "Where is he going?"

Jax grinned, shrugged. "Not my day to watch him."

"I knew having the two of you together on the set would be like herding cats."

"It wasn't my fault, Dad." Jax lifted his hands in innocence. For as much as Jax had worked with the man over the years and as good as the man had been to him, Russ had probably been more of a dad to Jax than his own father—who'd been too busy making movies and having affairs around the world to participate in his family. "I'm right where I'm supposed to be."

Russ had always been a phone call away. He'd given Jax some of the best advice of his life. Russ's mention had gotten Jax some of the biggest roles of his career. He'd been at every one of Jax's award events, even if none of Russ's own films had been nominated. Russ had been to the emergency room with Jax at least half a dozen times. Not one member of his family had ever been around to take Jax to the hospital. Even as a kid, the nanny had been the one to take him.

"Son," Russ played along with the role, wiping sweat from

his face with his forearm. "Go get your brother. I've got enough trouble with these damn cameras."

"He's such a pain in the ass," Jax called as he turned the direction Ty had gone. "Why'd you and Mom have him when you already had perfection in me?"

Russ's laughter followed Jax as he cantered into the trees. It didn't take Jax long to find Ty. He just followed the high-pitched female squeals. Ty had ridden over to the fence line and was off his horse, signing autographs. Jax pulled up, still within the trees. He didn't need to get any closer to that screeching than necessary.

Pulling his cell from the saddle, Jax checked for a text from Lexi first—nothing—then texted Ty.

> JAX: Your fifteen minutes of fame are over, kid. Grab the phone numbers you really want and get your ass back to the set or Dad's going to ground you.

Jax looked up from his phone, wondering why Lexi hadn't texted him back. Then wondered why he cared. He'd gotten a killer blowjob out of the deal. She was the one shortchanged if she wouldn't see him again.

But uncharacteristic doubts slid in. Had he been a disappointment? Not what she'd expected? Not rough enough? Not crude enough? Should he just have fucked her? Or maybe she'd been expecting more romance. Something slower, sweeter.

His phone chimed.

> TY: Come out here. See if anyone remembers you.

> JAX: Tainted cross section of the population. You've already told them I'm here. I don't need an ego boost.

> TY: I haven't. I'll prove it. Then you come out here and prove to yourself that chick is lying about not knowing who you are.

"I have a friend with me today," Ty yelled to the crowd, "who I think will make the ladies happy."

The women erupted in screams and cheers again. Despite

117

Jax's denial about the need for an ego boost, warmth and excitement spurted into his chest the way it used to at the sound of applause. That love of recognition sure as hell died hard. Especially since he'd lived with it his entire life—acting before he could walk. Theater until his late teens, when he'd transitioned to film. Just like Ty.

"Fucking idiot," Jax muttered.

"But he thinks," Ty yelled over the crowd, and they quieted to hear him, "I've told you who he is. So if anyone knows who's here with me today, I want you to yell out his name."

The names of a few of Ty's costars floated out of the audience, but not Jax's.

"Come on, ladies. I'm upping the ante. I will *kiss* any woman"—screams of excitement interrupted Ty—"on the mouth, *with tongue*"—more screaming, cheering, women jumping up and down— "who can tell me who's hiding in those trees over there."

When no one guessed correctly, he offered to have dinner with the woman who gave the right answer. When he had dozens, maybe hundreds, of women frothing at the mouth, Ty offered to *sleep* with the woman who knew.

"For God's sake." Jax rubbed sweat off his face and texted Ty.

JAX: You made your point. Get your ass back to the set now.

"Dude!" Ty yelled toward the trees. "Your fans await."

Jax sighed, frustrated as his tired legs tried to control the antsy Friesian. "Guess it's time for the kid to learn just how fast those fans forget you once you've left the box office," he said to the stallion. "Let's do this, buddy."

Jax released the pressure of his legs on the horse's sides, easing him into a canter toward the fence line.

His last big film had been over three years ago, and Jax steeled himself to the disappointment of being unrecognized. He told himself he was simply acting. Just running a scene.

When he broke the tree line, riding into the open, the sun blinded him. Before his eyes adjusted, his name filled the air in a chorus of shrill screams.

"Oh my God, it's *Bentley Chamberlin*! Bentley! Over here, Bentley!"

The name took him off guard. Jax hadn't heard anyone scream Bentley in so long, he experienced a complete disconnect of past and present, reality and memory.

By the time he reached Ty, the true movie star was back up on his horse and local cops were physically holding fences in place against the surging crowd.

The commotion freaked Jax's horse. The stallion pranced in circles, rearing. Great drama for the fans, might make for some stellar photographs too, even kept a steady adrenaline drip to Jax's blood, but it also wore him the hell out. This horse was higher strung than a wannabe starlet at the Academy Awards.

"I love you, Bentley," came from women in the crowd.

"We miss you," shrieked someone from a different direction.

"When are you making another movie?" another woman screamed.

Ty turned his horse in a circle, waving to the crowd. "Time to get back to work."

He and Jax cantered along the fence line together to continued, but fading, screams.

Ty's shit-eating grin didn't sit right with Jax. "Still think she doesn't know you, Chamberlin?"

He didn't answer. He didn't know what to think anymore. Everything he thought he'd come to believe over the last twelve hours was tangled in his head.

They slowed to a trot as they neared the edges of the filming area.

"I'm not telling you not to see her, bro," Ty said. "And she may very well be as sweet as you think. But we both know how these women operate, and you've taken enough hits for the team.

I'd like you to see what's coming for a change."

"Ty," Russ yelled. "What did I tell you about sneaking out to meet your girlfriends? You're looking at the ceiling of your room the rest of the night, boy."

"Aw, Dad…" Ty slumped his shoulders in a perfect imitation of a scolded child and walked his horse forward. "I didn't plan it. She was just…there. I didn't even kiss her."

The rest of their exchange dimmed as Jax's mind drifted to Lexi. To everything that had passed between them. But he couldn't make any solid truth out of anything.

And even if she was still at the hotel, even if she would see him again tonight, Jax doubted anything would help him see what was coming with this woman. She seemed to prefer keeping him in the dark.

TWELVE

Jax stared out the side window of the Lincoln from the backseat on his return to Spencer's. The driver was probably in his midseventies, courteous and quiet. Which worked great for Jax. Because he needed to think.

He looked down at his phone and read the message Lexi had finally sent around five p.m.

> LEXI: Sorry it took me so long to answer. The meeting went long—you know how women can talk—I went shopping after, picked up a surprise for you and then fell asleep when I should have been working. Thank you for leaving your jacket. I napped in it—naked of course. Can't stop thinking about you. Can't wait to hear about your exciting day. I'll be waiting.

At the end of the message, she gave him her cell number, one he could actually see on his phone, and said she'd removed the secretive application that had hidden it from view.

"Shit," he whispered and dropped his head back against the seat.

There were half a dozen sweet comments in that one message. And now every damn one was tainted by the revelation of just how instantly recognizable he still was. He had to either confront the issue head-on or drop it and let things play out, and he couldn't decide which.

He hadn't told Ty about the message. Had been looking for an opportunity to get Russ alone, but when he'd found himself standing at the cooler with the man, chatting about the loss of the Bond contract, Jax hadn't been able to bring Lexi up.

He pocketed his phone and looked out the window again. The sun was setting. Jax was exhausted. His muscles ached. His ass was killing him. Sex would be an interesting proposition, though

121

he'd make it work if…

If what?

"This is ridiculous."

He rested his elbow on the edge of the window and his forehead in his hand. He made small circles on his temples. Twenty-four hours ago, he hadn't even been interested in fucking anyone. Twelve hours ago, he was perfectly fine with a simple one-night stand. Now he was considering *not* sleeping with a woman who'd kept him hard all day because of the possibility she knew who he was?

"I'm insane."

He pressed his fingers to his eyes. He was just tired. Stressed. Still reeling over what Veronica had done. Hell, hard to put it behind him when everyone kept bringing it up. What difference did it make if Lexi wanted something from him, anyway? She was great. It wouldn't kill him to introduce her to someone or help her out in some other way.

"Fuck." The thought made his stomach knot.

Yeah, actually, it would. What would kill him was knowing she'd come on to him with the favor in mind, not because she'd been attracted to *him*. He was sick of being used. Worse, of being fooled into being used.

The car slowed, and Jax decided he'd let things play out. Take everything one step at a time.

He tipped the driver and dragged his filthy, sweaty self through the pristine, marbled lobby. He felt like a snail leaving a trail and darted self-conscious glances toward the sunken lounge and dimly lit bar. A number of beautiful women dressed the tables, a few of those blonde. But of course he had no way of knowing if any were Lexi.

He vowed to take the stairs if anyone else got on the elevator with him. No use in subjecting others to this sight or smell—but the car was empty, and Jax stepped in. He glanced at his reflection on the mirrored wall, winced at the grime, the way his hair stuck out all over, the cut on his forehead, then turned and hit number seven.

At his room, he slipped his key card into the door, turned the handle, then paused. This was where Lexi had stood a little less than twelve hours before. She'd been nervous, he'd been sure of it at the time. Now he wondered if he'd been projecting his nerves onto her. Or if she'd been reading him and playing off those nerves to see if he'd respond to them.

"I'm a lunatic." Jax pushed open the door, forcing his mind away from what he'd done to Lexi right there in the hall that morning. He flipped on the light and tossed his key card on the side table while glancing at the sofa, commanding his mind not to remember what Lexi had done to him right there.

Which, of course, didn't work. He saw her shadow lower to her knees. Saw her head between his legs. Blood roared that direction.

He growled, pried his gaze away from the sofa, and turned toward the bedroom while stripping off his T-shirt. Pulling it over his head, he sighed, anticipating the feel of the shower. He tossed his shirt on the bed but was already dragging clean, folded clothes from his freshly washed duffle, which the staff had set on the dresser.

Something crinkled when his shirt landed.

Jax turned and lifted his shirt. A paper bag indented the comforter. A handwritten note on the front in ink said, *In case you didn't get time to eat. ~ Lex*

She must have had the staff deliver it, the same way he'd had them deliver his jacket. A painful, tingling burn erupted high in his chest, as if he'd been stung by bees, and the emotion that followed tightened his throat. He blinked quickly to clear his eyes, reached down, and dumped the contents of the bag on the white down comforter.

An apple, a protein bar, cashews, a small plastic container of fresh blueberries, and a four-piece box of Godiva chocolates.

Warmth spread through his body as he stood and stared at the food. He huffed a pathetic laugh and murmured, "This is what it feels like?"

Or what it *would* feel like if it were real. To have a woman think of him during the day. Anticipate his needs and fill them before he even realized they would be needs. This was what it would feel like to know he mattered to a woman. Really mattered.

Jax ate the cashews while the shower water warmed and he undressed. Took the blueberries into the enclosure with him and devoured them while the hot water pounded his muscles. He tossed the carton into the sink across the room and dropped his head back under the spray. With the edge of his hunger sated, relief streaming through his muscles, and a beautiful woman waiting for him, a deep sense of…rightness filled Jax. A sense of comfort. A sense of peace. A sense of… He opened his eyes. Water droplets dripped off his lashes.

Happiness. Deep happiness.

"Don't set yourself up, dumbshit."

If nothing else, Lexi had shown him what he was striving for. Now, at least, he knew what it looked like—metaphorically speaking. Knew what it felt like—or could feel like.

He dried off and pulled on clean underwear and jeans. Drying his hair with one hand, Jax sat on the bed and picked up his phone. He tapped Lexi's name, and options came up. Instead of texting her, he hit the button to dial and held the phone up to his ear.

On the third ring, the phone picked up, and a soft, sleepy, female voice said, "Hello?"

Jax opened his mouth to speak and found his throat closed.

"Hello?" Lexi said again, more alert this time. More query in her voice.

"Hey," Jax finally got out, then swallowed and shook his head at himself. "It's Jax."

"Hi…" She drew out the word, her voice lifting with pleasure and surprise. "I'm sorry. I wasn't expecting to hear your voice. What a nice surprise. I…" She laughed softly. "Fell asleep again. I haven't slept this much in months. Sexual satisfaction seems to do a lot for me."

Jax couldn't keep the smile off his face.

She let out a long, languid sigh and moaned softly. Jax pictured her—as much of her as he could picture—rolling around on a bed just like the one Jax sat on, in nothing but his leather jacket, stretching the sleep from her gorgeous body.

"That's a nice visual. Still in my jacket?" he asked.

"Yes. God, it smells so good. Like you and leather."

A hot streak of lust speared his belly and stung his spine. Jax clenched his teeth to hold in a moan and dropped his head back to stare at the ceiling. If he saw her now, there would be no talking. His mouth would be way too busy tasting her body. He licked his lips, and the mint of toothpaste made him think of the snacks he'd eaten before he'd brushed his teeth.

"Thanks for the food. I was starving when I got back. It was perfect."

"I'm glad. Did you just get in?"

"About twenty minutes ago. Just out of the shower." He had to force himself to say, "Are you hungry? Do you want to get something to eat?" when he really wanted to order her to his room.

"I'm starving." The tone behind those words said exactly what she was starving for, and Jax's already half-hard cock swelled against his jeans. "But what I'm hungry for can only be found on the other end of this phone."

"Lex." He groaned her name. "You're too good to be true."

"No," she said, her tone deflating. "Unfortunately, I'm not. But it's nice to have the opportunity to show my better side."

He didn't know what that meant, but he didn't want to talk about it over the phone anymore. And he didn't want to argue to get her here. He wanted to look into her eyes, wanted to see her smile, wanted to watch pleasure wash over her face. But even though they'd already been so very intimate, not seeing each other kept a personal distance. There was something unique and connecting about a person's face. No two people looked exactly alike, after all. And expressions told a lot about what was happening on the inside, in the private spaces.

Jax didn't know if that was why she didn't want him to see her, or if she thought he'd recognize her, or if she had some kind of deformity or scar she didn't want to show. But he knew that if she wasn't going to change her mind about seeing him in LA, he didn't need her face haunting him. Especially given these strange, intense feelings he'd developed for her.

He'd get her here, then decide if he should try to chip away at the last barrier between them or not.

"The door's unlocked, bathroom light is the only one on, door is open halfway. Don't even think about negotiating," he said before she could speak. "This morning was...amazing. Exciting, hot, mind-blowing, but I'd like to at least be able to see shadows of your gorgeous body."

He pressed his lips together, closed his eyes, and waited.

Lexi hesitated. "Okay. I'll be right up."

She disconnected, and Jax lowered the phone, staring at the floor. *Okay?* Christ, he didn't know what to expect from this woman anymore. He set his phone on the dresser and moved around the suite, turning off lights, opening the door a crack. The curtains were open, but the sheers were closed, filtering the city lights. Jax pulled out a chair from the dining room table and sat. He rested his elbows on his thighs, threaded his fingers, and rubbed them over his mouth as he stared at the door and waited.

***

Lexi tossed the phone on the bed and rolled to her feet, sliding off Jax's jacket at the same time. She couldn't keep the smile from her face or the excitement from sweeping through her. When she turned to toss the jacket behind her, the sketch pad and the dozens of images she'd been drawing nonstop all day came into view.

She knew Jax had been the key to unlock the door on her

creativity and had it flowing so freely she couldn't sketch ideas fast enough. Or, rather, sex with Jax. The fact that the images were all of erotic designs and sexy lingerie had to be some mental block she'd put up against the new urgency to design those bridal gowns for the Luxe Bridal Show.

She forced the whole sordid thought from her mind, unwilling to let that sweeping disappointment ruin her night with Jax.

Lexi tossed down the jacket, pulled on the lace shelf bra and matching string bikini she'd bought—all in deep crimson. She'd realized how stupid it was to buy something so pretty when Jax wouldn't get to see much of it. But he'd get the effect, and that was the important part, along with the way it made her feel beautiful and sexy and made her want to do erotic things to Jax. Just dressing and thinking of him touching her hiked her heart rate.

Her sex was pounding by the time she slid her feet into heels and slipped her arms back into his jacket. She grabbed the massage oil and slid it into the jacket pocket. With her hair in a hasty bun, she grabbed her key card and her phone. The jacket was twice her size, but the short length hit high on her thighs, barely covering her butt cheeks. She found herself slouching from her walk to and from the elevator in case she ran into anyone in the hallway.

Then she was outside Jax's door. A whip of panic snapped through her, followed by a stark, surrealistic moment of *What the hell am I doing? This isn't me.*

But it was. It was a part of her she loved but had rarely been able to express. Never found a man who'd made her feel the desire to express it the way Jax did.

She closed her eyes, took a deep breath, and unzipped the jacket. Straightening to her full height, Lexi shook out her shoulders and arms to relax. The jacket fell open, exposing her cleavage, belly button, and sweet spot.

She tapped lightly on Jax's door and pushed it back. Not much more light filled the space than it had that morning, and Lexi relaxed a little. She moved slowly into the room tonight. Much slower than this morning. She knew Jax was watching, and she let the hallway light outline her silhouette so he knew just how little she was wearing.

By the time she closed the door, her heart hammered in her chest. Her lungs squeezed too tight for her to gather enough air, and her head went light. Lexi leaned back against the door to get her balance and her bearings. The room was so silent she could have believed she was alone.

"Tell me"—Jax's voice came from somewhere deep in the room, somewhere behind the sofa. It was rough, strained—"you have something on besides my jacket, Lex."

Lexi smiled. Excitement surged in her chest, and she closed her eyes. "Why?"

A sound came from his throat. Something needy, lusty. Pained.

She pushed herself two steps forward, out of the darkness of the short hallway leading into the suite's living room. With one hand pressed to the wall, she used the other to ease aside one edge of his jacket, giving him a better peek. "Would it make you feel better to know I have on a bra and panties? Ones I bought today, while I was thinking of you?"

From where she stood, she could make out his shadow. He was sitting in a chair, leaning forward, arms resting on his knees. He'd left the curtains open, and the lights of the city turned the sheers a soft blush.

"You've..." he started, his voice thick, "...modeled."

The excitement twisted on her and pinched. Lexi's past included many men who she'd come to learn had been with her for the sole purpose of telling buddies they were sleeping with a model. She'd never wanted or enjoyed the superficial lifestyle, but it had paid well. A handful of years modeling on the side had given Lexi enough cash to launch Lexi LaCroix Designs.

"I have," she admitted. "A long time ago. How could you tell?"

"The way you move, the way you stand."

Lexi swallowed and asked him what she'd asked in a different way at the airport. "Have you modeled?"

He laughed. The sound slid over her like a touch, and need rose to the surface. "You didn't get a good look at me, did you? I'm thinking your lights-off idea is a good one. I…dated a few models."

She echoed his laugh. "Models don't date unattractive men, Jax. And I have fifteen-fifteen vision. Rest assured, your looks may have been an initial draw, but they aren't the reason I'm in your room dressed in next to nothing, ready to do anything you want until my plane leaves in the morning."

Jax's breath left his chest in a heavy whoosh, followed by silence. Lexi could swear the air in the room grew heavy. Thick. Tight. And not in a good way.

The shadow of Jax's head lowered, and a muffled curse filtered through the room.

Lexi's stomach pinched. She stepped forward with an urge to fix—mend whatever tear she'd just made between them.

"Then why?" His frustrated question stopped her. The hurt anger in his voice chilled all the heat in her belly.

He stood and came toward her. Lexi fell back a step. As soon as he rounded the arm of the sofa, the distant light from the bathroom whispered over him. He was shirtless, jeans unfastened and hanging low on his hips. His hair lay flat, pulled off his face, probably wet from the shower. The dim light hit on his straight nose, angled jaw, broad forehead. The hell he wasn't model quality.

And that body… God, he was fucking *built*. The shadows hinted at ridges of muscle from his shoulders to his belly, some of which she'd already felt, but seeing it… The hunger she'd suffered all day tried to break through her fear.

"Why?" he asked again, standing close enough to touch. "Why are you here, dressed in next to nothing, ready to do anything I want until your plane leaves in the morning, Lexi?"

Her stomach clenched. But his tone wasn't angry as she'd thought. He was hurt. Suspicious. Jaded.

Lexi tried to search his expression but couldn't see any more than his flexing jaw. She swallowed back regret and reached up. Ran her thumb over the rigid, pulsating surface. "What happened today? You didn't question me this morning."

"I was reminded that you and I seem to have a similar problem—having people want us for reasons other than what they give up front."

Lexi remembered his friend's words at the airport. *"It's not a good time for him."* Yet she'd started a flirtation, accepted an invitation, then tossed in her own stupid mind games on the guy. Guilt tainted her excitement. She was always trying to please everyone else, always trying to anticipate what a client would want, need, love, and give it to her. But she hadn't done that here. She'd only been thinking about what she wanted, not how it might affect him.

"I'm sorry. That's…never a good feeling. But that is the beauty of anonymity, right? People can't want something they don't know you have."

He didn't immediately respond, then asked, "What happened at your meeting?"

"I'd really rather not talk about it, but since I can tell it's important to you…" She shifted on her feet, trying to figure out what she wanted to say. "It…didn't go as smoothly as I'd hoped." She let out a breath, all the frustration and worry and disappointment flooding back in. "I was under the impression I was specifically chosen for this partnership. But I found out at lunch, while the designer really wants me to join her, she has a board of directors who are interested in a couple of other top designers. They've decided to turn this into a competition, which doesn't please me at all. Not because I can't win, because I know I can—"

She stopped suddenly, realizing how conceited that sounded. "I mean…I'm not saying that because I'm full of myself. I know because I've participated in so many to get where I am, that I know how they work, I know the ins and outs. I know what judges like to see, how they score, how to present pieces in a unique way. I know how to win competitions the way some people know how to take tests.

"Anyway, I'm already operating at my limit. I don't have the bandwidth to stretch myself even thinner." She could feel the stress rising again. Just talking about it made a strap of steel tighten around her chest, forcing pressure to her head. "But if I don't take this opportunity, I'll continue to be overwhelmed."

This wasn't a good time for either of them. "I'm sorry, Jax. I…have too much going on to be a good…" A good what? A good fuck?

Jesus, she was twisting her own mind into knots. She shoved her hands into the pockets of his jacket. "Do you…want me to go?"

"No." He reached out and gripped her arms. Firm but not painful. The light touched on his tattoo—something she'd forgotten all about. "No, I don't want you to go. I'm just…I just want to know why you want to be here with me. The real reason. The truth."

She collected her scattered thoughts. "I'm here because I like you. Because you're fun and thoughtful and interesting and sexy. Because you make me feel more than I've felt in what seems like forever.

"I've already made it clear I'm not looking for anything beyond tonight." Her nerves kicked up as her mind spun. "I don't know what else there is to want. What do you have that other people want from you?"

He hesitated. "Connections."

When he didn't say any more, she tried to connect the dots. "With who…movie people? Producers, directors, actors? That kind of thing?"

"That kind of thing." His answer held a bitter edge.

"Well, that's of absolutely no interest to me, Jax. I have a lot of the same people as clients. I have all the contacts I could want in Hollywood, and I don't need any of them. As far as I'm concerned, people are people, and their value stems from their character, not their popularity or notoriety." She leaned into him, and he let her, releasing her arms and sliding them around her. Combing his fingers through her hair. "Besides my clients, I wouldn't know a star if they walked up to me on the street, and I like it that way."

She slid her hands over his muscled torso from belly to chest, loving the way his hands fisted in her hair. The way his nipples tightened under her fingers and a moan rumbled in his throat.

"Everything I want is right here, beneath my hands." She leaned in and kissed his chest. Loved the way a thin dusting of hair brushed her lips. "Are we good?"

"Not yet." He tilted her face up with one hand and covered her mouth with his, lips hot and demanding. His tongue forced her mouth open and took hers. She opened fully to him on a moan. Let go of all thought and took in the feel of his mouth and this passionate, hungry kiss.

His arms came around her again, pulling her hips to his, his cock already rigid and swollen against her lower belly. The hot skin and hard muscle of his chest pressed against her. Lexi whimpered and tried to push higher, tried to get him between her legs, but she was already in four-inch heels and had no leverage.

Jax answered her need by lifting her, and Lexi greedily wrapped his hips in her thighs, rocking her hips into place as Jax licked into her mouth.

"Jax, want you." She kissed him deeply. Scraped her fingers into his hair. "Need you."

He groaned, his hands moving over her like he couldn't touch her fast enough. His mouth eating at her mouth like he couldn't get enough of her taste. He pressed her against a wall, but she couldn't remember moving from the middle of the living room. His hips sank deep between her legs, and a fierce shot of pleasure arched her back. She broke the kiss on a moan.

Jax's mouth dropped to her throat. His hands to her ass. He

pumped his hips against her. His cock rubbed its hard length over her sex, and he used his hands to pull her into the movement. His teeth bit at the skin of her throat, then his tongue soothed.

"Oh God... Yes." She couldn't believe the intensity of this. "I've been thinking about this...all day." She put her hand to his face, tried to pull his mouth up from where it kept sliding lower. If he closed his mouth over her breast, she'd explode. "Jax. Inside me. Come inside me. Please."

His tongue slid over the exposed curve of her breast. "Soon."

Christ, the way he moved. He made her see stars. He didn't thrust. He rocked. Undulated. Varied pressure. Moved her hips to his strokes. Like a dance. The same way he kissed. This wasn't a fuck. It was an art.

His tongue passed over her nipple, and the friction spread fire through her breast, down her chest, and between her legs.

"Shit, Jax..." She fisted her hands in his hair, dropped her mouth to his ear, and whispered, "I'm going to come. Fuck me. Please."

He turned his head, and kissed her. A languid kiss, his tongue moving in her mouth the way she wanted his cock moving in her pussy.

He pulled back. "This is just the beginning. We have all night. A dozen different orgasms to explore. Let go and come for me, sweetheart."

He dropped his head back to her breast and sucked her nipple into his mouth. Picked up the lusty dance of their hips, his pace harder, faster. He spread his hands over her ass cheeks, his fingers brushing the sensitive skin near her opening that ached for him.

The pleasure swelled inside her like a balloon. Lexi groaned behind gritted teeth, dropped her head back against the wall, let the sensations peak. The orgasm rose to the sound of his pleasure-filled moans. But when it broke, the pleasure wasn't the low-level, languid heat Lexi expected. Electric fire shot through her hard, wrenching her muscles and prying a cry from her throat. The arch of her body pushed her against Jax. He took her breast harder in his mouth, her sex harder against his cock, intensifying the peak and wiping out all thought.

She shuddered hard. Tightened her arm around his neck and dropped her face to his head, breathing him in. Holding him close. The pleasure was sharp and sweet. Even more so with Jax's kisses against her throat, her cheek, her temple.

Her body softened, muscles loosened. She rested her forehead on his bare shoulder, one hand still tight in his hair. Lexi didn't have the strength to keep her legs around his waist, and they slipped down his thighs. He eased her feet to the floor. When she was steady, he lifted his hands to her face, whispered, "You're so beautiful," and drew her to him for a slow, relaxed, wet kiss.

The comment meant so much more to her knowing he didn't just refer to what showed on the exterior. Lexi smiled and rested her head against the wall as his mouth slid to her cheek, her jaw, her neck.

She sighed. "You are the best kisser on the planet."

"Takes two." He pushed the jacket to her sides, then took her breasts in his palms, pressing them together. He bent and snuggled his face to her cleavage, his mouth open and hot.

She clutched soft handfuls of his hair. Need ramped quickly again as Jax suckled her breasts, his tongue sliding, teeth nipping, hands massaging the mounds with slow, heavy pressure.

"I've never seen a bra like this." His fingers traced the edges of the lace that cupped the undersides of her breasts, supporting them for both visual appeal and easy access. "Whoever invented it was a genius."

"You're getting me all hot again."

His mouth curved against her skin. "That's what it's all about, baby."

He moved his mouth to the other breast and licked her nipple. She bit her lip to hold in another whimper.

He chuckled, low and dark. "You're so sensitive."

"You're so good. The way you touch and kiss and…everything is just so perfect."

"Everything?" he murmured, circling her nipple with his tongue until she arched her back, pushing her breast toward him. But he didn't take it like she wanted. "What else feels good?"

He wanted to hear her say it. She closed her eyes, as if the dark room wasn't enough cover. "The way you suck me."

His mouth closed over her nipple, but he didn't suck her as much as kiss her. "Like that?"

"Harder," she whispered.

"Harder what?"

"Suck me harder."

He growled and covered her breast with his mouth, rolled her nipple with his tongue, then tightened down with suction. Excitement flooded her body and stroked her pussy. She moaned and pulled her hands from his hair, slid them around his waist. She scratched her fingers over his skin and pushed them into the back of his jeans and under his boxers.

God, his ass was all tight muscle and hot, smooth skin. She pushed deeper into his pants and scraped. He growled, a frustrated, slightly angry sound. His hands dropped to her hips, thumbs hooked in the strings of her panties, and pulled them over her hips.

"You're right," he said. "The smell of the leather and your skin is fucking delirium."

He slowly dropped into a crouch in front of her as he kissed his way down her body while skimming her panties down her thighs, past her knees, over her calves, and off her heels. The sight of this strong, broad-shouldered shadow kneeling in front of her was such a turn-on, a fresh wave of wetness slicked her sex. His tattoo flowed over his left bicep, across his shoulder, up his neck, and down his back. She wished for light again, aching to watch that ink roll with the movement of his muscle.

"Well, look here," he murmured, his hands pausing on her thighs, his gaze on her pussy. "I've become distracted."

Jax's fingers tightened on her thighs and eased her legs apart. Lexi dragged in air. Jax's grip lightened, and his hands caressed their way up her inner thighs. She tightened the grip on his shoulders. Her sex clenched in anticipation of his touch. But his hands reversed direction right where she needed him most.

He shifted to his knees and edged closer. Pressed his lips to the front of one thigh. Then the other. Lexi closed her eyes. Then his mouth pressed between her legs, and she gasped, her eyes popping open.

"Oh Jesus."

One of Jax's big hands gripped her thigh just above her knee and pushed it sideways. He lifted her foot off the ground and pinned her leg to the wall, exposing her.

"My snacks must be wearing off," he murmured. "I'm suddenly starving."

Lexi reached for the corner of the wall for balance. His mouth pressed against her again. Kissing. Then exploring. Then licking.

She swore he was drawing pictures with his tongue. Tracing every ridge, every fold. Tension built quick and intense. Pressure rose through her entire lower body.

"Baby," Jax murmured. "You're ready again. I can feel you throbbing on my tongue."

He slid his fingers over her swollen folds and pulled them open. The touch of air against hot, wet skin tantalized. He licked directly over her clit—slow, hot, wet pressure in a spiral. The pleasure pounded her body. She moaned and squirmed.

"Jax—"

His mouth closed, his tongue moved, and Lexi's mind disintegrated in pleasure. Jax didn't just use a flick of his tongue or a little suckle of his lips. Jax *ate* her. He used his entire mouth in a fervent attack, taking her in, licking and stroking every inch of her until she thought she'd come apart, only to stop just before she exploded and slowly suck her out of his mouth. He stroked her with his hand, separated her with his fingers, then dove back in with his full, open mouth, repeating the exquisite torture until she was writhing against the wall, panting his name.

"You wanted me to savor you…inside…little Lexi." He released her hips. "Let everything go and ride my mouth."

When he put his mouth back to her this time, he thrust his tongue up inside her.

"Oh fuck." She grabbed the corner of the wall with one hand, his head with the other, and let his hands guide her hips to his mouth. He pulled her hips forward each time he drove his tongue inside, then held her against his mouth while he stroked and sucked.

"Jax." It was too much. Too damn much. It was crazy, amazing, blistering pleasure. "Jax. *Jax.*"

He thrust into her, hummed, and rubbed his face against her pussy. The friction sent her skyward, and she splintered. Pleasure knifed through every part of her body, filling, overflowing, then bursting.

THIRTEEN

Jax had been with a lot of women, but he'd never tasted pleasure this sweet. Every woman had a unique flavor, like they had a unique scent, and he could drink Lexi all night long. Her juices had a delicate sweetness, musky undertones, and a slight tangy edge that made him want to create more. Her aftertaste was spicy. A lot like he imagined temptation would taste.

He pulled his mouth from her pussy, and she shuddered. Her chest rose and fell with quick, heavy breaths, and she rested her head back against the wall. Her thigh rested fully in his hand, and he liked the feel of her relaxed and languid against him. Wanted her entire body lying on top of him like that.

But only after he'd finally fucked her.

Jax kissed his way up her body, caught her lazy mouth, and wrapped his arms around her. He lifted her and carried her to the sofa, where he lowered her to her feet again.

"Turn around for me," he whispered in her ear. She didn't question, didn't hesitate. She turned her back to him, leaned into his body, and wrapped an arm up and around his neck. The move arched her back and pushed her ass into his swollen cock. Jax gripped her waist. "You're so sexy, Lex. Kneel on the sofa."

She reached out and braced her hands on the back of the sofa, leaning over the cushions. Jax released her and pulled a condom from his wallet. Then pushed his jeans and underwear over his hips, let them fall down his thighs on their own, then kicked them off. Lexi looked over her shoulder, and Jax wished he could have seen her expression. He was sure it would have been a come-and-get-it look.

"I'll be able to get deeper if you kneel," he said, keeping his voice soft.

She made a delicious sound of desire and knelt.

He was so hard he hurt. His cock was thick and heavy, bowing away from his belly. He opened the condom and rolled it on.

"Take your hair down," he said.

She pulled something from her messy bun and shook her hair out. It fell down her back in soft shadows.

"Spread your knees," was his last direction.

When she had, Jax stepped forward. He combed his fingers through her hair. Pushed his jacket up her back, uncovering the luscious lines of her body—the taper of her waist, the flair of her hips, that perfectly rounded ass. Trailed his fingers down her back, hips, ass, backs of her thighs. Slid them back up her inner thighs. Lexi arched her back on a plea from her throat. Jax guided his cock along her opening. Once he was licked warm and wet by her pussy, he pressed the head of his cock inside her.

"Oh…" Lexi's head dropped forward. "God."

Her voice dripped with pleasure and hiked the urgency pulsing in Jax's blood. He'd thought this position would help him stay in control long enough to get her off one more time before he took her the way he really wanted—intimately. He ached to kiss her while he pushed into her. Longed to look into her eyes and talk to her while they drove each other toward the peak. But, he realized, there wasn't any way he could take her without making himself crazy trying to hold back.

Lexi pushed against the sofa, and her body eased closer to Jax, forcing his cock deeper. Pleasure gripped him. He closed his eyes and dug his fingers into her hips. "Ah, Lex. Fuck you're tight."

She eased forward, pulling him out, then pushed against him again, taking him deeper. Her body, so luscious, sucked him up and closed tightly around him. God, it was beautiful.

He leaned over her, pressing his chest to her back. "You feel amazing."

Her forehead fell against the back of the sofa. "You feel…unbelievable. I don't know what… I've never felt anything like…"

"It's the condom." He thrust, and his cock dug deeper.

Lexi gasped. Her head came up, hands fisted in the sofa. Damn he wanted to see her face. He used her hair to turn her head toward him so he could kiss her mouth. She gave back easily, erotically, sliding her tongue over his.

"A specialty condom," he murmured against her lips. "With ultrasmooth lubricant…" He bent his knees and eased out, dragging against her tight walls. Lexi's groan transitioned into a curse. "Studs on the length…" He contracted his glutes and drove in again. Again, Lexi arched, gasped, moaned. "Ribs at the base." He stroked his cock into her again. "And sensation tips, to hit you just right."

She was way out on the edge, shivering with her unreleased orgasm. Every sound she made pitched higher as she neared the peak.

"Too much?" he asked.

"No. Don't stop." She released the sofa with one hand, reached back, and dug her fingers into his hip. "It's so good."

Jax eased one knee to the sofa, between hers. Pulled her hand from his skin and pressed it against the sofa again, covering it with his. He wrapped his other arm low around her hips and held her still as he thrust slow and deep. She gripped his entire length, and Jax lost his mind. His body swirled with pleasure until control slipped and he surged deeper, faster.

A high-pitched sound came from her throat, then his name, part warning, part plea. "Jax…"

He used the leverage of his knee on the sofa for strength, his other leg for balance, and pushed up and in, up and in, hard, deep. Lexi arched, threw her head back, and cried out.

"Please… Fuck…," she pleaded. "More."

Instead of giving her more, Jax pulled slowly from her fist-like grip. The release seemed to allow blood to rush into his cock, and an unexpected wave of ecstasy plowed through his body. He used his knee to push Lexi's wider. Reentered her body with quick shallow thrusts until she growled out, "Please…"

Then he put power into his legs and drove into her hard, fast and deep, over and over, keeping his mind averted from the orgasm rushing at him.

Lexi rose fast, her body rigid. Pleasure drifted from her throat in a desperate sound. Then cut out as she hit the peak. A monster orgasm. Her muscles contracted, and her body went rigid, jerked, and shivered. But it didn't end there. The orgasm went on and on, racking her body with wave after wave of tremors.

Jax stilled and let the pleasure wash over her as he caught his breath. Her walls finally loosened, giving his cock a break from the relentless hold. He rested his cheek on her back. The chaotic beat of her heart in his ear made him smile. Made him yearn.

He turned his mouth to her skin. Kissed a path up her spine. Pressed both hands to the sofa flanking hers and scraped his teeth over her shoulder.

"One more, baby?" he asked between pants. "Can you give me one more?"

"Jesus…"

Jax pulled her hair to the side, pressed his mouth to her neck, and started moving. She whimpered but rocked with him. Her forehead dropped against the sofa, her fingers clutching and releasing the cushions. He wouldn't have to wait long.

Jax's world narrowed to the overwhelming pleasure building within his body, to the way Lexi moved against him, the sounds of pleasure she made, the taste of her skin. He wished he could make this last and last. She was delicious. Completely, radically luscious.

And he wanted more. More than just sex, more than just tonight.

Dammit, she'd gotten under his skin. Something basic and primal expanded inside him. Sweat slicked his chest, back, arms. His body shook with the growing need for release.

He pressed his chest to her back, whispered, "See me in LA,

baby. This is too good for one night."

"Beyond good," she agreed.

"You'll see me in LA?" he pressed, needing the words. The promise.

"Jax...I can't..."

Frustration sang through his limbs. Her earlier words came back around and hit him hard. He might be perfect for her fantasies, but he wasn't good enough to be included in her real life. No matter how perfectly they fit, or how much pleasure he brought her, it wouldn't be enough. He wouldn't be enough. The story of his life. The old, ugly disappointment melded with the dark thread of anonymous lust and raged through his body.

He slid his hand up her back beneath his jacket, gripped her neck, and added pressure until her chest pressed against the cushions and her ass angled higher into the air. Holding her against the sofa with one hand, he slid the other into her hair—the long, silky strands mirroring the long, silky length of her pussy. On every full, slow thrust, Jax fisted her hair, reveling in her sounds of deep, dark pleasure.

"Oh, so good." Her voice had grown tight, the thrusts of her hips back and into his harder. "So fucking good... Jax—"

Her pussy closed down on his cock like a fist, squeezing and convulsing, breaking Jax's control. Lexi's cries of pleasure filled his head, and he let go. Let his own orgasm slam through him—pure bliss bursting in his balls, blasting his cock, and radiating down his legs, up his chest. His brain shut down. No thought passed, only sensation. Waves of deep, staggering sensation he never wanted to stop. That was when another orgasm hit Lexi, and she pumped him with that velvet pussy, jerking what he could swear was another mini-orgasm out of him.

He used his arm against the sofa to keep them both upright. He'd never been able to attain that mythical multiple male orgasm. Had always believed it was an urban legend. But now...

Lexi's legs shook. She bent her knees and sank down until her thighs touched her calves. Jax's cock slid out of her slick heaven, but he kept his forehead on her shoulder and balanced on the sofa as they both drew quick, jagged breaths.

"Shit," she murmured. "You're so...*intense.*"

He couldn't think anymore, and all he wanted to do was float in this sweet euphoria longer, and he wished he could see her now, all flushed and sated. His anger over her rejecting his request to see her in LA dimmed to distant frustration.

Jax scratched his fingers down her spine lightly, and she sighed. The sound made his mouth quirk in a smile. And while he'd never been a touchy-feely kind of guy after sex, all he wanted to do with Lexi was hold her close, feel her body fit to the length of his. He wanted to taste her, smell her, feel her.

He eased to his feet and used the arm around her waist to lift her from the sofa. She was light and languid, and he set her on her feet, then turned her to face him. Lexi automatically wound her arms around his neck and Jax lifted her, allowing her to wrap her legs around his hips. She turned her head and put her cheek on his shoulder. And sighed again.

His chest squeezed hard, and Jax tried to shake it off like he would a hard fall on the job. He carried her into the bedroom, pulled back the covers, and leaned over to lay her down. But she held on to his neck.

"Lie with me," she murmured, soft and sleepy, then kissed him.

"Be right back."

He cleaned up in the bathroom, and when he returned, she lay exactly where he'd left her. He laughed softly and put one knee on the bed beside her.

"What?" she asked.

"You haven't moved."

"I can't."

The bathroom light cast a glow over the room, and the sight of her pale hair against the white sheets created a soft spot beneath his ribs. He couldn't see the details of her face, but he could see the oval shape, the way her features cast delicate shadows. Once he'd realized she'd modeled, he'd known her face was as gorgeous as her body. That combined with the fact that he was still so well-known turned the soft spot brittle.

But she didn't want to see him again, so it was a nonissue.

Trying to let it go, he leaned over her and kissed her lips. "I guess you'll just have to stay, then, won't you?"

She reached up and combed her fingers through his hair. "I'd love to. If I didn't have a customer fitting tomorrow, I'd change my plans."

"Can't you reschedule?"

"No. She's in a wedding this weekend."

Damn.

"You probably want to get out of this." Jax took the cuff of one jacket sleeve and tugged. She groaned and pulled her arm out. Jax reached for the other cuff and leaned over her, bracing himself on the bed. His hand pressed against a corner of his jacket, over something hard and cylindrical in the pocket. "What's this?"

Lexi's hand covered his, feeling around.

"Oh." She pushed her hand into the pocket and drew something out. "That's your second surprise."

"More like my tenth surprise. You've been delivering one beautiful surprise after another since you walked in." Jax sat back on his heels. "And I can't wait to hear what this is."

She pressed a small bottle into his hand. "Massage lotion."

He hummed at the pleasurable thought.

"Give me a little time to rest," she said, her voice languid, "and I'll work out some of your sore muscles."

Jax turned the bottle in his hand. "I *have* heard it called a love muscle before, but I happen to know it's not in the muscle group."

Lexi slapped his hand and pulled the bottle away, laughing. "It's not for *that*. It's for your shoulders and your legs. Aren't they sore after swinging a sword and riding a horse all day?"

He lifted her upper body from the bed to drag the jacket

from beneath her, then tossed it aside.

"Really?" he said, sliding onto his side next to her, propping his elbow on the bed and his head on his hand. He spread his free hand flat over her belly. "Sure you weren't trying to get a massage out if it yourself?"

"Smell it," she said, pouring some on her hands and lifting them to his face. "If it was for me, I wouldn't get something that was going to make me smell like a guy."

"Smells good." Warm, spicy, sultry.

"And it's edible," she said, her voice lowering with insinuation. "But I don't like massages, so I'll be doing the tasting."

Warmth flowed into his cock again. "What? *Who* doesn't like massages?"

"I'm ticklish, remember? And I don't like having a stranger's hands on—" She stopped suddenly, leaving the sentence hanging there in the dark. Then she laughed. "Well, that's a pretty ridiculous thing to say, considering…"

A place deep in Jax's belly softened. He slid his hand to the opposite side of her waist and pulled her close until they were skin to skin.

She flinched, squirmed, laughed. "See?"

Jax laughed and rolled to his back, taking her with him. He found more ticklish spots on her sides, and she laughed, screamed, wiggled. She was breathless when he finally stopped tickling her and draped her body over his, heavy and relaxed.

"Oh yeah," Jax moaned, closing his eyes as he ran a hand over her hair and down her back. "I've been thinking about this all day. This right here."

A moment of silence passed. Jax felt sleep try to tug him deeper into the mattress. He wished he could fall asleep with her in his arms. Wake up with her in his arms. But knowing this was the only night he'd get with her meant he had to savor every moment.

"Jax?" Her voice was soft.

A tiny flare of discomfort brought his eyes open. But it dissipated quickly. He tightened his arms around her and kissed her head. "Hmm?"

"Before I forget, or we get…involved in something and lose track of time and I have to rush out…"

She piled her hands on his chest and propped her chin there. And even though he couldn't see her face, he sensed her seriousness.

"Thank you," she said, voice gentle and sincere, "for the very best night of my life."

A cord of heat pulled straight down the center of his chest, and a wave of sweet emotion overtook him. He couldn't help himself, just combed his fingers into her hair and pulled her head down as he lifted into a half curl to press their mouths together. He'd intended the kiss to be sweet, but it instantly turned hot. Her mouth mirrored her body so perfectly—wet and hot. He hadn't even fully softened yet and his cock was already rising again.

"Baby," he said between kisses. "I know we agreed to just tonight, but you gotta admit we've got something amazing here—"

She kissed him harder, smothering his words.

In frustration, he pulled his head back. "Lexi, just think about—"

She pressed her fingers to his mouth. "Jax, I can't. I can't even consider it. Just giving myself that sliver of maybe with you is like a fault in a dam." She curled her fingers and brushed her knuckles over his cheek. "Tell me about your day. You don't have to go over the part that upset you again…unless you want to talk about it."

He grabbed her hand and pulled her palm to his mouth. After kissing it, he sucked every fingertip between his lips. "I want to talk about seeing you again."

"Jax…" she said, exasperation trailing his name out. "You don't understand. That's like offering an addict crack."

He burst out laughing, pulled her to him. "I'll be your

supplier, sugar."

"Shut up."

"Honey, do you realize how rare it is to be so comfortable together so fast?"

"Jax—"

"To be so explosive in bed, so fast?"

"Stop—"

"I just want to get to know you better. See if there's something more. Is that asking so much?"

She pressed her fingers to his lips again. Then removed them and pressed her lips there instead. The kiss was slow, sweet, filled with emotion. When she finally pulled away, she combed her fingers through his hair and said, "Tell me about your day."

He sighed. "It was great. I'm a lucky bastard. I've got the best job in the world. I get paid to play all day." He smiled just thinking about how much fun he'd had with Ty. Maybe opening up to her would help her open up. "Wanna see me being an idiot?"

"Of course," she said with so much enthusiasm, he laughed.

He kissed her and shifted her to the side. "Let me get my phone."

He slid out of bed and retrieved his jeans from the living room. Back in the bedroom, Jax pulled condoms from his wallet and put them on the bedside table, then tossed his pants on a side chair and stood at the edge of the bed, thumbing across screens to pull up the video. Lexi's hand reached out and stroked his hip, slid down the front of his thigh. The touch was more affectionate than sexual, and it made that soft place in his chest open wider.

When he'd found the video, he handed her the phone, climbed over her to the other side of the bed, and propped himself up behind her. She leaned back against him as he slipped his hand between her body and her arm, pointing to his starting image on the screen. "That's me. I was taking a break with the other guy while they moved cameras. I was trying to take my helmet off."

He adjusted the sound and tapped Play.

Ty had been filming well before Jax had known, and the first frames of the video showed Jax fighting with the helmet.

A muffled, "Who the hell…last wore this thing?" made Lexi giggle.

The sound drew Jax's gaze, and he realized the light from the phone cast a glow on Lexi's face. But she had her head tilted down and away, toward the phone. He pushed up a little, trying to get a better view.

He caught sight of just a portion of her face. Long, golden eyelashes over one crystal-clear blue eye and smooth skin. His craving to see her face intensified.

"How do you do that?" she asked without looking away the phone. Jax's gaze lowered to her mouth. Her lips were full, pink, pretty. "Ride like that with no hands?"

"It's just balance. And I've been riding since I was little."

She hummed, the sound impressed. "I bet you were an adorable kid."

In the video, Jax called Ty a piece of shit, and Lexi laughed. Crinkles appeared in the outer corner of her eye. He caught a flash of straight white teeth.

"Who are you talking to?" she asked. "Who's taking the video?"

"One of the actors. He runs his own stunts."

Another hum, but no real interest. And her laughter picked up at Jax's antics just before he finally pulled the helmet off. "Oh my God." She laughed the words. "Is he falling off his horse?"

Jax returned his gaze to the phone where the image was slowly tilting sideways, Ty's hysterical laughter booming from the speakers. "No, he's just screwing around. He's as good a rider as I am."

Jax returned his eyes to the tiny corner of her face. Took in the way her blonde hair lay softly against the part of her forehead and temple he could see. He wanted to turn her toward him and kiss her, eyes open and staring into hers.

"Did you grow up on a ranch or something?" she asked.

"No. My mother was very into horses, mostly because they were prestigious and allowed her to meet the people she wanted to meet. When I was old enough to decide whether or not to ride on my own, I stuck with it because it got me away from everyone before I could drive."

"Hmm, I'd have loved a getaway like that as a kid." She laughed at something on the video again, and he didn't get a chance to ask more. "He seems so fun. Do you like him?"

"Yeah. He's a good kid." A thought occurred to him, a way to test her. He clenched his stomach in preparation for a spastic response—he got that a lot when he mentioned Ty. "It's Tyler Manning."

She didn't react—at all. Just kept watching the video with a small shake of her head. "I don't recognize the name. Are you two always this funny when you're working together?"

If she'd known who Ty was, Jax doubted she could have held back a reaction. He had to admit, he'd been skeptical after the demonstration Ty had given today.

"Usually, yeah," he answered belatedly. "Like I said, I get to play all day."

On the video, Jax barreled toward the phone's camera, and Lexi gasped. Then the picture went dark as Jax's hand covered the lens, plucked it out of Ty's hand, and raced off. But his voice came over the audio: "Try, kid. It'll give me an excuse to knock your ass off that horse."

Lexi was laughing so hard tears gathered in her eyes. Then the video cut out, and the room went dark again.

"Oh my God, you two are hilarious. How old is he?" she asked. "You call him kid."

"Twenty-four."

"And you're twenty-nine?" she confirmed from their earlier texts.

"Yep. You?"

"Twenty-eight. When's your birthday?"

"July 7th."

"Mine too. July, I mean. The 14th. We're both Cancers." Her voice smoothed and softened. "Homebodies. We'd both rather be home, but…here we are."

Jax didn't really have a home. Not in the traditional sense. He hated LA as a city. Hated what it stood for. But it was the hub of the career he loved. His own family wasn't what people thought of when they thought of family. He was closer to the guys he worked with than his siblings or parents. And his house, while gorgeous, was big and empty.

"Home is where you make it and who you make it with." He reached down and turned her face toward his. He kissed her mouth, which was still curved with laughter. And now he'd gotten a glimpse of that mouth. A tiny flicker of her eyes.

Keeping the lights off was truly the way to go. He shouldn't have looked. Because when he put it together with everything else he'd learned about her in their short time together, he didn't want to let her go.

"Do you realize your birthday is 7-14?" he asked. "The same numbers as this room? I think you're right where you belong."

"Oh my God." She turned to face him, and he could imagine the wonder drifting through her eyes. "You're right. That's…"

"Fate," he whispered, rolling to his back and pulling her on top of him. "Tonight, baby, this is home."

FOURTEEN

The ring of Jax's cell pulled him from a deep, dreamless sleep. He blinked as the morning light hit his eyes. He was worn to the bone, and his mind wouldn't start.

He stared at an armoire with a flat-screen television inside. Another goddamned hotel. Christ, where the fuck was he now?

He rolled to his stomach and groped for his phone on the bedside table. Lamp, clock, hotel phone...no cell. Just as he realized the sound was coming from a different direction, the damn thing stopped ringing.

Jax let his arm fall. It missed the bed and dangled alongside. The stretch felt good, and Jax sighed. The sensation nudged his brain, but he resisted. Didn't want to think. Didn't know why, just knew he wanted to avoid it.

He pushed both arms over his head, stretched his shoulders, his back. And groaned. He felt good. Sore, but good. His mind nudged again. He let it float, and the memory came back slow, languid. Hands on his back, relaxing every overworked muscle. Sweet thighs straddling his hips, working out knots in his neck. His shoulders. His ass.

Lexi.

The entire evening came back to him at once, like an explosion. He flipped to his back and pushed himself up. "Lex?"

His gaze held on the door to the bedroom.

Please walk through that door.

He swallowed and called again. "Lexi?"

He already knew it would go unanswered, but sat there, propped up by his hands, waiting. Hoping.

The room remained silent. And he brought her exit back from his memories, the way she'd come to the side of the bed before she'd left.

"Lex," he'd whispered to her in the dark as she'd leaned over to kiss him good-bye. She'd been dressed in one of his T-shirts that hit her midthigh because she'd refused to take his jacket and didn't have anything else to wear back to her room. He'd slipped his hand up the back of her thigh and squeezed her ass. *"Please say you'll see me in LA."*

He'd kissed her long and slow and tender. Rolled his tongue with hers, eased his hand between those soft, toned thighs from behind and fingered her, still slick and swollen from his cock. She'd groaned, rocked that sweet pussy into his hand, then abruptly stepped out of reach. *"I'm sorry, Jax, I—"*

"We can keep it just like this, baby. No one has to know."

She'd thought about it for two full seconds before she'd denied him again and walked out of his life.

His one night with a woman as close to perfect for him as he ever hoped to find was over.

"Fuck." He dropped back to the bed and threw his forearm over his eyes.

His phone rang again.

"Jesus." Jax rolled toward the sound and groped for it on the opposite nightstand, eyes still closed. He answered with a grouchy, "Yeah."

"Dude, you out partying late last night?" Wes's voice registered instantly. "You sound like you just woke up."

"I did. I don't have to be on set until noon."

Jax glanced around the room. His gaze caught on the pillow next to his and a pair of red lace panties perfectly laid out on the white casing. His stomach clenched. Chest tightened. But a smile quirked his mouth as he reached for them.

He slid the fabric through his fingers, fisted it, wishing he could have held on to Lexi as easily. Her little memento didn't make him feel any better about not being able to convince her to see him again.

"Hel-lo. Chamberlin, dude? You fall back to sleep on me?"

"No. I'm here." Jax kicked the sheet off his legs and sat up on the edge of the bed. "What did you say?"

Wes gave an exasperated sigh. "Do you remember the conversation we had on the way to the airport, or are you missing too many brain cells?"

Jax winced. The airport. What did they talk about?

When he didn't answer, Wes prodded, "About finding you a girl like my Kayla?"

Wes's question temporarily rendered him completely dumb. What in the hell—?

Oh…that. Oh…*shit.*

"Uh, yeah," he said, "I remember." *Fuck.* "Listen, Wes, I don't think that's—"

"We found the perfect girl," Wes said. "She's absolutely fantastic. And, dude, I know your taste. You're going to like her. She's super pretty and really smart. And she's got a sweet streak that makes you want to eat her up."

Jax winced. This was so not the time to talk about another woman, because there was only one he wanted to eat up. "Hey, Wes, listen—"

"I know what you're going to say—if she's so great, why isn't she with someone? Well, she was, which, honestly is why *I'm* not dating her. Not now, I mean, 'cause I'm crazy about Kayla, but I met Tawna before I knew Kayla and would have totally gone for her, but she was in this long-term thing then.

"She's been out of it about six months now, lying low to make sure the guy was out of her system before she dates again, which I think is really smart, you know, balanced. And when Kayla and I told her about you, she was game.

"So what do you say? We'll double when we get back from this gig next week?"

Jax was staring at the beige carpet, Lexi's panties crushed in his hand. "Are you done?"

"Yeah, sorry. I was excited to find out Tawna was free. I

really think you two are a good match."

"Thing is, bud, I hooked up with someone here."

A beat of silence filled the line, then, "*What? I just* left you at the airport. You flew six hours, hauled your ass to the set for twelve, and should have been too tired to do anything but sleep for the rest. When did you have any time to hook up with someone?"

Jax rubbed his eyes. Dropped back to the bed. "I'm not really awake yet, Wes—"

"I imagine not, considering what you've been doing. Fuck, Jax, this is so you. You know, if you want to keep making the same goddamned mistakes, fine. Just don't bitch about the fallout. You pick up women so fast, you don't take the time to even get to know them. Then they screw you over and—oh shit, look at that, what a fucking surprise."

Jax sighed. "Why are you yelling at me like a mother hen?"

"Because you're my friend, asshole, and I'm sick of watching you let women walk all the fuck over you."

Guilt layered on top of his misery over losing Lexi. Wes was right. And Lexi was gone. She'd made the word *no* very clear in a dozen different ways.

"Look," Jax said. "You're right. It was a fluke thing. We started talking, hit it off. But it's...it's nothing. Just a one-night. I just...really liked her."

"Dude, you really like them all at the beginning."

"You really should let me have coffee before you gut me. Give me a fucking break. I haven't had any in over a month, she was hot as hell and offered. Don't tell me you wouldn't have done the same."

He needed to get Wes off his back, and that seemed to make the guy at least think a minute.

"So you flipped one, no big deal, right? You're not going to see her again, right?"

Jax hated that term. Wes applied the term flipped, as in flipping houses—getting hold of one, working it over, then getting rid of it—to one-night stands.

Jax looked at the ceiling and forced himself to say the words, hoping they'd sink in and he'd get over…whatever this was. "No, Wes, I'm not going to see her again."

"Okay, then, no big deal. You can still meet Tawna. Right?"

"Right," Jax said. He'd deal with this later. "Sure, why not, right?"

"Right. Now you're thinking. I'll bring pictures of Tawna with me. You won't even remember the other girl by the time I get there."

Jax disconnected, dropped his phone to the bed, and raked his hand through his hair. Wouldn't even remember her? Jax wondered how he could possibly forget her. He closed his eyes, brought the panties to his nose, and pulled in her scent. The spicy, floral, musky smell of her burst at the center of his body and radiated electric waves outward. Memories of every minute with her flooded his brain. Her laugh. Her playfulness. The way she'd fed him the Godiva, bite by bite. The way she'd licked every inch of his body just as she'd promised. The way she'd kissed him good-bye, as if she didn't want to leave him.

He knew, without a doubt, he'd never wanted a woman like this. Which he understood, somewhere in his psyche, stemmed more from the fact that he couldn't have her than the fact that she was as perfect as she seemed. Had to be. At least it had to be what he told himself.

His phone rang again, breaking into his memories. "Fuck. I can't even wallow in my misery in peace."

He sat up, glanced over at the rumpled sheets where Lexi had been lying just a couple of hours ago.

"I told you in the very beginning, Jax. I just can't have any complications in my life right now."

He'd gone from an asset that every woman wanted to use to a complication Lexi wanted to get rid of.

"I need to find some kind of happy medium," he muttered

as he picked up his phone and answered, "What now?"

"Whoa." Ty laughed the word. "Dude. Who stole your mojo this morning?"

"Oh, sorry, Ty." Jax pitched the underwear across the room. "What's up, kid?"

"Things go south with Miss Anonymous?" Ty asked, his tone surprisingly compassionate.

Jax laughed. "Not exactly. I just have a hard time accepting I'm not going to get what I want."

"Spoiled Hollywood brat."

"That's me."

"Hey, sorry, dude. I know you were into her."

"Thanks," Jax said, feeling better just talking to Ty. "What's up?"

"We got some awesome new ponies in this morning. Come in early and we can run them along the bay."

Now that made Jax smile. "That is exactly what I need today." The kind of adrenaline rush he would need every day for however long it took to get Lexi out from under his skin. "I'll be there in half an hour."

FIFTEEN

"Lexi." Martina's smooth voice took on a too sweet tone over the phone, obviously trying to make up for the news she'd just delivered. "I know it's never easy to take criticism, but I thought you'd want to know. And, to be honest, I wanted you to know because I desperately want you to win over the hearts of the board the way you stole mine years ago."

Lexi had been tapping the pen tip against the notepad on her desk when their conversation had begun. Now she was stabbing it. At one a.m. on a Wednesday morning, after working eighteen-hour days for the last three weeks straight—exactly three weeks from the day she'd met Jax—Lexi had little patience left.

"You're right, Martina." To hell with tiptoeing. "And it's especially not easy on this project. I've put an exorbitant amount of time into those designs, but I do appreciate your honesty. And to be perfectly honest in return, your board is wrong. I know this demographic. They're strong, empowered women who enjoy living life. Getting married later has allowed them to sow their oats and they're secure with their sexuality. A lifetime of living with the overexposure of American media has made them comfortable showing off their bodies.

"I know Galliano is more on the conservative side, but your whole purpose for bringing youth on board is to pull in a new clientele. That won't happen if you don't step out of Galliano's current mold. I've passed on several big clients to give myself time to design these gowns. They're already in production. I've already made a deep investment in this partnership, Martina, with no guarantee of getting it. I just don't know how much more I can give."

More than that, Lexi had come to realize over the last three weeks she'd given up a hell of a lot more than time, money, and clients. She'd passed up on a pretty good bet at a winner with

Jax—something she'd only fully realized as time passed and he continued to cling to her every thought.

"You're designs are stunning, Lexi," Martina said. "There's no doubt how much time you've invested. I don't think the alterations need to be drastic. I'd suggest simply making some of the small changes we discussed and resubmitting them on new boards. A different display will make them look like all new designs. It would really probably only be a day or two's worth of work. Surely that's worth the future opportunities this partnership would bring you."

Martina's voice expressed her excitement over the idea, as if Lexi should be thrilled. Instead, Lexi's throat grew so thick with frustration, she could barely speak.

"Resubmitting?" Her voice came out as a raspy whisper. Lexi dropped her pen. "You're asking me to *resubmit* the altered designs for...*approval?*"

She wanted to add, *I'm not a fucking intern* but stopped herself. Barely. Lexi gritted her teeth. She'd spent so many years struggling. Had busted her ass, sewn her fingers raw, worked for free, gone days without sleep for every accomplishment, every accolade. She'd broken in a long *fucking* time ago.

Martina sighed. "I know it's tedious, Lexi. I'm sorry. It's just—"

"The board," Lexi finished, frustrated, angry, disappointed. Again.

"Yes."

Lexi warned herself not to say anything she'd regret later. "I'll do my best."

After saying good-bye, Lexi jammed her finger down on the disconnect button. She slammed the phone on her desk and swiveled toward her cutting table where she'd been preparing yards of French-woven jacquard for a twenty-thousand-dollar wedding gown. Which made her realize once again how much this potential partnership was costing her.

All her fury, her doubt, her loneliness, her confusion from

the past three weeks expanded beneath her veneer, creating hairline cracks. With an animalistic growl, she picked up the phone and chucked it across the studio. It floated over the balcony, punched an armoire with a clack, clattered against the travertine floor of the main salon, and clinked to a stop against a rack of gowns—right beside the front door and Rubi's sparkling high heels.

Poised there, holding the door open, Rubi gazed at the phone for a long moment, then her eyes lifted toward Lexi. No other part of her body moved. "Bad time?"

All Lexi's problems crashed like a wave. Failure and embarrassment tangled into a web and wound around her like a straitjacket. She braced her head in her hands. "What the fuck is wrong with me?"

By the time Rubi's heels clicked on the stairs, Lexi's tears poured, completely beyond her control.

"I knew this was coming." Rubi wrapped Lexi in her arms and held her tight. "When are you going to realize it's not you?"

Lexi pulled away from Rubi when all she wanted to do was sink into her. She wiped her face, covered her mouth, and choked back the awkward sobs for air as she tried to force herself to stop crying.

Rubi crouched in front of her, hands on her knees, her friend's big eyes swimming with concern and sympathy. "Honey, let me just go drop my friend off and I'll be right back—"

"No." Lexi's hands popped off her mouth. She wiped her face again and sniffled. "Don't mess up your night, Rubi—"

"This is not messing up my night. You're my best friend—"

"I kind of need to be alone, you know?" She pulled open the bottom drawer of her desk and yanked tissues out, blotting her eyes. "I need to think about things. Make some decisions."

"About those?" Rubi tilted her head toward the cutting table and the sketches still sitting out.

Lexi nodded and sniffled again, then lifted a you're-not-going-to-believe-this look to her friend. "They're too *sexy*."

Rubi wore heavy eyeliner tonight and thick mascara that made her eyes pop. A slow grin spread over her face. "They are a bit...outside the box. But then...since New York...so are you."

Lexi's face flushed, burning so hot she put her hands to her cheeks again to cool them. "Stop. This is serious."

"I agree. These designs are a serious reflection of the shift you've made since your semi-anonymous rendezvous with Biker Boy. And a serious leap in your design process. A potentially serious leap in your career."

Lexi slid her hands up and over her eyes. She wished she'd never said anything about Jax to Rubi.

"I've noticed it in the way you dress, the way you walk, even the way you interact with your clients, Lexi. And now, here it is in your designs—"

The pressure of Rubi's hands released from Lexi's knees, and her heels clicked across the space. Lexi dropped her hands. The tears had stopped as suddenly as they'd started, leaving a hollow, dull ache at the deepest part of her. One she hadn't felt in decades.

The soft shift of paper drew Lexi's gaze up, but she was so tired, her vision blurred. "Rubi, I can't go over the changes she wants now, and you have someone waiting—"

"What are *these*?"

The thick insinuation and approval in Rubi's tone made Lexi fight to focus. Rubi had pulled a handful of loose sketches from her pad beneath the designs for Martina.

Lexi realized which sketches she'd found, and a burn of mortification erupted in her belly. She pushed from the chair and lunged for them. "Rubi—"

Rubi blocked her grab by turning her back. "Wowza, Lex." She fanned herself with one of the drawings. "Is it getting hot in here?"

Yes. Very hot. Lexi's face burned with embarrassment. Rubi had found the über-sexy, borderline erotic—okay, they *were*

162

erotic—sketches of women in highly suggestive positions wearing sexy lingerie.

"Come on, Rubi. Those are private."

"Good to know you keep them under wraps, except..." She shot a frown over her shoulder. "Since when do you hold out on *me?*"

Lexi reached around and tried to pull the sketches from Rubi's grasp—the sketches she'd started that night she'd met Jax and hadn't stopped doodling since—but Rubi just held them out of reach like an annoying sibling.

She finally gave up and waved at the notebook. "Shit, I don't care, go ahead and look at them."

She wasn't keeping the sketches from Rubi as much as she was keeping herself from having to recognize this hot little deviant streak in her current personal and professional persona.

"I was just...playing with ideas. But it's a complete waste of time, especially when Galliano won't even consider an asymmetric off-the-shoulder design showing cleavage or a transparent bodice, even when the fabric pattern hides everything important, for Christ's sake."

Lexi picked up the dress designs, her mind already reworking them at this stage of their production. Seams could be ripped out. New fabric cut and sewn in. Lexi could do absolutely anything with a piece of fabric. That wasn't the issue at all.

"What generation do they think we're designing for?" she murmured, shaking her head. She could look at all designs, her own included, with an objective eye. These were cutting-edge. These were breakout material. The suggestions Martina had made brought the designs right back down to average. Vanilla. Well within the box. That wasn't what Lexi LaCroix Designs was about.

Nor was it what she wanted to be about. Or had ever wanted to be about.

Inner turmoil raged.

"Is this partnership setting me up for success...or failure?"

As soon as the words were floating

in the quiet room, all Lexi's fears solidified. She lifted her gaze to her friend. "Am I... Am I selling out, Rubi?"

Rubi gestured with the images in her hand. "You tell me."

Lexi shrugged. "I've been on this track for so long. Shooting for this one goal, to move beyond the store, take that next big step that I've been living for nothing but this. Is that selling out?"

"Not if the end goal takes you where you want to go."

Her phone call with Martina made it clear the chances of that happening with Galliano were slim. Lexi looked away from Rubi, thinking of all the time and money and effort she'd wasted—when she had none to waste. The clients she'd disappointed by turning down their requests to design their wedding dresses.

The man she'd walked away from because he would have taken her attention away from her work. Because he had the potential to make her happy.

A familiar shame edged in. "I think I just...lost sight of..." Lexi shook her head, still confused. "...something."

"You just need to refocus. These are big-time breakthroughs right here." Rubi lifted the sketches again. "These are... I don't mean to diss your other work, because you know I think you're brilliant, but these might be the most unique work you've ever done. They're elegant, feminine, sexy, erotic, edgy...all at the same time. I'm thinking..." A slow smile grew and lit Rubi's gorgeous face. "Honeymoon line."

For a fleeting second, excitement darted through Lexi's system, leaving her high. Then reality crashed in, and Lexi crossed her arms, frustrated. "I've thought of that. I actually..."

"You actually what?"

"I actually feel like an idiot." Lexi laughed at herself, but not in a good way. She lifted her arms in a gesture of pure frustration. "I was so excited about this idea—I didn't even know how or where I was going to fit it into my business—that when I was at the fabric mart, I bought a bolt of"—she closed her eyes and pressed her hands to her chest—"the most exquisite embossed white leather. It was so freaking expensive. I couldn't afford it, shouldn't have bought it. I've been meaning to return it but haven't been able to part with it."

She sighed and let the creative pleasure linger. The height of pure self-expression through her designs was, honestly, the best feeling in the world. Instantly, the memory of Jax's mouth bringing her to an orgasm so intense her muscles bowed and gave and quivered filled her mind.

Right. Expression through her designs was the *second*-best feeling in the world.

"Let me see," Rubi said.

Another lick of excitement burned Lexi's chest as they walked to the fabric storage area. She untied the wrapping on the bolt and tugged the plastic back, then turned a corner to show the right side of the fabric.

"It was such an impulsive buy. And it's now just sitting back here."

"Spontaneous sex. Radical designs. Impulsive buys." Rubi crossed her arms, her eyes narrowing, expression growing serious. "I really like the effect this Biker Boy had on you. I'm thinking investing your time and attention in *him* would be a better business decision than dumbing down your amazing designs. And I'm dead serious."

The sheer validity of that idea turned Lexi's world on its axis.

Unable to process such an emotionally risky idea, she pushed it away as she fingered the ultrasoft leather. The fabric melted to the curves of her hand, as soft as rose petals. "God, feel this, Rubi. It's orgasmic."

Rubi ran her hand along the bolt with a gasp, then took the edge from Lexi and rubbed it between her fingers, her hands, and finally against her face. Rubi closed her eyes, took a deep breath of the rich, sweet leather scent, and hummed with intense pleasure. "What a wicked thrill." Her green eyes reopened and pinned Lexi with a serious gaze. "You've *got* to do this line, Lex. It will skyrocket."

A knot of anxiety tightened Lexi's chest. She knew that look in Rubi's eyes. That tone in her voice. They had preceded every breakthrough design. Rubi was like a fortune-teller when it came to Lexi's business. She could look at a design, touch a fabric, chat with a customer, and tell Lexi *that's the one*. That design, fabric, or customer inevitably went on to be the smashing hit or created an invaluable connection for the season. Rubi had pinpointed the design that had landed Lexi the spread in *American Bride*, which had in turn led to the partnership offer.

Rubi knew fashion.

But Lexi wasn't Rubi. Unlike Rubi, who had other software designers, Lexi was the only designer who could design what was in her head—and sometimes even she couldn't do it. But she was burning out. She couldn't keep up these hours, this intensity. She needed help beyond her secretary and sales associates. She needed more talent with designing and crafting. Needed someone as responsible as she was, as knowledgeable as she was, as skilled as she was. And she'd give her right arm to someone she could trust to handle the weddings and treat her customers like royalty.

But she didn't have any of that now. She certainly didn't have the time to create a whole new line of lingerie or the means to risk the investment required—mostly her time to design, implement, and oversee manufacturing, if not manufacture it herself. And if she was going to do it, the time to show it would be at the Luxe show—which would blow her chances with Galliano, something that had, at this point, more viability.

Rubi tapped her full bottom lip with one burgundy-tipped finger. "Have you researched the lingerie market?"

"Yes."

"And?"

Lexi pulled her own lip through her teeth. "It's a gold mine. Especially with my target market."

Rubi's face exploded with light as she smiled and pumped her fist. "Yes. I love it. The Honeymoon Line. It's such a perfect and logical extension of your gowns."

It was. And with her own clientele, it would be an easy transition into exposing her sexier side within the private setting of the studio. Lexi had been ecstatic about the idea since it first bloomed on the plane. But then Martina had pricked her golden bubble with a jagged blade, and Lexi just sat on the idea. Which ate at her.

"It would be," she agreed. "But now…" She gestured to the drawings she needed to de-sexify. "There's no way they would agree to a line like that. Even if I designed it for myself, having my name attached to a line so sexy might cause them to disassociate."

"That's probably true." Rubi's smile turned into a petulant frown. She crossed her arms, bit her thumbnail, and stared down at the drawings that needed alterations. "I sure wish you'd reconsider my offer, Lex, and let me in on this. We could do it any way you wanted. Silent partner, involved partner, straight loan with papers, unofficial loan between friends…"

Lexi stepped in and pulled Rubi into a fierce hug. "You're such a great friend." She stepped back and held a pouting Rubi by the arms. "It's really important for me to do this on my own. I've done everything up to this point without loans or favors. I'm not proud of much in my life, Rubi, but I'm really, *really* proud of that."

"You should be. It's amazing. *You're* amazing. It just kills me to see you work so damned hard and then have someone restrict you like this. And think about it, Lex. If they're not letting you express yourself, build yourself through your fabulous designs, why are you partnering with them? For the money," she answered before Lexi could. "And if you're doing it for the money, how is that any different from partnering with me?"

Lexi rubbed her forehead. "You've just confused the hell out of me."

Rubi grinned and waved one sketch. I think you're confused because you've got an internal struggle going on. "You've got this side of Lexi emerging…" She let go of the erotic lingerie sketch, and it floated down to cover the sketches she'd need to alter into a more conservative design if she was going to go through with the competition. "And struggling for control over another side of Lexi."

An uncomfortable heat twisted low in her stomach. Rubi was voicing something Lexi's psyche had been fighting with from the day she left Jax.

Rubi smiled, reached out, and squeezed Lexi's arm. "I have faith those sides will eventually reconcile and merge into the woman you were meant to become."

Reconcile... Lexi stared down at the sketches lying together with something churning in her subconscious. *Merge...*

Rubi leaned in, kissed Lexi's cheek, then swiveled toward the front of the store. The click of her heels broke Lexi out of her trance in time to see Rubi shoot her that million-dollar smile.

"I'll be checking on your progress."

When the key turned in the lock as Rubi left, Lexi's mind was already stirring, searching for the elusive idea hidden somewhere in the deep recesses of her mind.

SIXTEEN

Jax tapped the truck's steering wheel and bounced his knee to the beat of Fall Out Boy's "The Phoenix." His mind zigzagged all over the place, unable to concentrate on anything—including whatever Tawna was talking about in the passenger's seat. A movie, that's right. Something she'd seen a couple of nights ago.

But Jax's mind drifted to his shoot that day. Had there been too much sand blowing in the valley? Would they need to retake the shots after the producer reviewed them again? If they did, it would put him behind schedule for the fall he was doing on the Paramount set next week. He couldn't send any of the other guys to do it because they weren't certified to fall over sixty feet. Wes would be soon, but not soon enough for Paramount. Maybe one of the guys could take over for him on this job if it ran long—

A hand pressed against Jax's thigh. He jumped and turned, feeling like an idiot when Tawna grinned back at him. She'd moved to the middle of his truck's bench seat.

"You've been distracted all night." She squeezed his leg. "Something bothering you?"

God, she smelled good. Filled his truck with scents that should absolutely not be in a man's truck, but that when mixed with the leather and oil and metal, just…shit, turned him on. But it wasn't really Tawna that turned him on, even though she could have if he hadn't been ruined three weeks ago.

But he just wasn't going there.

"Uh, no." He laid his hand over hers, which had risen too close to his groin. "Just work stuff. Busy, you know?"

She lifted her other hand to his jaw. She stroked his stubble with the backs of her fingers before slipping her hand behind his neck. Her nails grazed his skin, and electricity burned down his spine, making him shift in his seat.

Shit, he just needed to take her into her apartment and fuck her. He needed it. She needed it. They'd been dating for weeks with nothing more than a few kisses. Not for lack of trying on Tawna's part, but due to Jax's inability to move on from his one night in New York. And she'd made her frustration with his lack of interest in sex plenty clear at the end of their date last week when he'd turned her down. Again.

He pulled onto her street and into her driveway.

Moment of truth.

His gut ached with dread. Dread that he had to have sex for the first time in three weeks with a beautiful, eager, young woman.

He was way more messed up than he'd realized.

He turned off the truck and released his seat belt. Tawny immediately took his face in both hands and pulled him down for a kiss. She had great lips. She was a nice kisser. If that night with Lexi had never happened, he'd have been balls-deep with this woman a long time ago. The kiss grew hotter as they always did, and while Jax was good at making the right moves and going through the motions, the true desire wasn't there. And there just was no way to will it to appear. He'd tried.

Jax opened his door and climbed out, then took Tawna's small waist and pulled her from the cab to set her on the ground. Instead, she wrapped her legs around his hips and her arms around his neck and smiled into his eyes. Hers were brown and beautifully shaped. Her hair long and deep chestnut. She weighed barely a hundred pounds and had a great, athletic body. She was funny and normal and sweet. She had a decent job, ambition for more, a normal family, everything Jax always thought he'd wanted.

Until he'd met Lexi.

Tawna kissed him long and hot, then whispered against his lips, "Come in with me, Jax. Stay the night."

He had three excuses rolling off his tongue that he hadn't used yet, but paused before answering. He set her down halfway up the walk and held her hand up to the porch. His mind pinged back and forth, telling him to go in, get what he needed, give her what she wanted. But it wasn't what he wanted, or rather, *she* wasn't *who* he wanted.

God, he was such an idiot. Lexi wasn't an option. She hadn't wanted him for any more than one night. He didn't fit into her world—whatever world that was.

And, if her silence was any indication—no texts or phone calls since she'd walked out of his room—she certainly hadn't changed her mind. It was over. Shit, it had never really started. He had to find a way to accept that. To move past it.

And then they were at Tawna's door.

Holding tight to his hand, she unlocked the door, pushed it open, and stepped inside, pulling on his arm. When he didn't follow, she turned a questioning gaze on him. Damn, she really was pretty. And as sweet and smart as Wes had promised. And...*damn* Lexi. *Damn her* for having some spark, some *something* that made it impossible for Jax to get her out of his mind.

The bright anticipation in Tawna's pretty eyes dimmed. Her smile faded. She propped her shoulder against the doorjamb with a new look of resignation and stared down at his hand, still in hers.

"You're not coming in," she said.

He didn't know what to say. He'd never gotten to this point with women and turned them down.

"What is it, Jax?" Tawna asked. "I thought we had something."

"Me too." Or could have. "The truth is... Before Wes set us up, I was with someone and– "

"I heard," she said, sympathy turning her eyes sad. "It ended badly. What she did was horrible, Jax."

His mind was so deep in Lexi, it took him a moment to climb out and realize Tawna was talking about Veronica. And he realized letting her think he was talking about Veronica might make this much easier for Tawna.

"I guess I'm more reluctant that I thought. I'm thinking you played it right," he said, referencing their discussion about her breakup and why she'd waited so long to start dating again. She smiled a sad, understanding smile and nodded. "I'm…really sorry, Tawna. Can I, I don't know, call you sometime? If you're free, great, if not, I totally understand."

"Of course."

She leaned in. They kissed. Jax walked back to his truck alone.

And cursed the shit out of Lexi.

Inside the cab, Tawna's perfume still lingered. Floral and sweet. She was a good person, and Jax hated himself for disappointing her. Hurting her. He slammed his palm against the steering wheel and laid his head back, closing his eyes.

Lexi instantly filled his mind like she did every time he closed his eyes. Which was stupid, because he'd never seen her. Not really. Yes, he'd seen shadows, silhouettes, glimpses of that one crystal blue eye, golden eyelashes, and full pink lips in the light of his phone. But that was it. And over the last three weeks, even those small details had faded from his mind. Now he was doing more imagining than remembering, because in reality, she was nothing more than a shadow.

He rubbed his face and swore. The tension in his cock was ridiculous, and he was getting tired of jacking off. "So fucking stupid," he muttered. "Should have just fucked Lexi and left it."

But no. He'd held on to her right up until she'd almost missed her flight. They'd made love all night—which he was sure was where his mistake lay. Once they'd made it into bed, the sex changed from wicked-hot fucking to…wicked-hot lovemaking. Sensual, deep, moving. The way she'd insisted on pleasing him touched a place he hadn't fully realized existed and made the sex ten times as intense, ten times as good as it had ever been. The way he'd needed to please her had been, in hindsight, absurdly important to him. At the time, it had felt crucial, and the payoff, a delirious high.

Yeah, it had been that damn bed. It had changed everything.

He turned the key and pulled away from the curb, his mind

turning toward home. An uncomfortable, heavy sensation coiled in the pit of his stomach. He loved that house, but it was so damned big. So damned empty. Usually, that worked for him. But tonight...

He'd go for a run on the beach. Yeah, that would help. Maybe jump in the ocean after. He could use a good cooldown after thinking about Lexi.

He'd taken far more swims than usual lately.

Forcing his mind toward work was easy. Business was great. He only wished he could clone himself. His guys were the best at what they did, real no-fear, no-shit, intelligent guys, but they all specialized in one area or another, making it difficult to schedule the work coming in. And Jax ended up spreading himself thin.

His work cell rang, and he picked it up. "Renegades."

"Jax." He recognized Russ Mathers's voice instantly. "What the hell are you doing picking up the phone at this hour?"

The last time he'd talked to Russ had been the day he'd met Lexi. He was beginning to think he was cursed to live with her inside his head. "I have no life, Russ. How's everything?"

"Good. What are you up to?"

"Just dropping off a friend. Headed home. Are you still in New York?"

"Yeah. The shoot's going great. Those scenes you shot with Ty are *epic*. Seriously, Jax, wait till you see them on the big screen. You do such great work. And as much trouble as you and Ty are to have together, like two little kids loose in a damn candy store, what we got from it was worth the trouble."

"Give it up, Russ. You love having us together. We make you laugh your ass off."

"Speaking of, remember when you and Ty were screwing around and you poked him with the lance when he was looking at some babe over his shoulder and he fell off the damn horse? Then while you were laughing your ass off, he grabbed your lance and yanked you down with him?"

Just remembering the incident had Jax laughing so hard, he had to pull over before he took the freeway on-ramp. He put the truck in park and wiped his eyes. All the fun and happiness he'd had between working with Ty and Russ and being with Lexi came rushing back and filled him so completely, he hurt.

"The masters in the studio messed with that digitally," Russ said, "and turned it into a gnarly fight scene."

"Oh man," he said, his gut burning. "I needed that."

"I could hear it in your voice when you picked up," Russ said. "I could tell something was bothering you weeks ago. What's going on?"

Jax sighed, wishing he'd been able to talk to Russ about this when he'd tried—when Lexi was still with him. "Nothing, Russ. Life's good. Work's kicking my ass."

"It's not that Veronica shit, is it?"

"No, man, I'm way over it."

"That's not why I called, but did you hear—?"

"Woods got fired as the stunt coordinator on the Bond film? Yeah, believe me, I've heard—numerous times." Jax had also been dodging calls from Veronica for a couple of weeks as well. "Looks like Veronica isn't going to get that chance to drive after all."

"You're saving her life, Jax."

"Don't go all dramatic on me. She'll just go fuck someone else, eventually get her ass in a car, and kill herself. She isn't the kind to learn from experience."

"You didn't used to be that kind either," Russ said, "but I do have to say I'm proud of the way your changes over the last few years have stuck."

Jax's throat tightened. It shouldn't matter so much, but it did. And he couldn't afford any more emotion pulling at him. "Thanks, Russ. I'm a work in progress."

"Aren't we all? Don't be surprised if Rimer calls you," he said, referring to the producer on the Bond film. "The director is trying to take over for Woods, and it's not working out very well.

They're about twenty million over budget on stunts."

"Christ."

"No kidding. Rimer knows you can pull it into the black for him, but I think he's trying to save face."

"I don't care what he's doing. I'm not all that interested. Even less now that I know I'm going to be pulled in to clean up someone else's mess." Especially a mess that was Veronica's making.

"Don't throw the baby out with the bathwater, now."

Jax laughed. "Haven't heard that in…like… Well, I don't think I've ever heard it used seriously."

"Shut up. I'm old. I'm just saying that stuffing your pride and taking the job if he offers it, pulling it out of the fire for him will earn you one hell of a lot of gold stars. It could really shoot you ahead in an industry that's already as competitive as it gets. Take it from someone who knows, Jax, you won't be young forever. Build now, while you can. You may not need the money, but you'd be a hell of a miserable man sitting home in your old age with nothing to do."

Jax grumbled a reluctant agreement.

"But, like I said," Russ said, "that's not why I called. Poe changed a few things around. He's jockeying, repositioning, you know how he is."

Jerry Poe was the producer of the *Robin Hood* remake. A really brilliant man. But brilliance, Jax had noticed, often came with eccentricities. For Poe, that meant rewriting the movie on the fly.

"He wants to run a few more fight scenes," Russ said. "We were hoping to get you back here for a week. What do you think?"

His mind immediately darted to Lexi. He propped his elbow on the windowsill and slapped his palm to his temple. *Idiot. Lexi lives here, not in New-fucking-York.* Flying across the country would not get him any closer to her.

"I'm really tight, Russ. I'll be running across speeding trains and fighting assassins for another couple of days, and I'm taking a hundred-foot fall in downtown Chicago first part of next week."

"I heard about you getting dirty for Cruise on that Barcelona flick. Hear he's pissed the insurance company's keeping him on the ground."

"You sure hear a lot for an old man. I'm letting Cruise do everything but run on the train. He knows he's more valuable than I am. He's dealing with it. But you can bet your ass I'm going to make it look as fun as fucking possible for the torment."

"You sonofabitch." Russ laughed the words. "Can you come play with us after you jump in Chicago—providing you live? You'll make your brother happy. He gets sulky when you're not there to entertain him."

"I'll live, and for you and Ty, I'll make it work. How long do you need me?"

"Four, five, eight...ten days," he said with a smile in his voice.

Jax chuckled and rubbed his eyes. "I'm pretty sure I can squeeze in five. I'll call you later and let you know for sure."

He said good-bye, disconnected, and sat there a moment, staring at the phone. Slowly, he slid it back into the case on his belt, moved his hand to the phone sitting right next to it, and pulled it into his hand.

One half of his brain was yelling, *Don't do it. Dooooon't do it.*

The other side was laughing like a mad scientist and rubbing his hands together, whispering, *The perfect excuse.*

He looked at his iPhone. Tapped into text messages. Lexi's last note was still on his list of recents because he did a lot more talking than texting.

LEXI: On the plane. Miss you already. XO

He'd asked her to text him when she'd boarded so he knew she was safely on her way home. The rest she'd added on her own. And every time Jax looked at the message, he ended up reading twenty different things into the words.

Jax looked out the windshield. He almost wished she hadn't

done that. Maybe it would have been easier to forget her if she hadn't left that *miss you already* dangling.

He watched the cars speed by on the highway, their lights blurring.

"...stuffing your pride and taking the job if he offers it, pulling it out of the fire for him will earn you one hell of a lot of gold stars."

And Jax was considering. For the benefit of his company. For the men who worked for him. For the sense of accomplishment. The sense of validation.

Which was just what Lexi had been doing for her company. For her employees. For herself.

Granted, Jax didn't like being her sacrifice, but he understood it. And he understood her. They were, in fact, a lot alike in a lot of ways. He believed they were even more alike in ways they didn't even know yet. If he could just spend some more time with her...

He looked down at his phone and shook his head. God, he knew he was setting himself up for heartbreak. *Knew it.* Yet he was like a moth hypnotized by the flame.

"She's not going to be in New York the same days as I am," he told his phone.

Jax so badly wanted to fool himself into believing that was the reason he was going to text her.

"Great," he muttered to the phone. "My subconscious has already decided I'm going to do it."

His phone didn't comment. Just stared back at him sending telepathic *Text Lexi, Text Lexi* vibes.

He shut off the engine and rolled down the window, letting the cool Los Angeles pollution roll in.

"Okay," he told his phone. "It'll be an easy way for her to brush me off, and I can stop thinking about her, right?"

He really was going out of his mind.

"Or it could open the door in case she's been feeling the

same way I have."

Chances were not good. He'd never met a woman who had that kind of self-control. If they wanted a guy, they found a way to get the guy. Which usually included subterfuge, lies, betrayal…stealing six-figure contracts.

"Fuck me."

That was just what he was doing by starting this. He was asking to get fucked again. Maybe he was more like Veronica than he was like Lexi after all, because he certainly wasn't learning from his mistakes.

He jerked out his work phone again, checked his calendar, and called Russ back. After finagling with him for ten minutes and promising the man another five days of his life, Jax hung up and tapped into his messages.

Then created a new one to Lexi.

SEVENTEEN

Lexi closed the lid of her computer and wandered to the other side of the loft and her bed, pulling off her shirt as she walked. She was exhausted. The mental stress was killing her. The crazy hours were draining her. Instead of feeling invigorated by her business as she had for so many years, she felt sucked dry. Like it aged her a year every month.

This wasn't what she wanted. But she also knew she had to go through the rough spots to get to the good stuff. And she hadn't decided whether this partnership with Galliano was one of the rough spots or a black hole. She'd fallen into some of those along the way too.

Already in bare feet, she tugged off her jeans, untangled her hair from the ponytail holder, and rummaged through her drawer for Jax's T-shirt. She'd brought it home from New York and had been sleeping in it ever since.

Her phone vibrated against her desk, signaling a text message.

Lexi glanced toward it and sighed. Rubi, sending her some follow-up inspirational note or shooting her an idea, she was sure. Rubi was such a good friend. Lexi was lucky to have her.

She dragged her sorry self to the desk, picked up the phone, and returned to her bed, where she fell into it with a groan. She lifted the phone to read her message.

A hot burst of shock slammed her stomach. Lexi gasped and sat up, holding the phone with both hands, scanning the message again and again, trying to convince herself she was mistaken.

But she wasn't. The message was from Jax.

Jax.

"Oh shit," she murmured.

> **JAX:** Hey, Lexi. Hope I'm not bothering you. I'll be heading to New York next week. Would love to see you if you happened to be in town.

"Oh my *God*."

She put a hand to her chest, bit her lip, and scraped it between her teeth. Her heart beat hard and erratic. She couldn't believe it. Jesus, she couldn't freaking *breathe*.

Okay, this was fate. Just like he'd said in New York. It had to be.

She hit REPLY. The message box opened, and the cursor blinked inside.

Lexi's mind went as blank as the box. What did she say? How did she say it? Why had he texted her? After all this time? What did it mean?

She closed her eyes. "Stop," she commanded herself. "Just stop."

Pulling in air, she texted slowly, writing and rewriting the message, suddenly tongue-tied, if there was such a thing in texting.

> **LEXI:** Hearing from you is never a bother. And, amazingly, I will be in New York next week. Are you staying at Spencer's? What are your dates?

She finally got sick of trying to read every possible misrepresentation the message might present, and with her lip between her teeth, hit SEND.

Then she sat there, holding the phone in both hands like it was made of jewels, her stomach somersaulting as she waited for a return text.

When it came, she still wasn't ready. The vibration startled her, and she dropped the damn thing.

Laughing like an idiot, she scooped it up and read.

> **JAX:** That's amazing. I'm doing a few more scenes on the same movie. I'll be there Tuesday through Sunday. I couldn't

get in at Spencer's this time. I'm at the Four Seasons. What do you think?

"No," she drew out the word in a whine. "I think I'm screwed." Her stomach dropped and burned with something far more intense than disappointment.

She set the phone down, pulled out her file drawer, and clawed through her receipts for the travel information. Spread it out on her drawing table. Her phone vibrated, and she startled. She closed her eyes for a second. Then read his message.

JAX: That good, huh?

LEXI: Looking at my schedule now. Trying to figure something out. It's not pretty. You're in New York the days I'm in London.

JAX: Why are you going to London?

LEXI: Fabric-and-fashion expo.

He didn't text back, and anxiety rose in her chest as if she had a limited time to accept the offer before it disappeared. As if she would never get the offer again if she couldn't figure out a way to accept. Worse, that she'd explode if she missed him by a few days.

"Dammit." She dropped her head into her hands. "Okay, how can I do this?" She was moving dates and appointments around in her head like a puzzle, and they were falling together about as easily as a Rubik's Cube.

Lexi's phone chimed, signaling an incoming call.

"Shit. Not now, Rubi," she muttered and picked it up. "Hey, Rubi, can I call you back? I'm trying to work on something—"

"Lexi?" Jax's voice took her by surprise. She sucked air and froze, unable to find words. "It's Jax. I, um…hope it's okay to call." He suddenly sounded guilty, like he thought he might have interrupted something. "I just thought it might be easier to figure out our schedules if we could talk them over together."

"I… I mean, of course. It's fine." She put a hand to her

stomach, as if that would settle it. "I'm sorry. Rubi was here a little while ago, and I thought— Never mind. I'm just looking at my... Oh, I guess I already said that."

Jax laughed, the sound soft, deep, and smooth. Lexi's body flashed hot with memories of those sure fingers sliding over her skin, his hot tongue behind her ear. The luscious, bone-deep craving she suffered whenever she thought of him created a heaviness between her thighs, and Lexi had to sit down before her legs went out.

"You sound like I feel," he said. "I've been sitting on the side of the road for fifteen minutes working up the nerve to text you."

All her muscles relaxed. She dropped her head into her hand. "Jesus, it's great to hear your voice."

"You just made my week, baby." His voice felt like a purr in her ear. "Let's work out these schedules so you can hear it in person. Though..." His voice deepened with suggestion. "I *am* sitting in my truck just off the intersection of Highways 110 and 5. At this time of night, I could be just about anywhere in the county within twenty minutes. All I need is an address, and we can spend all night looking at the fine points of these schedules...in the flesh."

Desire drilled through her body, making it difficult to think. On the fringes of her mind, his situation registered. "You're...on the side of the freeway?" She fought to clear her head. "Are you okay? Do you need...help...or something?"

"If I said yes..." He hesitated. "Would you come to me?"

Something about the way he said *come to me* made Lexi's blood bubble. Still, the question hit her wrong and cooled the growing heat. Not because he'd asked, but because he had to ask.

"If you needed something, you could always call me. I'm sorry..." Her throat squeezed with regret.

Jax waited a beat. "You're sorry...for what?"

"That I've created a situation between us that made you feel like you even have to ask."

But even through her frustration, his location sank in. He was awfully close to her studio, and she couldn't help but wonder if that was sheer chance. One glance at Google would have told him everything he wanted to know about her career. About who she was. What she looked like. She'd thought about researching him at least a hundred times but hadn't. Had wondered if he'd done the same.

"Jax...?"

"Lexi," he answered, his voice smoky.

Her mind and body warred—her brain suspicious, her body needy. She couldn't just forget about the men in her past who'd been difficult to shake. At the time, she couldn't have imagined any of them acting so immature or insecure. If she just put those instances out of her mind and believed it wouldn't happen again, she'd find herself right back in that hot seat.

She forced air into her lungs. "What are you doing at the intersection of 110 and 5 at this time of night in the middle of the week?"

"I was dropping a friend at home, stopped to talk on my phone, got the job in New York and...thought of you." He paused. His voice came quieter. "I must be close. You sound nervous."

She closed her eyes. Oh God, that voice. He could be caressing her through the phone. She replayed the sexy words he'd said to her that night.

"Tell me what you want, Lexi."

"I'll do anything."

"You feel so good, baby."

"Fifteen minutes," Jax whispered, pushing her toward the edge. "I'll speed."

Lexi dropped her head back to look at the ceiling and swore.

"If you're not with anyone," Jax asked, his voice growing contemplative, "and we both know how good it is between us... Tell me again why you're resisting this pull."

Her stomach seemed to float, giving her a giddy queasy sensation. "The truth is nothing's very clear anymore."

A moment of silence hung before he murmured, "God, I miss you, Lexi."

The underlying vulnerability in his voice ripped her open.

"I know that sounds crazy," he went on, "considering how little time we spent together, but... I can't stop thinking about you, and knowing I can't see you again...it's just..."

"Hard," she finished. "I know. I miss you too."

He breathed out, heavy and sharp, like the wind had been knocked out of him. "Baby..."

The almost-groan rippled over the connection and prickled Lexi's skin. She grasped at her last strands of safety.

"I don't want to hurt you." Even if Lexi could push all the image issues aside, even if she could forget about the partnership, her long hours and dedication to the business had always caused major problems in her previous relationships. And she certainly couldn't cut back. Not now. "This is a critical time for me. The shop demands more of me than there is to give. I just...don't have anything left."

"I understand what it takes to run a business on your own. And I'm a big boy, Lex. Let me worry about me. If you want me, take me. I'm offering."

"Christ." Lexi ran a hand over her face, caught her finger between her teeth.

"Just meet me, Lexi," he said, that imploring rasp in his voice that made it impossible to say no. "Just talk to me, face-to-face. At least give me a face to go with my fantasies."

She grimaced with the certainty this would not end well. "Do you know where The Recovery Room is?"

"On Sunset?"

"Y-yes." *Fuck, what am I doing?* "I'll meet you there."

Another breath whooshed out on his end of the line. "Wh—? O-okay. When?"

"Now. Before I change my mind."

"I'm there." In the background, an engine turned over. "Or I will be—fifteen minutes. Maybe ten. But, Lex, how will I know—?"

"I'll find you," she said and disconnected.

***

Jax couldn't ever remember being this nervous. Couldn't ever remember being this edgy. Not on his first date. Not during his first time having sex. Not on his first movie shoot. Not even on his most dangerous stunt.

He'd finished his second beer and ordered a third, just to have one sitting in front of him when—if—Lexi showed up. He'd been at The Recovery Room over thirty minutes and had already been hit on twice, been asked for an autograph once, and almost gotten into a fistfight with a guy over holding the stool next to him open.

A popular local band played on a stage in the back room, filling the bar with edgy music carrying a heavy base. The singer had a great voice, and his songs were filled with sexual lyrics. None of which helped the thick heat of blood pumping through Jax's veins.

The front door opened again, and he glanced over his shoulder from his seat, rubbing one damp palm down the thigh of his jeans. Two couples entered and drifted toward the only open table, closer to the music in the back. The door continued to open and close, customers continued to flow in and out of the busy club, but no Lexi.

Jax was caught between worried, angry, and disappointed. He spun his phone on the bar, switching gears from melting the ice between them when she got here to how he wanted to handle her no-show. He propped his elbows on the wood, ran both hands through his hair with the worst ache in his gut he could remember. Worse even than when Veronica had betrayed him and taken hundreds of thousands of dollars from his company and his guys.

After being chased by starlets, hounded by paparazzi, and

dogged by talk shows and tabloids, Jax had to admit Lexi's disinterest in seeing him based on his appearance had been a nearly lethal stab to his ego. But what really nagged at him—more than all the rest combined—was how Lexi's conviction to keep him out of her pristine "real" world brought up all his mother's ugly echoes—the disapproval and disappointment. The unfavorable comparisons to his brothers. The label of black sheep.

Lexi didn't know about any of that. And Jax truly believed she was too sweet to mean him any disrespect by placing these limits on their relationship. But somehow...the logical and the emotional were not meshing. And it had everything to do with how intensely he wanted Lexi. Had to be, because he'd gone through life not giving a bloody rat's ass until it kept him from her.

"Hi." A woman's voice brought Jax's gaze up and made his heart kick.

A blonde had walked up to the bar and stood near, casting him an uncertain smile. At least the fourth blonde of the night he thought could have been Lexi. All the others had been attractive. This one was so beautiful she struck him stupid for a moment. Her eyes were huge and deep crystal blue. Her lips fantasy plump, her nose sleek, cheekbones pronounced enough to edge her past sexy to a freaking knockout. Jax tried to pull up those moments of Lexi's face in the phone light.

No, this wasn't Lexi. Which was fine. One thing he'd learned by dating Tawna was the huge benefit in dating someone pretty and not gorgeous.

A man crowded the blonde on the opposite side. "Hey, sweetness. Let me take care of that drink for you."

She glanced away from Jax, leaving him with a strange sensation of familiarity. Not Lexi, but...he'd seen her somewhere before. Then again, this was a bar in LA on Sunset Strip. He'd probably seen her on some movie set.

That was exactly what Jax was not missing about the beauties he'd once dated—come-ons from other guys. A constant sense of needing to guard his territory or finding his chair taken when he came back from the restroom.

Jax put the blonde and the guy out of his mind, turned on the stool, pressed his back to the bar, and crossed his arms. Now what? He could call Lexi, but hadn't he groveled enough just getting her to agree to come? Or was that just his perception because he'd never really groveled before?

"Listen," the blonde said to the man, an edge in her voice that drew Jax's attention again. "If you want to buy my drinks, why don't you pass it through my date first?"

Her hand landed on his shoulder, and Jax didn't even flinch. He'd played this role so many times he could have freaking predicted it. He spoke without bothering to turn and face either of them. He wasn't in the mood. "Right. She's with me, dude. Back off."

The guy grumbled some bullshit Jax didn't even listen to. As soon as he was gone, Jax glanced at the beauty, then scanned the bar and looked at his phone. But the blonde kept tempting his eye as she slid onto the stool beside him. She wore something lavender, filmy, and short that showed every inch of her legs in his peripheral vision as she crossed them. Long, tan, and shaped in luxurious soft strokes of toned muscle.

If any other woman had stood him up, he'd have jumped at the opportunity to pick up a jackpot like this one. But Jax truly only craved one woman.

"Listen," Jax said without looking at her, "if you have more trouble with him and I'm still here, I'm happy to help out, but if you don't mind sitting somewhere else, I'm saving that seat—"

"Jax?"

He froze. A strange tightness clenched his gut. His gaze blurred over his phone's screen. His mind darted a million different directions in half a second, but nothing made sense.

He jerked around on the stool, startling her. Her eyes went wide, and her hand came up.

"L…Lexi?"

No. This couldn't be Lexi. His gaze traveled over her body—his only real reference point. The top of her dress was sleeveless, with just two thin straps on each shoulder. The fabric was sheer, everything underneath hidden only by the subtle similarly colored sequence across the bodice, fading as it moved down the front and belted in a solid row of sequins at her small waist. Her breasts swelled beneath the fabric, making the sequins wink and tease the eye that direction. Simple sequined sandals matched.

"Yeah, it's me." She smiled and the expression softened her from a knockout to a heartbreaker. Her eyes sparkled, teeth glimmered, and a dimple hinted deep in one cheek. Jax's heart stuttered.

"Holy fuck," he murmured. A familiar craving took root at the center of his body. One that flared quick and hot and made him suddenly, almost uncontrollably, ravenous.

But something dark had layered beneath the desire and blocked his affection. Jax zeroed in on her face again. This woman might be the Lexi he'd slept with, but this...situation...wasn't right. *Something* wasn't right. He wasn't sure what, but he'd been screwed enough to know when it was going to happen again.

He pushed off the stool and stood, a flurry of emotions whipping through him, but the one leading was hurt. A deep hurt that signaled Jax had let himself put way too much hope into this woman—a woman he knew nothing about.

"Jax, what's wrong?" She reached out, put a hand on his arm. The touch spread heat along his skin, and his heart rate sped. Then she laughed, the sound nervous while pulling her phone from a small purse. "You probably have women coming on to you all the time, and I know I'm late. I was so nervous I stood outside... Here, look..."

She turned her phone to face him. His own words from his last text to her letting her know he was at the bar, waiting, stared back at him.

He kept his gaze on them, his insides a total mess. He didn't question her identity, at least not since he'd recognized that dimple. That smile. He only questioned her motive. But...no...he'd initiated the conversation that had brought her here.

Shit, he was really confused.

She lowered her phone. Her smile flickered, and nerves darkened her eyes. "I guess you didn't Google me after all. Thought for sure..." A look of fragility hinted in her face. "Disappointed?"

He narrowed his eyes. No, he hadn't Googled her, but the fact that she'd brought it up meant she'd probably done some digging of her own. Had probably linked Bentley and Jax. Something about her expression, the nervous smile, the look in her eyes...

Bam. It hit him like a horse's kick in the gut.

The Ferrari outside the airport.

The scene played over in his head in a fraction of a second, and he murmured, "Rubi."

The name had struck something with him when Lexi had said it over the phone. He hadn't thought anything of it. Figured it was someone she'd mentioned when they were together. But that wasn't where he'd first heard the name—an unusual name that didn't come up very often.

Her smile fell into a confused frown. "What?"

"Rubi is your friend, the one you mentioned on the phone. Rubi Russo."

Her head tilted. "She... How do you know—?"

"She dropped you off at the airport. I saw you. In the Ferrari." He stepped back, his entire system reeling with the realization. A Ferrari. Two gorgeous women in a Ferrari. Rubi with her glaring flirtation. They'd had *wrong way, Chamberlin, go back* written all over them. Something Wes had to remind Jax of when he'd been unable to tear his gaze away from Lexi.

The sensation that flooded Jax went way beyond

disappointment. This was a dark, sucker punch of tar. "Fuck. Me."

Her eyes flashed with shock first. Maybe a touch of panic. He could see her mind working, putting puzzle pieces together. She put up her hand. "Jax...wait—"

"You're...wow, you're really good." He pressed one hand against the bar and gripped it hard, picked up his third beer with the other and drank.

"I don't know what you mean by that," she said, "but you're right, Rubi dropped me off at the airport. And I did see you. Then you showed up at the gate, and we started talking. I wasn't...*stalking* you. I *was* flying to New York. It was just—"

"What was your last job?" he asked before downing more beer. God, he was the biggest fucking fool.

Her lips parted, brow pulled. She eased to her feet, coming within easy reach. Her heat, her scent wrapped around him. Jax's throat closed.

He stepped back.

"I don't know what you're talking about," she said. "Last job for what?"

"Acting. What was it? An extra? A minor role? A commercial?"

Her gaze lowered to his beer. Darted toward the bar, then back to him. "I told you I wasn't in that industry. I told you—"

She stopped suddenly, her lips still parted, words still on her tongue. Her eyes scanned his. God, they were so clear, such a beautiful blue. His gaze lowered to her mouth. And oh fuck, that mouth. What she'd done to him with that mouth...

"It doesn't matter what I told you, does it?" She asked the question so softly it seemed as if she were asking herself. She slid her lower lip between her teeth and stepped away from the bar. Swallowed, and met his gaze again. "I'm...sorry, Jax. This is my fault. I shouldn't have... I didn't realize..." She pressed her lips together and curved them over her teeth. She glanced at him again, her gaze filled with regret and guilt and pain. "I'm sorry...for everything. I'm going to go."

She started toward the door.

No. Jax wasn't ready to let this go.

He sidestepped into her path, and she stopped just short of running into him. Her body was an inch from his. The familiarity of her scent, her heat made him weak. He lowered his head, tilted his face until his nose touched her hair.

He couldn't ever remember wanting anything or anyone this badly in his entire life.

"I…" she said, voice weak. "Didn't mean…for this to happen. And I don't understand…" She struggled but couldn't seem to find the words.

Jax let his eyes close, but he didn't let himself pretend Lexi was anything other than what he'd come to realize.

"Here's the thing, beautiful," he murmured. "You've scammed someone who's been scammed enough to know what it looks like." He pressed the palm of his free hand to her waist and felt the slightest flinch. "I'm street smart enough to recognize why a hot ticket like you is interested in me. And, baby, we both know it's not sex when you could get that anywhere, with anyone you wanted."

She put a hand on his forearm and leaned back. Jax slid his arm around her waist and pulled her up against his body. She gasped in surprise. Her hand tightened on his arm. Jax's mind blurred with the pleasure streaming through him.

"After that night with you," he whispered, "I swore I wouldn't do this again. But…" He exhaled heavily, growled with the frustration of how perfect she felt, how badly he wanted her… He nudged her hair off her neck with his face and opened his mouth on her skin. One taste was all it took—he caved.

"Tell me what you want from me," he murmured. "And I'll tell you if I can ultimately fulfill your wish. That way neither of us will be disappointed later. What is it? An introduction? A part in a movie? An investment?"

A sound came from her throat, and her hand swept up his arm, over his shoulder, around his neck and pulled him close. She pressed her body to his, and *God damn* she made Jax's blood boil. He groaned. Squeezed his eyes against the pain of disappointment.

"I'm so sorry," she whispered. "I never thought... I'm just...*so sorry.*"

She pulled away, but Jax held on. Frustration growing with his desperation. "Just tell me, Lex. I wouldn't go out of my way for anyone else, but I want you so badly—"

"Stop." When she looked up, her eyes were smoky blue and swimming in unshed tears. "Just stop, Jax. I'm not an actress. I'm a damn dressmaker. I don't want anything from you. Nothing but the man I was with a month ago. I'm sorry you've been scammed in the past. I'm sorry I somehow remind you of others who've done that to you. And I don't blame you for thinking the worst. It's completely my fault for starting our relationship the way I did. It was stupid of me to hope something good could come of something started that way."

Tears escaped her eyes. She stretched up and kissed his cheek. "Please think before you sell yourself out to another woman like that. You deserve better."

She pulled away from him with force and pushed the exit door open by slamming the metal bar. Then she was gone.

Jax's heart rate picked up. His brain pinged. Go after her? Was that what she wanted? If it was, this was the most elaborate scam anyone had ever used to get a favor.

By the time he pushed the door open, she was gone.

EIGHTEEN

Jax went back inside the club and straight to the bar.

"Hey," he called to the bartender. "Do you know the woman who was—"

"Looked like you knew her well enough." He gave Jax that you're-an-asshole look. "Why are you asking me?"

He blew out a breath, pulled a hundred from his wallet, and put it on the bar. "Where is her shop?"

"Two blocks north. Lexi LaCroix Designs."

Ah, fuck. Jax had been half expecting him to say, "What shop?"

Jax ran the two blocks, cursing himself. He stopped across the street from Lexi's storefront, a corner spot in a series of new, quaint, stand-alone stores. Her front window was curved around the corner, huge plateglass windows displaying the most ornate wedding dress Jax could ever imagine as the centerpiece, a red gown on the right, a blue gown on the left, each a different design, each exquisite. The kind of dress his mother, sister, or date would wear to the freaking Oscars.

Haute couture. On Sunset Avenue in Los Angeles. Across the street from a Jaguar and Bentley dealership. A *Bentley* dealership. How ironic was that?

She hadn't been lying or kidding or even exaggerating. She was exactly what she'd told him.

He swallowed, pressed his hands to his hips, and shook his head before he crossed the street. The shop was dark except for the lights in the window illuminating the dresses and highlighting signs declaring the store protected by surveillance cameras and a professional security system.

She'd probably gone straight home. Jax had no idea where she lived. He could call her, but she wouldn't answer. Not that he deserved to have his call answered after what he'd just accused her of. He wandered to the edge of the building, glancing into the windows.

A sound behind the building caught his ear. He went around to the back, and found the typical small parking lot, packing boxes, trash cans...and Lexi leaning against the back door, fighting with the lock. Sobbing.

His heart broke. He was a fucking fool all right, but not in the way he'd first suspected.

God, how had this all gone so bad?

"Lexi."

She jumped, turned, but Jax stood in the shadowed area between two streetlights. She started working frantically on the lock again, sniffling. "You know the parking lot is off-limits. This is private property. If you don't get out of here, I'll send your picture from the security cameras to LAPD. And you'll get nailed with another fine. I'm not going to tell you anything more about my clients at two in the morning than I do at two in the afternoon—"

"Lexi, it's Jax."

She gasped, stopped struggling with the lock, and pushed the hair out of her face. The light over the back door made the tears shine on her skin. The sight made Jax ache.

"Baby, I'm so sorry," he said, knowing it wasn't enough. Realizing how screwed up he was.

"It's my fault." She sucked in a choked sob and hammered the glass door with both fists, then dropped her forehead against it. "Fucking door."

And started crying again.

When Jax reached her, she'd melted against the door. He pulled her back, turned her, and eased her against his body, holding her gently. "Aren't we a couple of fucked-up messes?"

She heaved a troubled breath and tilted her chin back. Her mascara had smeared, and Jax ran his thumb along the corner of her eye, wiping the shadow away.

"I—" She hiccupped. "I've had a r-really rough d-day."

"I'll say," he murmured, feeling like the biggest dick on the planet. "I'm sorry I made it worse." He ran his thumb over her plump lower lip, unable to tear his gaze away. Needing to feel it between his own. "Can I take you home? Make it up to you?"

"I am home." She pulled back and looked down at her keys. "If I can just get inside."

"You live here?" Jax asked, confused.

"My apartment's in the loft above the shop."

He had a million questions. "Let me get you inside." He held his hand out. "Let's talk a little."

She pushed a wad of keys into his hand, her own shaking. "It's two in the morning, Jax. Don't you have to work tomorrow?"

Her concern pinched his chest. "Let me worry about that. Which key? Why do you have a thousand of these things?"

"The red one. Everything inside the store is locked in case someone gets past the system."

He frowned as he held the door open. "This might not be the safest place to live, Lex."

As she passed, her scent touched him. Invited him to touch her. Taste her. "Since I spend almost every hour here anyway, it only makes sense."

Beside the door, Lexi uncovered a hidden keypad and punched in a code. She re-covered it with a snap and shot Jax a sad lopsided grin. "Now I have to kill you."

He matched her grin, mesmerized at how her face was already so familiar to him. She locked the door, her gaze searching the exterior through the glass without turning on a light.

Jax eased up behind her, put his hands on her waist. "Who did you think I was?"

"Photographers," she murmured. "Or a reporter. They're always around, but they hover when I've got high-profile clients."

"Who were they watching for?"

"Jessica Love, mostly. But Bailey Simmons came this week too." She shook her head. "Bad scheduling. I'll never make that mistake again."

"Daughters of the biggest producer and director in Tinseltown? Yeah, probably not the best ladies to have in the same location in the same week without a LeCroix security force."

"If I could afford one, a lot of my stress and problems would disappear."

"Maybe you need to raise your prices. Jessie's daddy would buy her the moon if it were for sale. Bailey's daddy is still negotiating with God for the deed to the universe."

She tilted her head back and looked up at him. "How did you know she goes by Jessie?"

"I've worked for her father, Stan."

He'd actually had dinner with Stan and his family numerous times. He'd coached with Jessie's future husband on several big films, and they were friends. He'd been invited to Jessie's wedding this weekend. But that would probably be overwhelming and unnecessary information at the moment.

She searched his eyes, but then nodded and gazed into the dark again. "He's a nice man. Stan, I mean."

"I knew who you meant. No one would ever mistake Simmons as nice."

She hummed in agreement. "My prices are already high. My biggest problem isn't getting what the dresses are worth, it's cloning myself. There aren't enough of my bloody fingers to go around."

She lifted her hands, palms facing them. Even in the dim light, Jax could see her torn, roughened fingertips.

"The price of success, huh?" he murmured and drew one of her hands to his lips, kissing each fingertip.

Lexi sighed, and as soon as he lowered her hand, she turned in his arms. "I really don't want you tired while you're working. That's dangerous. You need to get some sleep. We can talk tomorrow."

He loved the way she tried to take care of him. "I've got a night shoot tomorrow. I won't go into the set until late." He eased the backs of his fingers over her high cheekbones. "God, you're crazy beautiful. Why did you want to hide this?"

"I've had some bad experiences…" She looked away, her golden lashes sweeping down to hide her eyes.

Jax's mind filled with the words she'd spoken shortly after she'd stepped into his hotel room. *The truth is that men are attracted to me for my…body."*

God, it all clicked. Men wanted her for her *beauty*, not just her body. Men used her as window dressing, the same way women used Jax—for dressing, a reputation boost, favors.

A dry huff of laughter drifted from his throat. "Baby, we are far more alike than you know."

Pulling from his arms, she walked toward a wall and flipped on a bank of lights, filling the store with soft spot lighting.

Jax found himself standing in a near replica of his mother's living room—every surface marble, chrome, smoked or etched glass. Overstuffed furnishings dressed in thick jacquard or leather dotted the small series of rooms. A fountain drowned out the exterior noises with a tranquil gurgle. Dresses on mannequins and hanging on racks sparkled like fireworks.

His gaze skimmed the space, taking in all the detailed woodwork, paint, displays. A few things struck him at the same time. He suddenly felt overly big and bulky and rough in the delicate, refined space, and terribly out of place. He realized what caliber of people Lexi must deal with every day, people far above what she believed of Jax's life. And he recognized how much she'd accomplished. More than probably any other woman he'd dated.

"Let me just clear a few things up before they become problems." Lexi strolled up beside him, arms crossed, then continued past and into a room with carpet so thick it swallowed her small feet and sparkling sandals. "Everything here is mine. Everything you see I've created, designed, sewn myself. I have a few seamstresses that help me out. They work out of their homes. But the work is so specialized and my clients so particular, I have to do all the finish work myself."

Jax met her eyes. They looked as dark blue as the Pacific in the dim light.

"I've been building this business since I could draw. I didn't go to college. Don't have a fancy degree from a design school. I grew up poor. Dirt poor. So every success for me is that much sweeter. I've never borrowed a dime. Never had a financial backer. Everything about Lexi LaCroix Designs is one hundred percent...mine."

"*Fuck*," Jax whispered, rubbing a hand over his eyes, wishing he could take his impulsive words at the bar back. "Lexi, I'm sorry. I didn't..."

"I know," she said. "That's why I'm telling you. I don't need anyone to do or give me anything to succeed. I'm already there. I'm trying to refine that success to give me a better quality of life. But I have everything I need to do it on my own terms, in my own time, through opportunities that come to me because of all that hard work. I'm proud of that.

"And with how little I know about you, it's hard to imagine what you could possibly have that you fear I would want. Money is the obvious answer, since as I told you in New York, Hollywood contacts hold no value for me. So let me just set your mind straight right now. My friend, Rubi, has been trying to push millions on me for years. I've had three different investors approach me. I've turned everyone down. I don't want to leverage my business. I want to build it. Grow it. Myself. That's what the business opportunity in New York was about. And that's not panning out very well either."

"Your rough day?" he asked.

"Partially, yes."

Things were starting to fall into place—making him want her more and pushing her farther away at the same time.

He ran his tongue over his lower lip and looked around the

shop. "And the reason you wouldn't see me here in LA is because…" He gestured to the surroundings, his gut aching. "I don't fit into that image you've worked so hard to create."

She dropped her arms and raked both hands through her hair, then turned and wandered away, toward a rack of pristine white gowns, each sealed in a clear plastic cover.

"I've trapped myself. I didn't realize it until I met you. I was just building a business, doing what I loved to do, growing with the market, meeting demand. Slowly, my clients became wealthier, more important, higher profile. It looked like success to me. I was so caught up in becoming what I'd always dreamed, accomplishing what everyone said I couldn't that I didn't see how limiting it had become.

"Now I feel like I live in a bubble. Cameras follow my clients into the shop; reporters dog me for the inside scoop. I've had reporters try to pay me off, seduce me, threaten me. They are relentless."

She sighed and turned back to him. "Now how clean my personal image is becomes a factor in whether this billionaire will have me design his daughter's wedding dress and the dresses for her eighteen bridesmaids to the tune of half a million dollars. Whether this big New York designer wants to take me on as a partner and distribute my work in stores I can't even imagine reaching on my own."

Jax nodded slowly, raked his bottom lip between his teeth, but it didn't ease the growing knot in his chest. "And it doesn't matter who I am as a person. Your biggest clients would take one look at me—my leathers, my tattoos, my too long hair, my motorcycle, the cuts and bruises and occasional black eyes—and jump to their own conclusions. Then judge you based on those. And take their business elsewhere."

And based on how much of this she'd done on her own and the fact that she'd grown up poor, he'd bet this was all she had.

He huffed a humorless laugh. "Yeah, I get it."

And he was disgusted with the whole superficial scene—one

prevalent in the entire LA area, not just Hollywood. More, he hated the way it kept him from what he wanted most. Lexi.

She clasped her hands, threaded her fingers, and looked down at the floor again. "It's that, yes. But, it's also…" She swallowed. Her hands twisted. "I've just come too close to losing everything because I trusted. I hoped. And it's, I don't know, scarred me…or scared me…or both."

She started laughing, an exhausted, disheartened sound, and pressed her hands to her cheeks. "See, aren't you glad I didn't tell you all this last month? You'd have thought I was psychotic. 'Cause…well, I kind of am…"

She covered her face and made a sound Jax couldn't decipher between a laugh and a sob.

"I'm glad you didn't," he said, "but not because of that. I'd have been freaking intimidated. I think… No, I know, I'm still intimidated. I know a dozen corporate executives who can't handle their personal and professional lives so well, Lex."

She dropped her hands and gestured to her face, wet with tears again. "I'm obviously not handling it all that well."

He grimaced. "You were until I messed things up."

"No." She approached him and gripped his arms. "This is not your fault. This is not about you not fitting in. This is about me putting on a face to be what others think I should be to keep my business going."

She heaved a sigh and slid her hands down his arms until her fingers wound around his, then pulled him toward a corner of the shop. He followed, hoping she was going to drag him into a chair in some corner, raise her little dress, and straddle his lap, bridge this growing distance between them. But she started up a set of stairs in the back.

Even better. Her apartment. His mind drifted away from all the problems between them and straight to getting her naked, filling her, and staying there the rest of the night.

At the top of the stairs, an open space stretched the length of the shop. One glance and Jax could see this wasn't an apartment. It was an office and a workroom with a bed in the corner.

She had a drafting table on one side of the room, another long table with fabric bolts lined up, pattern pieces stacked, sketches layered everywhere and lining the walls. Three different mannequins stood in a corner, each wearing partially finished dresses in different states of completion beside an industrial sewing machine, it too covered in pattern pieces and stray fabric and trim.

Her bed was pushed up against two walls, the only other furniture a nightstand and a small dresser.

"This is me." She gestured to the chaotic space. Messy but clean. The space of a creative genius. He'd been around enough artists and writers to know what kind of spaces produced the really radical, ground-breaking shit. This was it.

She walked to the banister and gestured to where they'd just been. "That is who I have to be to do…" She waved to her drawing table. "…that. To make a living at what I love to do. The only thing I know how to do."

The same way Jax had to live in LA to make a living at what he loved to do. He understood. He did. But he wasn't finding any easy solution to the issue.

She turned back to him with so much worry and pain and regret in those gorgeous eyes, his mind flickered toward becoming exactly what she needed just to be able to look at her forever. He had the breeding, the knowledge, the skill. He'd have an entire fucking fan club in his family alone.

But he wouldn't be himself.

"I'm not too good to be true, Jax. I may look good on the surface, but on the inside…" She winced. "I'm really a pretty ugly mess."

Jax scraped one hand through his hair. He wasn't going to try to argue with her here or now. "Honestly, babe, I'm digging this ugly mess. But…Lexi…Jesus, living here? Do you even have a closet?"

"Across from the bathroom." She pointed to the corner opposite her bed, "Through that door."

Jax crossed the space, peering into a dark room. "Lex, this is not a bathroom, this is a hole in the wall." His entire living room was the size of this freaking store, and he suddenly wanted to spoil her in his luxurious house that went to waste, empty most of the time. He turned out of the space. "How much do you charge for the dresses?"

"Anywhere between fifteen and fifty thousand, depending on the work involved."

Jax made an involuntary sucking sound in his throat. He finally choked out, "Fifty thousand *dollars?*"

"No, grape seeds," she said, hand on her hip, mouth quirked in a little smile. "I find they're far more valuable than dollars."

The spark in her blue eyes, the look on her beautiful face, the sass in her tone floored Jax, and electricity sparked through his body. "You smart-ass little—"

Her laughter made him pause. Made him focus on her. Feel her. Made him realize he was holding her, one arm low on her back, one against the base of her neck, looking down at her smiling eyes. Fire flared inside him so fast he stopped breathing. Lexi's gaze softened. One hand rose from his bicep, rested against his cheek, and a look of longing in her eyes that made him forget everything but her.

"Fifty thousand dollars a dress," he said, "and you're living in this lunch bag?"

"Not every dress sells for that, each dress takes a long time to make, and I have one hell of a lot of overhead. Besides, growing up poor has made me…frugal. I don't see the point in paying two thousand dollars a month on a lunch bag of an apartment to do nothing but sleep there a few hours a night."

He ran his hand through her hair and smiled. "You need a life outside work, Lex. It's not healthy." He laughed. "Christ, this is like lecturing into a mirror."

"You're so handsome. I wish…" Emotion flooded her eyes.

She swallowed. Smiled, but the expression was sad. "I know it's stupid to say when we really don't know each other..."

"You're not listening to me..." But he let her slide. "And say it anyway."

"I've missed you so much."

An emotion Jax couldn't identify flooded him. It started at the middle of his chest and washed outward until he ached with it. Desire flowed in its wake. Deep and hot and strong. But different from anything he'd ever felt before. Far more intense.

He closed his eyes and pressed his forehead to hers. "What do you wish, Lexi? I'm in the mood to make your wishes come true."

"I wish I could have made love to you...looking into your eyes."

The feeling in his chest magnified. A sensation of both pleasure and pain mixed until Jax felt fused to Lexi. Like he'd go insane if he had to let her go.

"Tell me what I can do to make this work, baby."

She laughed. "I'm the last person to be giving advice on relationships, as evidenced by the lousy way I've handled this one from the start."

"I'm no gem either." Pulling back, he took her face in both hands and met her gaze seriously. "But I've been through enough relationships to know when I've found someone I want to keep. And I want to keep you." Tears gathered in her eyes. She bit her bottom lip. "What about you, Lex? It has to go both ways."

"Want? Yes," she whispered, her eyes sliding closed. "Yes, I want to keep you more than I want to breathe."

***

When Jax's lips covered hers, Lexi whimpered with relief. With lust. With need. She hadn't realized how badly she needed him until his strong arms pulled her up against his hard body. Until his lips were sliding against hers. Until his tongue touched hers and his taste filled her mouth.

They groaned at the same time. She sucked at his lips, licked into his mouth. Jax pulled her hips up against his. The jeans he wore were medium blue and deeply worn. They cupped his sex like a far softer fabric than denim, and when he rubbed against her, his heat burned through all their clothing layers.

Jax's hand clawed into her hair from the base of her neck. The strength pulled at the strands, shooting a delicious tingle through her scalp.

He pulled her head back, breaking the kiss. Lexi opened her eyes to his, heavy lidded and hot. They were a smoky blue-green. Not hazel at all.

"These have been the longest fucking three weeks of my life." His lips slid over hers again, as if he couldn't keep them away for more than a second. His tongue did sweet, erotic, wicked things to her mouth. He groaned, pulled back again. "I need you, Lex."

"Yes," she murmured, barely able to stand.

She fisted his shirt, a soft cotton T-shirt that melted beneath her hands, molded to his muscles as she touched him. But it wasn't enough. She needed skin and yanked the bottom edge from his jeans. Slid her hands under and groaned at the feel of him on her palms.

He broke the kiss. "Fuck, Lexi, I don't think I'm going to be able to go slow."

She smiled. Laughed Pressed her mouth to his throat. Hummed with pleasure. Took a deep breath—

Lexi froze, but Jax was still moving. Hands pulling at the belt on her dress. It fell to the floor when she finally leaned back.

He glanced down at her, took one scan of her face, and stopped moving. "Lex?" His hands slid over her arms. "What's wrong?"

She lowered her gaze. Her eyes held on the pulse beating in his throat. Her own throat thickened with turmoil. Emotion and regret tore through her stomach. She closed her eyes and pressed her nose and mouth to his shoulder. The fabric of his shirt caressed her skin as she took another deep breath, hoping she'd been wrong.

But no. Her head filled with perfume. A woman's perfume. She closed her eyes and pushed back.

"Honey?" he said.

She forced her eyes open and lifted them to his. Her mind ricocheted for an innocent reason he'd smell like another woman. His mother, his sister...a hug from a female friend. There could be a hundred reasons other than the one tormenting her.

"You...smell like perfume."

His heavy lids widened. Surprise flashed in his pretty eyes, then guilt, and his eyes slid closed. Head lowered. "Fuck."

Disappointment hammered her stomach, but it was her own damn fault for letting him go in New York. She waited, a sliver of hope still struggling to shine deep inside. "It's not exactly a surprise. You're hardly the kind of man who's going to stay available long—"

"Lex, it's not like that." His head came up, gaze fierce, but still guilt-ridden.

She bit the inside of her lip, her past demons trying to force their way into her heart. Her instinct was to push back, walk away, get out of this before he really hurt her. But she'd invested more of herself in Jax than any man in years, so she stayed put and raked her fingers through his hair one more time. "What is it like?"

"I was dating someone...for a few weeks—"

"Okay." *Ouch. Dammit.* She shook her head as her eyes fell closed. "That's all I need to know. You don't owe me an explanation." She opened her eyes but stared at his chest. The thought of him with another woman burned through her. "You have every right to see whoever you choose—"

"Then I choose you," he said, tightening his hands on her arms. "Lexi, I didn't sleep with her. I haven't had sex with anyone since you left me."

"I didn't *leave* you. Not the way you're making it sound. We agreed—"

"You're right. We did. And when you stuck to your end of it, I tried to move on. My buddy set me up with a really nice girl, but it didn't work because I haven't been able to get past *you*."

The admission coupled with the imploring look in his eyes made her heart squeeze, then open. But she left one last barrier in place. "Then why do you smell like her perfume?"

He sighed and took her hand, leading her to the bed. Lexi's body lit with desire, but she pulled her hand back. Jax didn't let her go. He wrapped her in his arms, picked her up, sat on the bed, and pulled her atop his lap so she straddled him. Lexi kept her weight on his thighs, her hands against his chest. They had to get this other-woman thing straight before she completely caved. This was complicated enough without adding other people into the mix.

He leaned his back against the wall, his feet hanging off the bed. "Because I was with her earlier tonight. We went out to dinner. When we got back to her house and she wanted me to come in and I couldn't, wouldn't—again—we both knew it wasn't working.

"After I left her, I got a call from the director of the film in New York for more work. And I thought of you, though it's not like you've left my mind very often in the last three weeks, which is when I texted. And was floored you'd even consider seeing me. I thought I was going to get the big brush-off."

Relief expanded inside her until her entire body felt tight. She chewed on her lip and forced her gaze to blur over his tanned, ribbed abdomen peeking at her from beneath the edge of his shirt.

"Stop that." He pulled at her lip with his thumb. "It makes me crazy."

She laughed and lifted her gaze to his. "Why?"

"Because it reminds me my lips aren't on yours, and they want to be." His thumb stroked her lip one more time. "What are you thinking?"

She curled her fingers in the soft cotton of his shirt, her gaze on his chest. "That if I was a good person, I'd send you back to that nice girl and tell you to try again."

His hands closed on either side of her face and pulled her eyes up to his. "If you were a good person, you'd give me that gorgeous body of yours. If you were a good person, you'd love me like you did in New York and put an end to this misery." He pulled her mouth to his. Kissed her dizzy, then murmured, "If you were a good person, you'd be a very naughty girl right now—with me."

She huffed a laugh and dropped her head back, looking at the ceiling. "I am a good person," she reminded herself, knowing she should push him away. Let him find someone far less complicated. "I am."

His lips skimmed down her throat, pumping banked need through her bloodstream. "Prove it."

She leaned back, lowered her head, and took his mouth. He opened to her on a groan. Pulled her head to him with one hand, deepening the kiss, searched for the hem of her dress with the other.

"Tell me…" she said as she tilted her head to the opposite side and kissed him again. "She isn't expecting to see you again."

"No." He answered the same way. "I broke it…" His tongue rolled over hers. "Off."

Lexi sighed into his mouth and sank into the kiss. Fisted his hair. Let go to pull his shirt over his head. Ran her hands over him. So warm. So muscled. She struggled with his belt, her hands shaking with excitement and need.

Jax chuckled. "What happened to those smooth hands, Lex? You undressed me faster than I could undress myself in New York."

"Shut up and kiss me."

He laughed again, this time against her lips. "I am…kissing you."

"Not enough if you can still talk."

This time Jax pulled back purposefully to drag her dress over her head. His gaze scanned her body in the strapless, sheer, barely there bra and matching tiny panties, which should really have been considered a thong because there was so little to them. His smile vanished. His arms dropped, bunching her dress in a pile on the bed, and he fell back against the wall.

Lips parted, he just kept looking, those eyes scanning, rescanning, and so heavy lidded she didn't know how he kept them open.

"Great...color..." he finally managed without ever taking his eyes off her body. "Stop abusing your lip, or I'm going to take it over, and you'll never breathe again."

She hadn't realized she'd been chewing on it and pulled it from between her teeth to tease, "Great *color*? That's it?"

She shoved his shoulder, and he fell to the bed on his back without any resistance.

"Purple. Love it." He made a show of wiping his mouth with the back of his hand. "I'm drooling, right?"

She started working on his jeans again. Belt, button. Couldn't keep herself from stroking her hand over the bulge beneath his zipper.

Jax siphoned air, squeezed his eyes and pushed his head back into the bed on a deep groan.

The move tightened the muscles of his chest, arms, abs. Now she was the one drooling. She needed him. All of him. Yesterday.

She jerked his jeans open, moved her hands into his underwear, and hummed when she pulled his erection out. Without waiting, asking, teasing, she closed her mouth on the wide head and sucked his length deep.

Jax's entire body shuddered. "Fuck, Lexi...*God*..."

His body arched, hips lifted, pushing Jax deeper until his head touched her throat, dragging a louder groan from him. He fisted one hand in the sheet, slammed the other flat against the wall. "Lexi...please..."

Oh God, the sound of him begging shot an insane dose of adrenaline through her body. The extremity of his pleasure made her suck him harder, deeper. His taste flooded her mouth, his scent filled her head, the texture of his delicate skin covering heated steel teased her tongue. She groaned and feasted.

"No, no, no..." he murmured, gripping her face and pulling her off him. His cock left her mouth with a pop, making her grin. He gripped her jaw in one big hand, firm, almost painful with his slipping control.

"Not doing it right?" she murmured, tilting her head until she could take his thumb into her mouth and suck, rolling her tongue around his rough, salty skin. "Do it for me. Use your hands and make me do it the way you want it."

She bit down on his thumb until his eyes opened. The intensity of his desire made her so needy she was offering him a freedom with her she'd never felt safe or confident enough to offer another man.

He closed his eyes, his chest heaving. "Condom. In...my wallet."

Lexi whined a complaint, but she reached for his back pocket. He gentled the hand on her jaw as she moved. As soon as she had her fingers on the leather, she licked the head of his cock, barely within her reach.

He choked out a laugh and pulled her away. "You little cheat..."

"You wanted naughty."

His eyes opened to slits. "I forgot my limitations."

"I like being able to push you to them." She kissed his palm and sat back, pushing her fingers through his wallet. "Where are they? And do you have any without the studs? I want to try something."

"Baby...you're asking...questions of a man with no...blood in his brain."

"Ah-ha!" She whipped an ordinary condom from his wallet

and grinned.

"Oh hell," he said. "That look on your face…"

She ripped it open, figured out which side was up, and grinned at him. "Okay, no promises, but I've wanted to try this since Rubi mentioned it."

"Wait. What? I'm a guinea pig now—?"

His teasing ended when Lexi popped the condom into her mouth, positioned it in an open O between her lips. But the look on his face—part shock, part confusion—made her laugh, and she had to take it out again. "You can't make me laugh, or it's not going to work."

"Baby," he said, low, throaty. "It won't work anyway because I'm not gonna last until it's on."

He reached for it, and she pulled back. "Do your best. I have faith in you."

"It would be easier if you put it on the tip first, then rolled it with your mouth."

She frowned. "I can see this isn't a new trick for you, which only means I have to do it better."

Remaining out of his reach until she had a good grip on the condom with her mouth was harder than it sounded and she grabbed his hands when he tried to reach for her again, pinning them at his sides. She landed a perfect shot over the head of his cock on the first try.

She'd planned on grinning up at him in triumph once the rubber was seated over his head, but the way his hands fisted in the sheets beneath her own gave her such a thrill, she couldn't stop. Jax was growling and writhing on the bed beneath her by the time she reached the base.

His hands broke from beneath hers. He sat up while pulling her mouth from his cock and reached for her panties, pushed them over her hips, down her thighs. With one arm, he wrapped her waist and lifted, pulling the panties free of her legs with the other.

Then he pulled one knee wide and settled her back over his

hips, dragged her down for a kiss, and whispered, "Ride me hard, naughty girl."

Lexi reached between their bodies and wrapped her fingers around his length. He groaned her name as Lexi rubbed his head over her opening. She ached in anticipation and rocked his head slowly into the swollen, wet folds. The muscles all over his body clenched. His fingers dug into her hips.

"You're going to come...*so*...*hard*," she said, dragging out the last two words, smiling into eyes that had gone so dark she couldn't separate the pupil from the iris. "Is that what you want?"

"Yes." He lifted his hips and pushed deeper. "God, yes."

Now it was Lexi's turn to agree, the word hissing from between her teeth as he pulled her hips lower, pushing his thick cock deeper, stretching her and offering delicious counter pressure to the ache she'd been living with for weeks. "Yessssss..."

NINETEEN

There was no way Jax would last beyond one mammoth climax. Lexi was the most beautiful thing he'd ever seen, inside and out. Beyond that, he finally felt like he'd found a woman he understood, a woman who understood him—or could, once he'd told her everything about himself. And, just as it had when they'd been in New York, the emotions he felt for her made the sex electrifying.

Jax held the orgasm back with every trick he knew—forcing his mind somewhere else, focusing on something less sexual than the fact that his cock was forging that unused path again through her tight body. Yep, that was working.

"Lexi…I'm not going to last."

Her hair had fallen forward over one shoulder and spilled across her face in a gorgeous display of raw beauty. That sight wasn't helping him hold back either.

She rose and lowered on her knees in short, quick movements, teasing his head with her tight opening. "But you feel *so good.*"

He lifted and pushed deeper. Lexi's lips parted. Her eyes closed. Her head tilted back. And with every passing moment, he grew more and more desperate to mark her as his. To own her. To make sure she never wanted another man like this.

He'd never wanted that before. Didn't understand the fierce, growing need now. Knew, logically, he couldn't own her. Or mark her. Or ensure she never wanted another man. But deep down inside him, he needed all those things.

"Lexi…come on, baby…give me everything."

She pushed him inside her one more time, then stilled. Sank lower.

And lower.

And lower.

"Fuck…" He lost it. Dug his fingers into her hips and drove upward.

He and Lexi both cried out at the same time. Jax stilled, giving her a moment to adjust. The look on her face was part pleasure, part pain. But Jax couldn't control it anymore. The need overwhelmed him. His body shook from the effort of holding back the climax, and Lexi was so perfectly snug around him.

"I think…you lost your patience somewhere…over the last few weeks," she said, hands pressed to his chest, balancing herself as she started to ride him in long, excruciatingly slow strokes.

"I think"—he slipped his hands beneath hers, threaded their fingers, pulled them off his chest until they were palm to palm— "you picked up a control habit."

"Nope. I've always had it."

"I noticed it in New York." He lowered his gaze from her beautiful face, those light blue eyes glazed with the heat of sex, scoured her breasts, jiggling gently under the transparent lace, the undulations of her soft, flat belly. "I see it all over this studio."

He continued scanning, to the erotic thrusts of her hips and his engorged cock sliding in and out of her pussy. He wanted to let go of her hands and guide her hips to a faster release but didn't want to lose the contact.

"You keep a very tight hold on everything you touch." He covered her hands with his, and pressed them to the curve of her spine. "I think it's time you learned to let go."

With her arms stretched behind her, Lexi's back arched. Her pelvis tilted, forcing him deeper.

"Oh God…" she moaned, head dropping back.

With her hands on her own skin, his guiding them, Jax spread their fingers, reached farther around her to cover her ass cheeks, lifting and pulling her into the thrust, forcing Jax balls-deep. The head of his cock hit her cervix on each thrust.

"Jax…God. That's so…good."

Reckless

"Sometimes, letting go of a little control…" he said, holding a partial curl until his abs screamed, "…has a lot of benefits. Relax, Lexi…" he panted, "…and feel me finishing this off my way."

The tension drained from her arms, allowing Jax to pull them farther behind her, reach deeper between her legs, and brush the nerve-lined skin high on her thighs bordering her opening with twenty fingers—hers and his.

She made a high-pitched sound in her throat.

He added strength to the pull, to the thrust. Waited until her eyes were squeezed closed, her mouth dropped open. Her hair spilled down her back, a few loose strands crossed her face. When she cried out with each thrust, Jax rolled forward a little more and closed his teeth around the lace-covered nipple.

"Oh God…"

He curled all the way up, pulled her arms completely behind her, forcing her breasts forward and against his chest.

"Open your eyes." When she did, he said, "You wanted to make love looking into my eyes. Keep them open."

He dragged her fingers over her own hot, wet skin as he stroked her, thrust, rubbed, rocked, pulled out, started over. "You're going to come *so…hard…*Lex."

At the first squeeze of her pussy, her eyes closed.

"Open your eyes."

She opened them, barely, little slits of sparkling, smoky blue, and Jax watched the intensity tighten her face. Watched her lips form his name as the orgasm broke. Watched exquisite pleasure rush over her beautiful features.

"God *damn*—" was all he got out before his own orgasm tore through him. Extreme pleasure gushed into his pelvis, burned up his spine, boiled in his belly. His hips jerked, and jerked and jerked, plunging into Lexi's succulent heat. His muscles contracted, released, contracted again, each squeeze nothing but pure pleasure rocketing through his body.

Jax let Lexi's hands slip from beneath his. He was sweating,

215

panting, his heart beating hard against his chest wall. Lexi went limp against him, her arms around his neck. She kissed his cheek, his jaw, his neck, then laid her head on his shoulder and grew heavy.

"Oh…my…*God*…" Jax wrapped her in his arms and lay back, propping himself up on an elbow to ease them both down.

And then she lay atop him, limp and loose, hot and sweet, while Jax remained deep inside her.

Christ, this was heaven.

Jax combed her hair back from her face and tossed it over her opposite shoulder. "What time does the shop open?"

Her chest was still rocking against his. She didn't answer right away. Then finally, "My receptionist comes in…at seven."

He rolled his head to the side so he could look at her without lifting his head. "Seven a.m.? Crap. I was hoping you'd say ten."

She laughed softly. "I wish."

She lifted her head and rested her chin on his chest. Her eyes were heavy, her face flushed, hair falling over her forehead. Jax had been with a lot of beautiful women, and Lexi was indeed one of the most beautiful, but her physical beauty wasn't what was doing all these insane things to his heart.

She pushed up on her hands and smiled down at him with such warmth and joy in her eyes, Jax's chest tightened. "It's so good to see you."

Then she lifted her hips and pulled his body from hers.

A pinch of panic burned his gut. That sounded like *great fuck, you can go now.* She leaned down, kissed him again, then rolled to her feet. Jax grabbed her arm. She gave him an expectant look as she lowered to her knees and pushed up one leg of his jeans to take hold of his boot.

Then paused. "I guess I should ask if you can stay—or want to stay—for a few hours before I get you all undressed."

"You're not kicking me out?" he asked, only half kidding.

Her head tilted in the cutest way. "Why would I do that?"

"Then I'll stay as long as you'll have me."

She tugged on the boot and slid it off his foot, then his sock. "That's a dangerous statement."

After taking off the other, she pulled his pants free of his legs, and he lay naked in her bed. When she straightened, she smiled down at him, her gaze raking over him with appreciation and hunger. Reaching up, she unfastened her bra and tossed it aside. Definitely not shy about her body, she stood completely naked in front of him. Glorious wet-dream material. His cock started to harden again.

Her gaze lifted to his face. "I'm going to get a warm towel and clean you up before that," she pointed to his growing erection, "gets out of control."

Jax's gaze was gliding over her body when the comment registered. When he lifted his gaze to meet her eyes, Lexi turned for the bathroom. His gaze lowered, taking in the beauty of her backside for the first time. And her ass looked as good as it felt.

The water ran in the bathroom, and as promised, she returned with a warm towel, sat on the edge of the bed, and lovingly removed the condom and wiped him clean. He was fully hard again by the time she was finished. His heart full. Jax had never felt so spoiled.

She tossed the towel aside and lay beside him, her head near his hip. He rested his cheek against her thigh and bent his knee so she could do the same to him, their position reminding Jax of a yin-yang symbol. Her hand floated over his belly, up his chest. Jax stroked her arm.

"I know you're tired," she said. "You can sleep. I'll wake you up before my assistant comes in."

He took her hand in his and brought it to his mouth. "And leave you alone to find eighteen ways to convince yourself this will never work by the time I wake up? Forget it."

She smiled.

He glanced around the space again. "Lexi, how do you eat?"

"I usually grab something from one of the restaurants nearby. There's a fridge in a break room downstairs." She pushed up. "You want me to get you some water?"

He pulled her back to him. "No. I want you to stay here, touching me."

"Well, I don't know." She melted against him. "That's a rough job, but...for you..."

He sighed, squeezed her hand. She'd agreed to tonight, exposed a lot of herself, but she was still holding back. "Okay, Lex, truth—am I going to be another one of your casualties?"

All amusement left her face. "What...does that mean?"

"It's obvious you haven't been with anyone in a while. With your looks..." Understanding filled her eyes. He didn't have to connect the dots. "I thought you were skittish in New York because you were sweet. Thought men took advantage of you. But I'm getting the feeling you don't let anyone close enough to take advantage."

Her blue eyes scanned him, serious, troubled. But she didn't answer.

"Who did this to you, Lex? Who made someone with so much to offer hide away in this five-hundred-square-foot box?"

Her gaze drifted away with the hint of a rueful smile. "It's over a thousand square feet, I'll have you know."

He stroked her cheek with his thumb. "What happened? And who did it happen with?"

She heaved a sigh, and her gaze drifted toward the darkened window above the bed. She seemed to think about it for a long moment before she spoke.

"A man I was dating, who, unfortunately, only saw me as part of his long list of accomplishments." She paused. Licked her lips. Still didn't meet his eyes. "When I realized what kind of person he was I broke off the relationship, but he wasn't ready to unpluck my feather from his hat." Her gaze lowered to his chest, her fingers tracing his ribs. "He was...wealthy, connected. Out of vengeance, he almost took everything I had, everything I'd worked for, and I realized how quickly I could lose my entire life by choosing the wrong man. How vulnerable I am against the rich and powerful of LA. Ironic that those are the very people who have enabled me to have all I have. Some of whom I love dearly. It's…a very convoluted, twisted web."

Twisted, all right. Especially when Jax fell right into that same category. He wanted to ask more about the guy, but Jax didn't want to push her too hard. Yet.

"How—and when—did that end?" he asked.

"Three years ago. My friend's father helped me out."

"Rubi?" he asked.

She nodded. "Her father is—"

"Rudolpho Russo?" he guessed.

Her gaze darted back to his. "How'd you know?"

"The Ferrari, her looks, Russo, LA," he said. "Doesn't take a genius."

"Rubi's amazing," Lexi said. "She's the best friend I could ever have. We met modeling and have been close ever since. She's nothing like her father. Though, he came through at a terrible time for me, so I can't say anything bad about him."

"Did your modeling lead you to fashion?"

"No. All my money from modeling went into this"—she waved her arm toward the rest of the room—"until it grew big enough to support me."

"How did you get started?"

A distant look came into her eyes, a small smile on her lips. "I used to get hand-me-down clothes from a local church. Really ratty stuff. The kids at school were pretty brutal, and I learned early to do what I needed to do to mesh. So I used to take the charity clothes, rip them apart, and put them back together in a way that either looked like everyone else's or in a new, trendy style."

"Why wedding dresses?" he asked. "Are you a closet

romantic?"

"Hardly. I've been through too much for that. But when I was young, I was infatuated with fairies and princesses. I thought I was born to live in a castle. I think it was my way of escaping reality. I guess I never really grew out of it, because I love everything ethereal and sparkly and feminine. Those have become signatures of my work."

She ran her hand over his chest. "Tell me about you. Where did you work today?"

"Desert. Riding bikes."

She lifted one brow. "Bikes?"

"Motorcycles," he said with a grin.

"Fun?"

"Hella fun."

She laughed.

He caressed her cheek. "Your eyes sparkle when you laugh, and that dimple makes me want to do crazy things to you."

Her smile softened. Her eyes grew heavy lidded with a look that made his cock ache. "I've never met anyone like you."

"I hope that's a good thing."

"Very. Are you working in the same place the rest of the week?"

When his mind veered, Jax's grin fell. "No. I'm there tomorrow, but have to jump on a flight right after for Idaho."

"Oh." She sounded disappointed. Jax was disappointed too. "What are you doing there?"

He was already trying to fit one of his other guys into the shoot, but none of them had the experience. "Couple days of rock climbing."

"For fun?"

"For work. Same thing. But I'll be back Saturday early."

"I've got two weddings this weekend, Saturday and Sunday."

"Oh, right, Jessie." He thought of the wedding invitation in his stack of mail on his kitchen counter. "How long does that take? What do you do, deliver the dress? Help her get into it?"

"No, for these I stay the whole time. As long as they're wearing the dress and want me there, I'm there for any unforeseen disaster—lost bead, loose button, torn train, etcetera."

"So, like for the ceremony *and* the reception? Shit. That's going to last for days."

She grinned. "I'm not on loan for days. But, yes, her father spent over two hundred thousand dollars in my shop, so I'll be at their beck and call from sunup to sundown on Saturday.

"Two hundred grand? For what?"

That made her laugh again. "Jessie's dress, her bridesmaids' dresses—there are twelve—the flower girls' dresses—there are eight, and Jessie's mother's dress."

"How long does it take to make all those dresses?"

"Only Jessie's is haute couture. But the rest are couture, so I've had my hands on all of them. And I've been working on them for six months."

"Jesus, that's crazy." Jax put a hand to his forehead. "It would be totally selfish of me to ask if I can sneak some time in with you Saturday night, wouldn't it. You'll be exhausted."

"How about this," she said, then pressed her mouth to his belly. Closed her fingers gently around his erection, making Jax groan. "I'll keep you up tonight, and you can keep me up Saturday night. Because I realize I still haven't licked your tattoo."

She kissed her way up to his nipple, sucked it into her mouth, nibbled until he moaned, then soothed it with her tongue.

"That's not my tattoo," he teased.

"I'm getting there. You're just so…yummy. I have to taste everything along the way."

Jax lifted her mouth from his skin even though he didn't want to. She smiled up at him, but the grin dimmed after she scanned his face. He must have looked as serious as he felt.

"You know," he said, "I'd never hurt you, right?"

Her brow pulled. "What do you—"

"Like that other guy. I know how hard it is to get where you are, baby. I'd never try to take that."

Turbulence deepened her eyes to a smoky blue, but she nodded. "I know you're not the same kind of man, Jax. But I also know there's a lot more to you than I know. Things…I don't think I'm ready to hear."

He stroked her face. "Why?"

She turned her head and kissed his hand. "Because it will require some big leaps for me. And I'm trying to get comfortable with the ones I've already made."

He nodded but still feared he'd be asking her to jump right into the fire if he told her everything. Was almost sure he'd lose her.

She lowered her head and let her tongue follow the lines of his inked tribal pattern over the corner of his chest, over his shoulder. He'd figure it out. A couple of days away from her to think would be good, because he couldn't think of anything when she was near. Nothing but her. And how good he felt. How important he felt. How loved he felt.

Jax cupped the backs of her thighs, slid his hands up to her cheeks. Squeezed. Her teeth closed on his skin. Lust made his cock jump, and the shaft hit her thigh where she had it between his legs.

"Lexi…" He moaned her name, a sudden need to be inside her making him crazy again.

But when he tried to pull her hips over his, she climbed off him and pushed at his shoulder. "Roll over. There's more on the back."

He obeyed, relaxing into the bed. Her hands roamed his skin.

"God, you're just beautiful," she murmured.

He chuckled. "Never been accused of that before."

Her fingers hit a sore spot near his shoulder blade, and his muscles jerked.

"You're all knotted up again," she said. "I put a lot of effort into getting those out last month."

"Yes…" The feel of her tongue sliding over his skin teased his cock harder. The thought of her hands kneading out the discomfort in his muscles in New York spread liquid fire through his hips. "That you did, baby."

"Guess I'll need to work on them again." She leaned forward, rubbing her breasts over his back, and whispered in his ear, "You liked that, didn't you?"

He hummed, his throat growing thick at the thought of her hands between his legs.

She kissed the spot just below his ear and whispered, "I thought so. And I just happen to have that lotion right here. The scent reminds me of you."

With a hand pressed to his back, she lifted herself off his body and reached into the drawer of a small bedside table. She pulled out a bottle and pressed her breasts against his back, her chin to his shoulder, and popped the top. Above his head, directly in his line of sight, she poured oil into her palm, set the bottle down, and caressed the shiny liquid over her hands.

The sight and scent brought back a rush of erotic memories. "You look like an angel, but I love your devilish streak."

"So glad to hear that." She pressed her oiled palms to his back. "Because I want to do…things to you…"

He shifted his hips so he didn't break his cock. "I…don't know how long I'm going to be able to stay like this."

She reached over him and grabbed a pillow. "Lift your hips."

"Everything that comes out of your mouth twists into something dirty in my mind," he muttered, obeying as she laughed and slid the pillow under him and he readjusted.

"Better?"

He eased his hips down and sighed in relief. The cool room air bathed his cock where it hung off the side of the pillow. "Much. Thank you."

"All right, enough talking. I have work to do. And I'm going to work backward this time. Loosen *you* up before I work on those muscles."

She swept her oiled palms down his back, paused on his ass cheeks, and squeezed. Jax groaned in both relief and excitement.

"Your ass takes a lot of abuse," she said. "Have you ever realized that?"

"Only when you're squeezing the abuse out of it," he said, his voice tight with pleasure as her magical fingers rubbed deep into his glutes and released delicious sensations.

She pressed both knees between his thighs, spreading them. Her hands were strong, her movements slow, draining those sore muscles of tension. He could swear she was releasing lust into his body on every stroke.

His need flashed like a firecracker. She curled her hand and pressed her knuckles down the muscle running parallel with his spine. Each vertebra felt as if it released in turn, and Jax groaned in pure pleasure. "You're amazing."

"Pleasing you makes me hot," she murmured, her voice thick with desire.

Her mouth came down on one ass cheek, and he tensed. She hummed as she slid her tongue down to the junction of his thigh, where she bit down gently, then sucked. His entire lower body tingled like he had current running through his veins. His cock throbbed.

Both her hands squeezed his ass. Pleasure-pain rocketed through his glutes and straight into his cock, balls, and spread through his lower body. She caressed his cock in her hand, and his throat closed, cutting off his air. Then her mouth was there, her tongue sliding along the underside of his cock.

Jax gripped another pillow above his head, sinking his fingers in for traction as pleasure ripped through him. He pressed his face to the sheet and groaned long and loud from his throat, just holding on until Lexi took her mouth off him and he could think again.

But she added her tongue, her teeth, nibbling up the insides of his thighs, licking his entire sac, then sucking until Jax nearly screamed into the bed.

When she finally took mercy on him and poured more massage lotion into her hands, Jax tried to catch his breath. He pushed up on his knees and shaky forearms with the intent of flipping their positions and riding them both to a skyrocketing orgasm, but she pushed him down with slippery hands.

"Oh no, you don't."

"Lexi." Jax slid back onto the pillow. "This is torture."

Her hands rubbed circles of warm junk all over his backside, and the sensation brought terribly lurid visions to mind.

"I'm sorry you're finding it torturous," she said. "Maybe this will help."

She rubbed counterclockwise circles on his ass. When her hands met at the crease, she spread her fingers and dragged them toward his balls. She rubbed the very sensitive skin of his cheeks near his perineum on every sweep.

Then one slick hand eased between his legs and cupped his boys. God, that felt amazing. Jax groaned, until the fingers of her other hand followed the crease of his ass—right over the tight pucker and down to his perineum. He sucked air. A crazy kind of pleasure he didn't recognize flooded his lower half. A little dark. A little edgy. And Jax wasn't sure if he wanted to block the direction she was headed or press her foot to the gas.

The hand at his balls, moved to his shaft, and those expert fingers made him forget what he was thinking. His brain had flipped to that one goal, flashing like a red light: Screaming Orgasm.

And even as her hand, gliding so perfectly and smoothly over his head again and again before squeezing his shaft and pushing to the base of his cock, nudged him closer to that goal, he wanted to wait, to hold out. He wanted this ecstasy to last. But her hand moved back up those sensitive areas along the inside of his cheek, her slick fingers creating sensations that didn't just ease him skyward, they catapulted him there.

"Lexi…"

"Do you like this?"

"God, I…yeah."

"I love doing it. I love touching you in these secret places."

Her fingers continued to spend more time around the most sensitive, tightest area, and his body didn't know whether to open or pucker. It seemed to want both.

"It makes me so wet to excite you," she murmured, her tone filled with a sweet, dark thrill.

Need double, quadrupled, grew exponentially until he couldn't keep himself from moving and lifted his ass into her hand. Her fingers rubbed harder, and the excitement thrust his hips forward, pushing his cock through her tight, oily fist.

Fuck, that was amazing. The pleasure so intense he lifted again, thrust again. On every thrust, she shot the deepest, rawest pleasure through Jax's entire body twofold—through his ass on the way up, through his groin on the way down.

"God, that's so hot," she murmured. "Watching you move like that…"

A growl ground deep in his throat. He'd passed that tipping point. He couldn't stop now. It was too good. Too intense.

"Sonofabitch, Lex, that's so damn good." His voice shook. He sought the peak like a man possessed. Pushed up on his forearms to gain more leverage. And oh fuck, yeah, he clawed for that goal. "Don't stop, Lex."

"Ask nice," she said with that devilish tone that set him on fire. "I like hearing you beg."

"Fuck, I wish…I was…pumping into…your dirty mouth…"

She squeezed him harder, and Jax jumped straight to the edge of orgasm, but before he reached it, she released him, and he just hovered there on the edge of ecstasy, in unbelievable anguish.

"Lexi," he growled from behind gritted teeth. *"Please. Don't. Stop."*

"That's so hot. You can have my mouth next time." Her hands moved again. "I'll go as long as you do. Come on, Jax, *rock me.*"

His frenzy worked his muscles hard, thrusting up and back, her hands smooth, strong, erotic, until the orgasm came so hard, he screamed into the pillow and nothing but stars coated the backs of his eyelids.

TWENTY

Lexi checked her makeup in the bathroom mirror and replaced a stray strand of hair into the artful twist Jessie Love's stylist had created before the wedding. She glanced at the time on her phone—nine p.m. Then at the message Jax had just sent from his late arrival at the airport.

JAX: Sure miss you. When do you think you'll be free?

She sighed, smiled. He'd only been gone two days, and it felt like forever. This was going crazy-fast. This sudden relationship she'd never consciously agreed to but now couldn't face life without. Over the years, she'd heard hundreds of stories about how the couples she was working for had met. She'd listened raptly to every strange, funny, romantic tale. Knew these types of whirlwind, you'll-know-its-right-when-you-find-him kind of instant relationships happened. And thrived.

She'd just never expected it to happen to her.

Or with a man like Jax. He was both everything she wanted and nothing she needed. Or rather what she'd been telling herself she hadn't needed.

They'd been texting and talking on the phone nonstop since that night at her studio, and Lexi felt like she knew Jax better than any man she'd dated in years. Yet, she didn't really know what mattered most—who he was, how he could damage her life.

He'd been trying to tell her, bringing it up at every opportunity, but she'd been stalling, putting him off. When he told her about his past and whatever he felt this burning need to tell her, she wanted it to be in person. From the moment he'd told her he'd never do anything to damage what she'd built, Lexi knew, without a doubt, he had the ability to do just that.

She realized then that was where his subtle but deep sense of confidence came from. One that Lexi found both attractive and soothing on a subconscious level. On a conscious level, she knew too well it also lulled her into a false sense of security.

LEXI: Miss you too. Unfortunately the reception is showing no signs of letting up. Will keep you posted.

She slipped her phone into her wrist purse, took a fortifying breath, pasted on a professional smile, and headed back into the throngs.

The rock band on the northernmost patio of Greystone Mansion played a really great rendition of "Heaven" by Theory of a Deadman and made Lexi ache for Jax. She turned toward the patio on the opposite side of the complex to check on the mother of the bride.

The click of her heels on the marble terrazzo drowned in the music of voices and laughter floating on the soft summer Beverly Hills air. She nodded and smiled as she passed guests she recognized. Everyone who was someone was here, including some very big movie stars, billionaires, musicians, and the mayor. The level of security was almost stifling.

She squeezed between one of the mayor's guards and the doorway onto the patio, patting his arm. "Excuse me, Emilio."

"Yes, ma'am." He turned with a serious expression, met Lexi's eyes, and smiled. His dark gaze heated and skimmed over her body. "Oh, hey, Lexi." He put a gentle hand on her arm. "Can I grab you for dinner next week?"

He'd asked her out every single time he'd seen her. Her path tended to cross with the mayor's relatively often at these events. "No, but thank you—"

"For asking," he finished, his grin sparkling in his handsome dark face. "One day, Lexi, you're going to say yes."

She squeezed his arm and skirted the patio slowly, searching for Jessie's mother. The woman stood among a group of rich and famous, a glass of wine in one hand. Lexi scanned her slim body, searching the gold dress for any imperfections. When she found none, she spotted a bridesmaid in crimson and continued around the patio toward her. This woman had very large breasts and was pushing the design of the bodice to its limits—even though Lexi had reinforced the fabric with a corset-like structure.

"Lexi." A hand closed over her arm. She turned and faced Stan Love. "I haven't gotten that dance you promised."

The musical quartet assembled near the fountain started playing "Somewhere in Time," a piece that always reached into Lexi's heart and tugged. She smiled, took his hand, and walked to a small area alongside the band.

"One of my favorite pieces." She sighed as the older man took her smoothly into his arms and picked up an elegant, slow waltz.

"For one of my favorite women." He smiled down at her, his gaze she could only describe as paternal, even though she'd never known her father and had never had a paternal source in her life.

They danced for a few moments in comfortable silence. Stan was strong, well-built, and smelled of spice and citrus.

"What a beautiful day, Stan," she murmured. "You must be so proud."

"She's my baby," he said. "They're all gone now. I don't know what I'm going to do with myself."

Lexi laughed. He was one of the busiest producers in Hollywood. "I'm sure Claudia will keep you plenty busy," she said of his wife. "But I don't know what I'm going to do with *myself*. With no more of your babies to marry off, I might go out of business."

He chuckled. "I happen to know of a young man who would like to take up a lot of your time."

Oh Lord. She'd had two dozen people try to set her up in the last twelve hours. Still, she feigned mild interest.

"Jax asked me to put in a good word for him."

Lexi stumbled. Stan smoothly carried her through the step

until she'd fallen back into the rhythm.

"He thought that might be your reaction," he said, grinning down at her.

She lowered her gaze to Stan's open collar. He'd taken off his tux's bow tie the second they'd left the church. Lexi's gut burned with an automatic flight reflex. And when all she'd been able to think about or want for the last three days was Jax, the reaction both confused and troubled her.

"He mentioned that he'd worked for you." She finally managed to say something coherent. "He had great things to say."

"It's mutual."

She glanced up, tried to read his clear blue eyes. They were sparkling with amusement. Lexi relaxed. "That's it? He asked you to put in a good word for him and that's all you can manage?"

"He said not to overdo it."

She narrowed her eyes. "Do you always take direction from your stuntmen?"

"From this one, always."

"Stan, you look like a cat that just emptied the canary's cage."

He laughed, head thrown back, eyes closed. The sound bounced off the mansion's stone walls and drew every gaze on the small patio. Stan stepped back, turned her in an underarm twirl, then swept her right back into his arms.

"What is so funny?" she asked, grinning up at him, wishing he had been her father. Or wishing she'd had a father half as wonderful. Or had a father at all.

"Nothing, nothing. I admit, I had hoped Jessie would catch Jax's eye, then Connor swept her off her feet and, well, there's no accounting for who you fall in love with, is there?"

That comment knocked her on her ass. The song ended, and Stan released her, but Lexi held fast to his hand.

"Wait…what…? You can't just say that and walk away."

Stan cupped the back of her neck and pulled her close for a

kiss on her forehead. He whispered, "Try not to let this place run your life, Lexi."

She pulled back and found his blue gaze filled with affection and…wisdom. "What are you trying to tell me?"

"I'm telling you what I've told every one of my kids—as long as you rule LA and LA does not rule you, you'll find success."

Claudia stepped up to them, then wrapped an arm around her husband's waist and Lexi's shoulders. "Don't try to make me jealous, you two."

Lexi stepped back, and Stan pulled his wife into his arms but kept his gaze on Lexi. "He said his plane came in late, but promised me he'd show."

Then he pulled his wife into a spin, a dip, and kissed her. Applause erupted around them. Someone's hand slid over Lexi's arm. She startled, glancing up into Emilio's rich brown eyes.

"I got a break. If you're not going to have dinner with me, at least let me have one dance."

Lexi did her best to be mentally present for the dance with Emilio, but a new fear had taken root. Jax would be here. In the midst of her biggest, wealthiest client pool. And now, her apprehension over being associated with a bad-boy type dimmed, as her other bigger fear took shape—the confirmation of Jax's power in these circles. He was far more capable of taking her business under than Steven had ever been, and in a far more subtle way. A few targeted comments and the word would spread. Rumors would grow.

Even as she tried to tell herself Jax would never try to trap her that way, never manipulate her that way, her damn flight reflex had Lexi searching for excuses to escape. But she'd never left a reception before her bride. Never. And she certainly wouldn't desert her largest client of the year thus far over an irrational fear.

The song ended, and Emilio switched topics from his security detail for the mayor to Lexi. "I'd like to get you away from all this. Be able to talk to you when you're not so distracted."

He kept an arm around her waist well after they'd cleared the dance area. She didn't mind the touch when they were dancing, but now, it made her skin tight with discomfort.

"I've got to check on my bride," she said, smiling up at him. "Thanks for the dance."

Emilio reluctantly released her with a grin and a soft, "Someday you're going to say yes."

Lexi paused in a quiet area of the gardens and shook out her arms. Suddenly, pins and needles stabbed her neck and spine. Her heart beat a little wildly. She couldn't think straight. Her mind, always so open with the big-picture view at an event, narrowed to pinpoint focus, and she couldn't widen it past Jax. Past seeing Jax at an event like this. Past what he might do when he saw her. Past how he could try to control her if he chose.

She was sweating. So nervous she was shaking.

Lexi walked to the edge of the balcony that looked out over Beverly Hills. Lights sparkled in the distance. She pressed her palms to the concrete banister and breathed long and slow. Tried to assure herself he wasn't that kind of man. That he'd promised he wouldn't hurt her.

In her clutch, her phone vibrated. She swallowed, unzipped the bag, and pulled out her phone.

> JAX: You look mouthwatering. I hope you don't have a gun in that little purse. I have a feeling if you did, you might use it on me.

Lexi stared at the message. She couldn't even lift her head to search for him but slid her eyes closed and swallowed a ball of nerves rising in her throat.

She felt him come up next to her. Smelled him—that mix of subtle spice and leather. Unbearably sexy.

"No one's around." His voice touched her ear like a caress, low and rough and familiar. Delicious. "It's safe to talk to me."

"Don't." She shook her head. "I love being with you. Don't make it sound like I..."

She couldn't say the words.

"Like you're embarrassed to be seen with me? Baby, it's not a new situation for me."

"This isn't fair. Just ambushing me like this."

Her frustration overflowed. She wanted to love him and hate him with equal parts. Then she made the mistake of looking at him and knew she could never hate him. His hair was still too long, still mussed in that terribly sexy way. His jaw still covered in a couple of days of beard growth. And he sported a new cut down the left side of his jaw. A bruise high on the same cheek.

She ached to throw herself into his arms. Kiss him until they couldn't think. This mental straitjacket binding her forced all her air from her lungs in one gust. She reached up to touch his face. When she stopped herself and drew her hand back, Jax's smile turned sad.

"Did you have that looked at?" she asked.

"Medics on the set said it was okay." He sat on the banister, angled toward her, wearing another leather jacket, this one all black. His jeans were also black. His boots black. The only concession he'd made toward dressing up was the light blue button-down shirt under his jacket and the tear-free denim.

"Why didn't you tell me you were invited to the wedding when you told me you knew Stan?" she asked.

"If you're reacting like this now, imagine how I thought you'd react then."

She felt tears rising to her eyes. Tears of excitement and relief to see him. Tears of fear for what he brought. What he might still bring.

He extended one hand, offering her a glass of champagne. "This will help."

"I never drink when I'm working." She took the flute and downed the entire glass in one swallow. Barely without tasting the expensive alcohol. And murmured, "Never."

Jax's laugh was low and smooth. "Seems I tend to make you

do all kinds of things you've never done before."

She hissed air from between her teeth. "I'm not ready, Jax."

"We both know you'll never be ready, baby."

"That's not true." She turned her head to look at him. "I was going to talk to you about it this weekend when we saw each other."

"Somehow, I had a feeling that no matter what I told you, you'd need reinforcements from others you respect. So I made a call." When she started to shake her head, he said, "*One call*, Lexi. Stan would never say anything to anyone. I knew you'd have to see that I'm not a total outcast to believe it, so I decided this was as good a place as any."

But her fear wasn't focused on his lack of social standing now; it was focused on his power within those social circles. One call now. When things went bad, how many calls would he make? Even as she thought the worst, another side of her mind refueled her belief in his character. And her mind continued to ping between past bad experiences and the desire to believe Jax was different.

"Chamberlin!" The call came from a pathway nearby, and Lexi recognized it immediately as the groom's. "It's about fucking time, dude."

Lexi clenched her teeth as Connor neared.

"Oh, sh-shoot," he amended his curse. "Didn't see you, Lexi," Connor said, grinning the euphoric grin of a man who'd just married the love of his life. "Sorry. I'm sorta—"

"Smashed?" Jax finished with a smile for Connor so filled with brotherly affection, it tightened Lexi's throat.

"Shut up. And get rid of that frilly stuff." He gestured to the champagne. "My new father-in-law gave me a case of Ladybank at my bachelor party."

"No shit." Jax laughed the words.

"No shit." Connor wrapped his arm around Jax's neck in a drunken bear hug. "Get me over there and you've earned a bottle.

And leave Lexi alone." He gave her a drunken wink. "She's way out of your league, troublemaker."

Jax tossed back the champagne, set the glass on the railing, and wrapped an arm around Connor as he stood. But his gaze was steady and intense on Lexi, reminding her of the first time they'd looked at each other through the windshield of Rubi's Ferrari.

"You may be right, bro," Jax said, his voice impossibly disappointed. "But a man can hope."

"I know I'm right," Connor said.

Jax broke Lexi's gaze, turning Connor toward the pathway. "Like you know you're going to pass out before you make it to your bride's bed?"

"Shut the fuck up." Connor laughed, wrapped his other arm around Jax's neck as if trying to wrestle him to the ground.

Jax winced, but gently pried Connor's arm away from his left shoulder and guided the groom across the grass. "Take it easy there, bro. I had a disagreement with some rocks this week."

Lexi's chest felt like a hurricane. "Jax—"

He kept walking. "I'll find you, Lex. Let me get this man back to his bride."

***

Jax wasn't all that unhappy when Connor's bride pulled him onto the dance floor, because he wasn't all that anxious to have this talk with Lexi anymore. He'd been trying to talk to her about it for days, but she kept avoiding the conversation, as if she already knew what he was going to say. She claimed she hadn't done her own research already, but somehow she believed whatever he was going to say would interfere with what they had…and where they were going.

Jax stepped back and held Jessie's hand loosely as she turned under his arm, then took her back into the step.

"You're almost as smooth as my dad," she said. Her big brown eyes were made up heavily but tastefully and shone up at him.

"I take that as the highest compliment."

"Connor and I are having a barbecue at the new house when we get back from Bali next month. Will you come? He misses you."

"He just called me a bunch of names that says different."

"You took away his scotch on his wedding night."

"Only so you can get lucky later. And no guarantees. He may have already imbibed too heavily."

She laughed. "We're married. I already consider myself lucky. And we've got many, many years of luck ahead. One night won't make a difference. But thank you for trying. So, will you come?"

Jax was thinking about years and years of luck with Lexi. First time that thought had ever crossed his mind. He pushed it away.

"If I'm in town, I will absolutely be there." He pulled back and gazed down at her dress. "That's some gown, Jess. Did your daddy leverage the Maui vacation home for that thing?"

She laughed. "Probably. But Lexi's designs are amazing, and she made my sisters' dresses. My parents said it was tradition." She pulled back, made another slow twirl, and came back to him. "Mom says they're heirlooms. I like to think my daughter will wear it one day. Isn't it the most beautiful thing you've ever seen?"

Jax pulled Jessie into another turn and scanned the crowd for Lexi. She stood beside a table talking to five different men Jax recognized as financial wizards from Silicon Valley. His entire body warmed to life at the sight of her.

He smiled back at Jessie as she returned to face him. "Absolutely."

She laughed. "You're so full of shit."

"That's why you love me."

"Absolutely," she echoed.

Jax pulled her close to finish the dance while watching Lexi. Two other men had joined the conversation, both riveted to her, even though she wasn't doing more than responding to whatever someone else said. One of the men Jax knew as an up-and-coming actor. The other was a friend of Connor's. An investment banker. Jax loathed the insecurity welling in his chest.

He soaked in the sight of Lexi. Her dress was cream, almost entirely heavy lace. Cut low in the front, the design was both tasteful and sexy, showing just the inner curves of her breasts. A band of beaded lace circled her slim rib cage, and the rest of the simple design needed nothing but Lexi's body filling it out to look perfect. It molded to her flat belly, slim hips, cutting off at a respectable midthigh. The back created an open diamond exposing her delicate shoulder blades and the indention of her spine.

Just looking at her made an ache burn deep at the center of his body.

He was just about to drag his gaze away from her when Lexi looked over. She could have grabbed him by the collar, he felt her pull that intensely. Her eyes seemed so crystal blue in the darkness. Maybe it was the makeup that made them pop, but as soon as they touched his face, Jax's heart skipped and he couldn't look away.

"Do you want me to introduce you?" Jessie's voice pulled his gaze back to her face. "She's single."

His chest burned. "Who?"

"Lexi LaCroix. That's the woman you've been staring at since you got here."

He sighed. "You're worse than my little sister."

"I'm more of a little sister than your little sister ever was."

"You're right." He grinned and grabbed the tip of her nose between his fingers.

She cried out a soft complaint and slapped his hand away. "I can't believe you did that to me at my wedding."

"You'd have been disappointed if I didn't."

"Do you want to meet her or not?" she asked, rubbing her nose, still laughing. "She's totally sweet, obviously gorgeous, has her own successful business."

"Your husband thinks she's way out of my league."

Jessie made a scraping sound in her throat. "My husband is fall-down drunk, and he's always been jealous of you. He probably just doesn't want you bagging a woman prettier than his."

"Oh, stop. No one is prettier than you."

"You're a lousy liar. And I've never seen you *not* go after a woman you want. What's up with that?"

"She seems pretty...classy, you know?" He looked down at Jessie. "I think your husband might be right."

Jessie stopped dancing and gazed up at him with a what-the-fuck look. "Bentley Jaxon Chamberlin, don't make me flog you at my own wedding."

Jax laughed, but he wasn't feeling the humor. And as he looked down into Jessie's eyes, he was reminded that even she had chosen Connor over Jax one night long ago. Something Jax never thought twice about. Never regretted. In fact, he'd believed in a lot of ways Connor had taken a bullet for him. He'd felt pushed toward Jessie because of her father's not-so-hidden wishes and Jax's own drive for Stan's fatherly approval. Once Jessie had chosen Connor, Jax had been so relieved in so many ways, he'd never cared *why* she'd chosen Connor.

Only now, it was clear. Connor had respectable family, an outstanding Hollywood reputation as an upstanding guy. Walked the walk. Talked the talk. Shook hands and kissed babies.

A sick gurgle of a laugh came from Jax's throat. His mother would get such a thrill out of this moment. She'd always told him he'd lose out big someday, because in Hollywood, *image was everything.*

This was never something he'd ever fathomed losing. Probably because he'd never imagined falling in love.

Pain shot through his shoulder, and Jax finally heard Jessie talking to him, tugging on the arm he'd injured in Idaho to get his attention.

"Are you okay? Maybe you had a little too much to drink too."

No, but he definitely wasn't right either. Physically or emotionally. The longer he watched Lexi in this environment, with the upstanding businessmen flocking around her, the lower Jax sank.

The song changed, and another guest came up to claim Jessie for the dance.

Jax slipped through the other guests on the dance floor and leaned against the bar. A wave of dizziness made him sway.

"Are you all right, sir?"

Jax put his forehead against his hand. "I could use some water."

His cell rang. The Renegades phone, not his personal phone. Jax was suddenly exhausted, but he answered, "Renegades."

"Jax, it's Ted Rimer."

Jax's gut coiled tight. "Part of me was hoping you wouldn't call."

"But you knew I would."

"What else are you going to do? Sucky spot to be in, Ted. I'm sorry this happened."

"You'll keep your mouth shut in bed from now on I guess, right?"

Jax didn't appreciate the dig. "People who live in glass houses…"

Rimer sighed heavily. "So what am I going to have to give you to pick up this job? You've pretty much got a gun to my head here."

"You put it there. It's not my fault you tried to go cheap and ended up getting screwed."

"I'm twenty million over budget," he said, ignoring Jax's comment.

"I heard thirty."

"You heard wrong," Rimer said.

"Whatever." Jax didn't doubt it, and how much over budget they were didn't matter to him. "Since you didn't pick us up for your movie, I've found a lot of work. I'd be giving up a lot, taking my boys off sure things. You're the one over budget. Tell me what you can give us to make it worth the risk."

"I can pay you the minimum SAG contract rate."

The Screen Actors Guild minimum contract payment was far less than what Jax negotiated for a job. He made a low hum in his throat. "That's not inspiring. In fact, it's demeaning."

"I'm not done," Rimer said. "If you can pull us back into the black, I'll give you ten percent of the money you save us."

Jax paused. "I must have heard you wrong too."

"No, you didn't. You save me twenty million, and I'll give you two."

"Two million," he clarified.

"That's the deal."

Two million was one-tenth what he'd made on a movie at the height of his acting career, but it was a hell of a lot of money to a stuntman. Jax was pretty sure he could do it. And that kind of money would float Renegades for a while. Buy new equipment. Bring on new guys. Ease the burden on Jax. Maybe he could even have a life. "Send me the script and tell me where you're at in the filming process. I'll let you know."

He said good-bye and disconnected, then glanced over his shoulder toward Lexi. She'd moved to another table where two bridesmaids sat and eased to the edge of a chair, leaning in to hear something one of the women said to her. She laughed, her head tipping back, eyes sparkling. And that damned dimple appeared in her cheek.

Jax instantly returned to that night in New York, the front of his body pressed to her back, the feel of her hair against his chest, the sound of her sweet laugh.

He realized now that had been the very moment—when she'd laughed at Jax's stupidity on the horse—the moment he'd fallen in love with her.

She wanted for her business and her life what Jax had just

been offered for his. And he wanted that for her too. He wanted her to experience this sense of relief. Of hope.

Which meant getting the hell out of her way.

TWENTY-ONE

Just watching Jax move made Lexi ache. She knew he was hurting, yet he still danced with Jessie, hung out to bullshit with Connor and others. He knew one hell of a lot of people here. Most seemed to love him, though she'd noticed a few people move the other direction when someone in the circle initiated a conversation with Jax, but it didn't seem to bother him. And his earlier comment about being used to having people being ashamed of him cut at her.

Claudia Love stood with him now, her arm around his waist. He had his arm over her shoulders in a circle of Claudia and Stan's friends, giving Stan a ration about something. But Stan gave it right back, and everyone laughed.

The sound of Jax's laughter made Lexi's chest warm and her belly ache. An hour had passed, and he hadn't tried to talk to her again. He seemed so tired. As if the last hour had drained him of all his energy. She wanted to take him home. Wanted to undress him, make love to him, fall asleep with him.

Jax shook Stan's hand, kissed Claudia on the cheek, and broke from the group.

Panic prickled her skin. She didn't want him to leave, which didn't make any sense. He turned toward the bar, spoke with the bartender a moment. Lexi couldn't let him leave with this wedge between them.

She pulled one packet of ibuprofen and one packet of acetaminophen from her clutch and approached him at the bar. He'd only had two drinks—the champagne and one glass of Connor's scotch. She'd been watching him. So when he turned glazed eyes on her, she knew something was wrong.

"Hey," he said. "I'm sorry for coming here, baby. Stupid. Don't worry, I'm going home."

She wanted to touch him. Kiss him. "You look like you could use these."

She slid the meds toward him. His eyes lowered to the packages and his mouth turned in a smile. The bartender set a bottle of water on the bar in front of Jax. He thanked the man and lifted his gaze to Lexi. "Baby," he said, relief sliding through his voice as he reached for the meds. "If I were an investment banker, I'd kiss you right now."

She frowned as he opened the meds and swallowed them with the water. "If you were an investment banker, I wouldn't want you to kiss me. At all."

He set the water on the bar and met her eyes. "You are so fucking beautiful it hurts to look at you. Good thing I love what's on the inside too, or…" He made a cutting motion over his throat.

He seemed…drunk. Then another thought occurred to her. "Jax, have you taken something tonight?"

His eyes narrowed, then a slow, brittle smile turned his mouth. "Like…drugs?"

She didn't want to accuse him, but… "You're not right."

"But you wouldn't really know, would you?" He turned away from the bar, picked up the water, and walked away.

She deserved the cut. It hurt, and she took it, but she didn't let him go. He exited the mansion's front doors, skipped down the curved marble staircase with the help of the banister, and started down a long, tree-lined flagstone path toward a side parking lot.

Lexi paused at the edge of the patio. The path was lit only by tiny white lights where the flagstone met the grass, one side lined by one of the mansion's high stone patio walls.

"Jax?"

He didn't answer. Didn't stop.

Lexi glanced around, pulled off her heels, and started down the path. "Jax, wait."

A few yards ahead, Jax's silhouette stopped. His head tipped back with the bottle of water at his mouth. By the time he stopped drinking, Lexi had caught up and heard him crinkle the bottle in his hand.

"Don't worry, babe," he said, his voice low and hopeless in the dark. "I'm not going to out you."

"I don't care." She heard the words, but it almost seemed as if they'd come from someone else. "I mean I do, but...I don't want to. I care about you. I just...it's complicated. Can you give me some time, Jax? This is...terrifying."

He didn't answer, but he didn't walk away. Lexi moved closer. He was barely visible in the dark, and it brought back memories—and nerves—of their first night together.

"I missed you," she said, reaching for his arm and sliding her hand down to close her fingers around his. "And I'm stressed. And I wasn't prepared for this. But I..."

His hand closed around hers in the dark, the sensation so reassuring, the same way he'd been that first night. Every moment they'd been together since. Emotion swelled in her chest. Tears burned her eyes.

"There's no accounting for who you love, right?"

"I love you, Jax." The words didn't come out right. They sounded plastic. Fake. "But it's happening so fast, and I'm confused. I've been living so long one way—"

He pulled on her hand, drawing her close. His other arm wrapped around her waist. "What?"

"I don't..." Why did she feel like she was dangling over a ledge? "I don't want to lose you because I'm resistant to—"

"Not that."

His hand found her face, felt along her temple, her cheek, until he found her jaw, then drew her up. His mouth covered hers, and Lexi whimpered, kissing him back, seeking his tongue. He tasted her for one long moment, then broke abruptly.

"The other part," he said.

She knew what he meant, and the warm sensations flowed through her. "I love you. I know there's a lot I don't know, but I can guess. And all that matters to me is that I love who you are now."

"Lexi…" Her name was more of a groan than a word before his mouth closed over hers again. And so much emotion filled his kiss, Lexi could taste it. She was too short without her shoes on and stretched against his body to get more of his mouth, more of everything.

The hard ridge of him rubbing her low belly made her crazy, and she stroked him through his jeans.

"Lexi…baby…" He pulled her hand away.

She kissed his jaw, his throat, pulled at the buttons of his shirt. Jax might have been holding the hand that had been stroking him, but now he was rubbing his erection along her hip bone.

"Lexi, you make me insane."

She whimpered against his neck. "Please…"

On a growl, he picked her up by the waist and carried her toward the rock wall. Behind each large tree, the wall curved into an alcove of smooth sandstone. More marble floored the area, housing a piece of ornate pottery filled with plants.

He pressed her back to the cold stone, kissed her deeply as his hands ran up the backs of her thighs, raised her dress.

"Christ, Lex…" His hands roamed over the garters, her silk panties, gripped her ass. "That's so hot."

"I need you." Lexi opened his jeans, found his cock, and took him into her hands with a groan.

"Shh," he murmured against her lips. "Grab my wallet, baby."

She found a condom quickly, ripped it, rolled it on his hot length. It was one of the studded condoms, and the rubber nubs nipped at her fingers. Jax lifted her while she was still fitting it. Pressed two fingers inside her pussy from behind with a growled, "Move your hands."

Lexi had barely lifted them to his chest when Jax guided himself halfway into her, pressed his mouth to her neck, and muffled a deep groan of pleasure.

He filled her, stretched her, the extra friction from the condom raking fire along her walls.

"Jax, Jax, Jax—" She was so ready she rose to climax before he'd fully penetrated her. "Oh God—"

Jax's hand closed over her mouth, and his hips plunged just as the orgasm peaked. Her muscles squeezed. She arched against the cool limestone. Jax thrust, thrust, thrust, never stopping.

When her cries dimmed to moans, he exchanged his hand for his mouth and kissed her as if he were starving. "Lexi...feel so good...missed you...crave you...love you...so much..."

He drove into her, pulling her hips to meet his, fingers digging into her flesh. He felt so good. Filling her. Completing her. Feeding her craving. She hooked an arm around his neck, pressed one hand to the wall, and lifted into each thrust. His pelvis hammered her clit on every drive, his cock so deep she felt the orgasm build until her throat tightened with the thrill of it.

"Oh shit..." was all he got out before he broke, his thrusts coming fast and so hard and wild he pumped another orgasm from her. She completely lost herself in the intensity of sensation for long, long moments. Moments filled with Jax holding her tight, moving inside her, cool air washing her skin.

Perfection. Ecstasy. Bliss.

Jax collapsed, crushing Lexi against the wall. She didn't care. All she could feel was pleasure spiraling through her body.

She wasn't sure how he did it, but Jax lowered to his knees while staying inside her. She wanted to loll in the beauty of it, keep her head against his shoulder, kiss his jaw, but Jax was all business.

"Gotta get you cleaned up," he panted, leaning away and smoothing her hair as if that would help. "God, I shouldn't have done this."

"Jax..."

He pulled out of her, groaned as he removed the condom, then buried it in the nearby planter. Before he'd even zipped his pants, Jax was straightening her clothes.

"Shit." He bit out the word, more to himself than to her. "What the hell is wrong with me?"

Panic slid in and burned Lexi's chest. Her I-love-you confession was probably just sinking in, and he was freaking out.

"Jax, it's fine—"

"It's *not* fine. This is your work. This is your career. I told you days ago I'd never do anything to take it away, and what am I doing? Fucking you in some dark corner with the goddamned world on the other side of this wall."

She pulled his face to hers and stopped his mouth with a kiss.

He groaned, then kissed her back, sighing into her mouth. "God, I love you."

The words burned across the surface of Lexi's heart. She pulled back and pressed her hand to his lips. "You don't have to say that."

He shook her off. "I want to say it. I mean it, which is why I shouldn't be doing this with you."

Lexi's heart felt as if it turned over in her chest.

Jax straightened his own clothes, wrapped his arms around Lexi, and pulled her up against his body hard, as if he were afraid she'd disappear.

She was just relaxing into him when he swore and his left arm loosened.

"What's wrong?"

"Nothing. I just hurt my arm yesterday. It's sore."

God, how had he done what he'd just done with an injured arm?

"I'll walk you back." He put his right arm around her waist, but let his left hang limp by his side.

Bad feelings trickled into her gut. "I want to see your arm before you leave."

He stopped her as soon as they reached the light and turned

her to face him. With his right hand, he smoothed her hair, leaned down to tug at the hem of her dress. Glanced around the quiet gardens.

"No one's here. No one will know we were together."

His concern for her reputation made her stomach hurt. But she was more immediately concerned about his arm. She took the left wrist of his jacket but didn't pull. "Take your arm out and let me see it, or you're not leaving."

He tried to pull it from the sleeve, but pain ripped across his face.

"Jax?" Fear speared her belly. She lifted the left shoulder and pushed back that side of his jacket. Something dark stained his shirtsleeve. "Oh God. Are you bleeding?"

"It's just a cut from the rocks yesterday—"

"Goddammit, Jax. If you can't get out of this jacket, I'm going to take scissors to it." Panic bubbled up in her belly. "*Let me see your arm.*"

When he tried and failed again, she moved behind him and grabbed the collar. "Roll your shoulders back."

As he did, he growled in pain from behind clenched teeth. The jacket slid down his arms. And his left shirtsleeve was covered in blood.

Jax lay back on the gurney in the ER, staring at the ceiling. God, he'd done this a lot. Only he'd never had anyone holding his hand or smoothing his hair back from his face before. Even his nanny hadn't done that.

He'd tried to convince Lexi to stay at the wedding. Tried to get her to go home when there was an hour wait at the ER. They'd even gotten into an argument over it. Jax had given up when she'd threatened to stitch him up herself.

The nurse had already numbed the laceration, and without the pain, Jax was feeling pretty good by the time the metallic curtains slid back and Doctor Pete Hale walked in.

"Nice to see you again, Jax."

Lexi now knew Jax's first name was Bentley. Knew his last name was Chamberlin. She'd reacted stronger to the fact that he didn't have health insurance than to his name. She'd already decided that not only did he need health insurance, but all his employees needed health insurance, and how could he *not* have health insurance with a job this dangerous?

Just thinking about how she worried made him smile.

"Hey, Doc," he said.

Pete held his hand out to Lexi. "Pete Hale."

"Lexi," she said, shaking his hand.

He peered down at the cut. "Nicely done. And you missed the tattoo. Keeping us in business, I see."

"Just doing my part."

"Upgraded your chaperone too." Pete grinned at Lexi. "Now my nurses are all huffy. Nobody's fighting over you tonight, bud."

Lexi laughed.

"Don't flirt with my girl, Doc. I still have one good arm."

"That's your job, Lexi," Pete said. "Keep him from slugging me, and I'll get this fixed up."

Jax turned his head and searched out Lexi's gorgeous face. She smiled at him, combed her fingers through his hair. He knew for a fact in that moment, he never wanted to lose her.

"Why didn't you get this looked at yesterday?" Pete asked. "You know better than that."

"Would have delayed my flight. I needed to get home to my new chaperone."

"Ah." Pete's grin widened. "Enough said."

"Baby," Jax told Lexi, "you don't have to stay for this."

"I'm fine. Stitched up my brother's split knee when I was nine."

Pete's hand froze with the needle in the air. His gaze darted to Lexi.

"I'm good with a needle, my mom wasn't much of a mom, and I didn't have the money or means to get him to a hospital." She said it simply, the same way Jax had made the offhand comment about his father and scouting. She glanced up at Pete as he started to stitch. "Jax is still pale and dizzy. How long will that last?"

"He lost a little blood. A day of rest and lots of water, and he'll be fine. He's an ox."

Jax sputtered. "I'm feeling more and more like a lizard."

"You could always go back to acting. Far fewer casualties."

Jax winced and sneaked a look at Lexi.

She only raised her brows at him.

The stitches went fast. A nurse bandaged him and gave Lexi the at-home-care instructions Jax already knew by heart. Lexi wrapped her arm around his waist on the way to the car and opened the passenger's door for him.

Jax decided arguing would be wasted. Before he slid in, he took her face in both hands and caressed her cheeks. "If I didn't already love you, tonight would have clinched it."

He kissed her, long and slow. She pulled away with a moan, "Rest and water, Mr. Chamberlin." He winced at the use of his last name, knew what was coming. But when she got into the driver's seat, she laughed, then looked at him. "I have no idea where you live."

"Can we go back to the shop? My house is out of the way."

"Well, it can't be in Beverly Hills, because that's not out of the way." She sighed and started the car. "Do I want to know where?"

He hesitated. "Malibu."

She closed her eyes and pulled her lower lip between her teeth. Then stared out the windshield with a shake of her head. "This is what I get for living in LA without a television."

TWENTY-TWO

Jax woke to Lexi's soft voice. She was on the phone but still lying next to him in her bed.

He rolled to his side and lifted his arm to slide it over her waist. Pain erupted from his shoulder to his fingertips, radiated into his chest. He groaned.

Lexi leaned toward him, curled her fingers around his, and murmured, "Stay still, Jax."

He relaxed back into the bed. Opened his eyes. And knew there was something really wrong. He was sweating. His whole body hurt. "Fuck."

"He's taking them every six hours," Lexi said softly into the phone. "No, he's steady at one hundred and two. It's not breaking. Yes, it's red and swollen around the edges."

"Who are you talking to?" As soon as he spoke, he realized how dry his throat was.

Lexi sat up, put the phone between her chin and shoulder, and picked up a bottle of water beside the bed. "No, I don't see any. No, not bleeding." She turned back to him with a bottle of water and a wet rag. She handed him the water and murmured, "Drink." Then wiped his face and neck with the cloth. It was cool and felt heavenly.

He held the bottle against his chest and closed his eyes. Slid his hand down her thigh.

"Okay," she said. "Sure, okay. Thanks."

She disconnected the call and turned worried blue eyes on him. "How do you feel?"

"What's this? The flu?"

"Infection," she said. "You should have gone to the ER as soon as you hurt yourself."

"Ah, damn." His brain started spinning. He tried to sit up.

Lexi pushed him back down. "You're not going anywhere."

"I need my phone. I've got a shoot tomorrow—"

"No, you don't," she said. "I've already worked it out with Wes. He and Troy have at least the next few days covered. The doctor said it will take you that long to kick this."

He frowned at her, trying to drag their conversations to mind. He didn't remember mentioning Wes or Troy. "What…time is it?"

She glanced at her phone. "Almost one. Are you hungry yet?"

"One in the *afternoon*?" His gaze scanned her. She wore a T-shirt and jean cutoffs. Her hair was pulled into a messy bun. She didn't have a speck of makeup on. And she looked gorgeous. Like one of those homegrown, heartland beauties. He tried to push up again. "You have another wedding today."

Again, she pressed her hand to his chest. "One of my assistants is covering the wedding. If there is an emergency, she'll call. The ceremony and reception are twenty minutes away."

"Shit, I'm sorry." He covered his eyes with his good arm. "I keep fucking everything up for you."

"It's an infection, Jax. You didn't plan it."

No, but he hadn't been responsible about getting his arm checked either. He'd been reckless with his health, and now it was costing Lexi.

"Whose wedding?" he asked.

"Claire Beaumont." Lexi stood and redirected a small fan toward Jax's face and chest. The cool air hit his damp skin, and relief poured over him. "I've already talked to her. Told her I had a family emergency. She's a friend. Rubi and I modeled with her. She's absolutely fine with it."

Family. He released. Yeah, he could easily think of Lexi as his family. "Claire's cool. I didn't know she was getting married. To…God, what's his name?"

"David."

"Yeah." He dropped his arm. "How did you find Wes?"

"Your phone."

"But…"

"There are only five guys' names in your personal phone. The rest are women. It doesn't take a genius to figure it out. And by the record of your recent calls, I figured Wes was the guy who'd know you best. I lucked out that he also happened to be a guy who could keep things running while you're down. Good thing too. If I had to send guys out on stunt jobs, people might die."

A laugh bubbled out of Jax's chest. "Christ, where did you come from? And how did I get lucky enough to find you?"

"Kentucky." She grinned. "And *I* found *you.*"

Maybe, but he wasn't seeing that as particularly lucky for her.

He hadn't been able to stay awake once they'd gotten back here last night. They'd curled up together on her bed and fallen asleep. It had been the most peaceful moment he'd known in way too long.

"You haven't had anything but water," she said. "You might get some strength back if you eat."

He grimaced.

"I don't like to eat when I feel sick either." She brushed her fingers over his sweat-dampened hair. "What about ice cream? Ice cream makes everything better."

He laughed. "Way outside my diet, babe."

"Diet?" She looked at him like he was crazy. "You're joking."

"No. This body doesn't come easy." He made light of it, but he was very serious. He maintained a pretty strict diet to stay fit and healthy. Without those two things, his stunt career would be over. "And I'm not getting any younger."

"I, for one"—she ran her hand down his chest, leaned in, and kissed him—"greatly appreciate your efforts."

He sighed into her mouth, kissed her back. "Have I told you I love you yet today?"

She grinned against his lips. But when she pulled back, apprehension dimmed her eyes.

"What's wrong? Don't like me telling you?"

"It's not that. We just...have a lot to work out."

Yeah. They did.

She kissed him again, then stood. "I have to pick up your prescription down the street," she said. "If you won't eat ice cream, tell me what you want, and I'll get it while I'm out."

"Toothbrush would be amazing."

She laughed. "Fine, but you're going to have to eat something when I get back."

"You look really tasty. I'll take a whole lotta..." He scanned her body. "All that."

"Rest and water, Mr. Chamberlin," she said. "Speaking of which, give me the name of your favorite movie. I'll pick up a DVD. You can give me a play-by-play behind the scenes while we watch it."

He hesitated. "One of *my* favorite movies or my favorite movie?"

"Yours. Why would I want to watch something else?" She squinched her nose up, making her look so young. "But maybe one where you're not all over another girl. Don't think I'm ready for that."

Lexi put strawberries in a basket at the market and moved on to the mangoes. Her cell rang, and she answered without looking. "Think of something you want?"

"Details," Rubi said. "Lots and *lots* of details, girl."

Lexi frowned down at the bright bin of mangoes, discomfort tightening her chest. "About what?"

"I'm at Claire's ceremony. She said you had a family emergency. Since I'm your only family..." She trailed off, her voice thick with suggestion. "*Who's* your emergency?"

Guilt tumbled in. This was the first wedding she'd missed in her career. Jessie's wedding was the first she'd left before her bride. All for Jax, a man she barely knew.

Lexi released a breath of both dread and excitement. "Jax."

"Oh my God." Rubi's voice was filled with more surprise than true shock like it should have been. "I heard you tangled with someone at Greystone last night, but I didn't believe... I leave you for thirty-six hours and your whole life changes? Without consulting me first?"

"What did you hear? And from who?" Discomfort edged out her excitement.

"Just murmurings of you having words with some hot movie star. Is this Jax guy an actor or a stuntman? And what the hell happened to my steadfast, no-risk, OCD Lexi?"

"I don't know, and it freaks me out." She wandered around the little store, scanning the shelves for healthy, protein-rich food—something she didn't know much about. "This is going so fast."

"Tell me about him. What have you found out?"

Lexi pulled a can of cashews from the shelf, trying to remember if that was what he'd eaten first from the last snacks she'd bought him.

She pulled in a deep breath, then said, "Do you know who Bentley Chamberlin is?"

"Uh...duh. Who doesn't? Does your Jax know him? Work for him? A brother? A friend? Is he as hot as—? Oh. My. *God.*" Rubi barely paused before she started back in, her voice rising with excitement. "That's *him.* That's why he looked familiar. Oh my *God*, you're screwing Bentley—"

"Rubi!" She scolded her friend in a hushed voice. An older woman frowned at her. "Think about where you are and what you're saying."

"Wait, why'd he tell you his name was Jax?" she asked, hushed now.

"It's his middle name, what he goes by. He said he used

Bentley for acting, but he isn't acting—"

"I know. He quit to… Oh, this is *priceless*. Miss Perfect sleeping with Hollywood's bad boy in hiding. Hell, girl, when you go bad, you go all the way."

"I'm not Miss Perfect." Lexi tossed the cashews into her basket and found a quiet corner of the store. She set her basket down and rubbed her forehead. "And what does that mean? I know nothing about him."

"He's… Why don't you Google him? Or *ask* him? Where *are* you?"

"At the grocery store. Would you just give me the freaking highlights, please?"

"His entire family is in the movie business. Parents are huge actors, brothers have directed and produced, sister is an always-in-trouble wild-child wanna-be actress."

Lexi's stomach knotted tighter. "What about *him?*"

"Tabloids say he's been in an ongoing family feud since he left acting." Rubi's voice leveled. "And he gets around, Lexi. Shit, I bet he's fire in the sheets. No wonder you've been so messed up, girl."

Lexi muttered a curse. That familiar fear rose up her chest like a heating thermometer.

"Don't wig," Rubi said. "It's just sex, Lexi. Enjoy him while you have him. He's not known for staying with any one woman long. In fact, his last fling—can't remember her name—was some actress who fucked him out of a huge contract of some kind. Literally fucked him out of it. I'll have to see if I can find that story."

"When you do, keep it to yourself," Lexi said, "I don't need to hear it. I've got to go. I'll call you later."

Lexi wandered down the short aisle of toiletries in a fog. She stared at the toothbrushes until her vision blurred. Family feud. Womanizer. Bad boy. Malibu. "What in the *hell* am I doing?"

She closed her eyes. Forced her logical mind to churn.

Lexi knew how sensational the tabloids were. She knew what lengths reporters went to for stories. She herself had been pushed to the brink of making shit up just to get them to leave her alone. So she knew it wasn't all true. But she also knew a lot of the bullshit was seeded with fact.

She opened her eyes and pulled her phone from her pocket.

LEXI: Any preferences on your toothbrush?

She mused over the vast selection as she waited to keep her mind from turning her belly into a four-alarm fire. Bristle types, head sizes, neck features… "This is worse than buying a car."

JAX: The one that gets you back here fastest. I'm naked in your shower.

"Oh man." He probably had his phone sitting on the back of the toilet right next to the shower—that was what she did.

She clenched her teeth against the burn of need between her legs.

LEXI: I didn't need to know that. Now I can't concentrate. What a visual. Don't get your stitches wet and don't faint.

She pulled a toothbrush from the display, tossed it into the basket, and moved on.

JAX: I love the way you take care of me. Next shower will be together.

"Jesus," she muttered and paused at the ice cream display. Found an all-fruit peach sorbet and tossed it in, grabbed a quart of milk…and smiled as she picked up a can of whipped cream.

"Enjoy him while you have him. He's not known for staying with any one woman long."

Lexi's smile fell.

"Have I told you I love you yet today?"

Her mind spun. Her heart squeezed. She closed her eyes and

shook all the confusion away. They definitely needed to talk.

TWENTY-THREE

Jax paused the movie as Lexi answered her phone. He prayed she didn't have to go out, and from her end of the conversation, it sounded like his prayer had been answered.

When she disconnected, her blue eyes smiled up at him from where her head lay on his belly. "Claire and David just left the reception for their honeymoon."

He smiled, leaned down, and kissed her. "Congratulations on your first successful day off in fifteen years." Then he spooned peach sorbet into her beautiful mouth and kissed her again.

Jax was feeling a hell of a lot better now, eight hours after starting the antibiotic, but he could still feel the drag in his body. He was so grateful Lexi had taken care of covering his shoots the next couple of days. It was good for his guys and for him.

"I feel guilty," she said, "but I have to admit, it feels incredibly…decadent too."

She reached up and pressed her hand to Jax's forehead, then the side of his face, then his neck. And smiled. "Fever's down."

He covered her hand, sighed, and pulled it to his mouth for a kiss. "Your touch feels decadent."

When he opened his eyes, she smiled, but the look was still worried. "What's wrong? You haven't been the same since you left for the market."

"You're awfully sensitive," she tried to tease.

"I'm perceptive, and I've had enough people pull away from me to know when it's happening."

She shook her head. "I'm not. There's just a lot on my mind."

"What happened?" he asked again.

"Rubi called. She heard rumblings about me from Jessie's wedding and wanted to know what they were about."

It was starting. Not twenty-four hours after being in public together for the first time, and it was already happening. And they hadn't even truly been together at the wedding. He sighed, reached over to the laptop she had perched on her thighs where the movie filled the screen, and closed the lid.

"What did she say?" As if he didn't already know.

"I really don't care what she said. I'd rather hear about you from you."

"What would you like to know?"

She lifted her shoulder. "Whatever you'd like to tell me?"

Jax licked the spoon, then put the ice cream on the bedside table. He wound a piece of her hair around his finger and decided to start with what would be most important to Lexi.

"I've spent my life working hard and playing harder. Was caught up in the whole Hollywood scene for several years. I've been successful but not truly happy. When I started taking different types of roles, looking for that…satisfaction, that…elusive happiness, it caused a rift in my already shaky relationship with my parents."

"Also actors, I hear," she said.

Jax nodded. "An ugly web, really."

"I've heard uglier," she said. "Go on."

"As the rift with my parents grew, my life got shaky. My relationships with my brothers went south too. And even though my family roots were shallow, they were my only roots. Without that, I kind of…" He shrugged. "I just lost my way."

"How old were you?"

"Early twenties. Twenty-two, twenty-three. Decent looking with a truckload of money, a famous family, a famous face, and no one who gave a goddamn about me."

Her thumb cruised over his cheekbone. A small smile turned her mouth. "You're lucky you're still alive."

"Damn straight." He loved that she understood the deeper meaning. That she didn't make a big drama out of it. "I met Wes on a movie set. He was grabbing stunt gigs where he could. I loved doing my own stunts but ended up standing by, arms crossed, watching guys like Wes having all the fun because the insurance company on the films wouldn't let me do them.

"Then Wes would walk off the set like nobody, have drinks with friends, and go home to a sweet woman. No stalkers, no cameras in his windows, no interruptions when he tried to go out to dinner. Real people in his life. When that movie was over, I decided to drop acting and pick up stunts.

"In my own defense, since then, my only bad-boy tendencies have been related to riding motorcycles, playing with fire, and jumping from buildings."

"And picking up women," Lexi said.

Jax's mouth turned up in a lopsided grin. "Which was something I was trying to change when you texted me at the airport."

"That was what, then? Falling off the wagon?" She laughed, the sound soft but light. No jealousy darkened her face. Both refreshing and a little…unnerving. "Because you slept with me sight unseen."

"I don't remember much sleeping," he said, loving the way her eyes darkened with memories. "And that was a huge feat for me. Looks have always been important. Too important. It was one of the things I was trying to get over. That and choosing women who walk all over me and treat me like shit—or so Wes likes to say."

"Ah," she said. "That explains his attitude when I talked to him. He thinks I'm another one of those women."

"Not…exactly." Jax grimaced. "And sorry about the attitude. I'll straighten that right out when I talk to him. He's a good guy. Trying to look out for me, but I'm not exactly—"

"The perfect patient?"

"Something like that. He, uh…also set me up with the girl I was dating…"

"I see. It's all becoming very clear."

He tugged the strand of hair from his finger and touched her cheek. "I've also never been in love with a woman—other than you—and I've certainly never told another woman that I loved her. Ever."

Her smile was so sweet it made his chest tighten. He leaned down and kissed her.

"You're a good man, Jax," she whispered against his lips before she opened and tasted him.

Love flowed through him, swift and hot, whipping up a fierce desire. He groaned into her mouth, slid his hand around her waist, and pulled her to him with his good arm.

She moaned but pulled away. "You're just getting better. You should rest."

"I'll rest better after I've made you come two, three…six times." He kissed her again as she laughed.

The abrasive tap of metal on glass cut into his bliss. Lexi pulled back with a frown. She turned her head toward the balcony.

The sound came again, louder. *Tap-tap-tap.* "The front door?" Jax asked, sitting up with Lexi as a wave of protectiveness swept through him. "Rubi?"

"She has a key." Lexi stood and started toward the balcony. "And she knows you're here. She wouldn't bother us."

"Have the photographers ever done this?" Jax asked. Stitches or not, if that was a reporter knocking on her door, the guy was going to lose more than his camera.

"What the…?" she said.

"Who is it?" he asked coming up behind her.

Lexi swung around and put both hands on his chest. She walked him backward, out of sight. "It's Martina."

From the way she said her name, Jax knew this Martina was important. "Who's that?"

Tap-tap-tap, then a muffled, "Lexi? I need to talk to you."

"Shit," she muttered. "This cannot be good. Jax, please,

please, stay up here. I'll tell you about it when she's gone." She must have read the frustration in his face, because she said again, "Please."

Stay up here hidden from anyone who mattered to her career.

But he rubbed her arms and said, "Fine."

Lexi's beautiful face filled with dread, but she straightened her shoulders, and went to unlock the front door clad in bare feet, shorts, and T-shirt. He loved that she didn't rush to change for whoever this was.

Jax pulled on his jeans and sat on the corner of the bed, forearms on thighs. He could just see over the edge of the balcony as Lexi unlocked the front door.

"What are you doing in Los Angeles?" were Lexi's first words to the other woman. Martina. "And why are you here? Why didn't you call?"

Martina didn't smile, didn't greet Lexi, but she did say, "I'm sorry for not calling, but this was urgent, and I was nearby."

Jax thought she might be a relative, only Martina was dark skinned, dark haired. She carried a purse and a manila envelope.

In Jax's experience, manila envelopes were never good. Anything good was already out of the envelope. Things that stayed inside envelopes were time bombs. His chest tightened with apprehension.

Lexi was still locking the door when Martina said, "I was having dinner with colleagues. I just got into town for an event at the fashion center. I'm speaking for someone who couldn't make it at the last minute."

Lexi gazed out the glass door, searching up and down the street, before turning back to Martina. "Can I get you something? Water?"

"You can get her the hell out of your studio at nine o'clock on a Sunday-fucking-night," Jax muttered to himself. Who the hell did that?

"No," Martina said to the offer of water. "I'm here because someone had this delivered to my table at dinner." She thrust the envelope toward Lexi.

"Oh shit," Jax whispered, fisting his hands.

Lexi looked down at the envelope but kept her arms crossed. "What is it?"

"A photograph." She thrust it forward again. "Look for yourself."

Jax ran his hand through his hair and fisted it. His mind scoured his time with Lexi. When could someone have gotten a picture of them together?

Only about half a dozen times.

He held his breath while Lexi took the envelope, lifted the flap, and slid the photograph out. She stared at it for a long second when Jax couldn't read her body language. Couldn't catch enough of her face to see her expression.

When Lexi looked at Martina again, all she said was, "Who?"

"I don't know, but I told you about this in New York, Lexi. I told you that some of these designers are cutthroat—"

"I know the designers involved in this competition." Her voice was fierce. No one was going to push this woman around. And Jax was humbled by her inner strength. "None of them would stoop this low."

"I don't know what to tell you, Lexi. I have no intention of sharing this with the board, but who knows whether this person has already sent it to them or not?"

Holy fuck. Jax's stomach fell to his feet. This was the designer. *The* designer. The one who could make all Lexi's dreams come true. Make all Lexi's hard work pay off.

Lexi rubbed her forehead. "I can't do anything about this. Especially not if I can't confront the sender." She threw her hands out to the sides in exasperation. "What do you want me to do, Martina?"

The break in Lexi's voice turned him for the stairs.

"Stop seeing him." Martina's voice felt like a snap of cold electricity in Jax's gut. "You know this is suicide to your career, Lexi. Why would you do this?"

"Because I love him."

The words were barely out of her mouth when Jax stepped up beside them, startling them both. He put a hand on Lexi's shoulder while Martina backed away three full steps, eyes wide with fear, hand at her chest.

"Jax." Lexi turned into him with a hand on his arm. "It's okay, I can handle this."

"Let me see it." She opened her mouth to argue. "*Let me...see it.*"

Lexi handed him the envelope and lowered her gaze, but he saw the shame in her eyes.

Martina eyed Jax, standing there in nothing but blue jeans, with a dark glint of suspicion. He didn't care what the woman thought of him. He only cared how she could hurt Lexi. He kept a hard gaze on her until he'd pulled the photo from the envelope and lowered his eyes to it.

The image must have been taken last night. In the dark. It was grainy, but he could clearly see the image of him and Lexi pressed up against the alcove's sandstone wall, his tongue down her throat, hips between her legs, hands pulling up her dress.

"Fuck." He bit it out fiercely, jerking the photo down to his side and startling both Lexi and Martina.

"It's okay—" Lexi started.

"It's *not* okay." He turned his gaze on Martina. "I'll find out who did this and get it from them within twelve hours."

Martina shook her head. "It's too late for damage control. Whoever took this photograph has more. They won't stop taking them. And you can bet they didn't keep their mouth shut about you two either."

Lexi's gaze jumped to Jax's. He saw the realization in her eyes. Then panic. And finally...resignation. The kind of resignation that signaled defeat. And the loss of dreams.

Lexi turned back to Martina.

Before she could speak, Jax said, "This won't be a problem."

"How can you be sure of that?" Martina asked, more rhetorically since they all knew he couldn't be sure of anything.

"Because like I said, I will take care of whoever took this picture."

"Jax." Lexi put a hand on his arm, but he shook it off.

"And because we aren't seeing each other anymore," he said. "There won't be any more opportunities for pictures."

Lexi opened the door for Martina. She didn't have anything to say to the woman, and even if she had, Jax had just knocked the wind out of her.

Martina looked over Lexi's shoulder and up toward the loft where Jax had gone. "I think that's a good decision. Listen to him, Lexi. This is your future. Don't throw it away for one hot guy."

Lexi said nothing. Because saying nothing was far kinder than anything else that would come out of her mouth now.

As soon as Martina stepped out of the shop, Lexi locked the door and turned toward the stairs. She barely kept herself from running and reached the landing just as Jax was starting for it.

She put her hands up and blocked his path. "This is not your fault, and you're not leaving just because some idiot—"

"No." He said, resolute. "Not just some idiot, Lexi. All idiots. And there are plenty out there." He had pulled on the T-shirt Lexi had brought home from New York after wearing it back to her room after their first night together. His eyes were dark with guilt and shame and pain. "It won't end, Lex. And I won't be the reason everything you've worked for goes to shit. I don't know how I ever thought…"

"Jax." Lexi had never felt so desperate. It was completely illogical but so very real. She couldn't lose him. "I don't care. I don't care about the competition. I don't care about the partnership. I was already considering trashing the idea—"

"Make your decisions. Do what you're going to do. But they won't be based on whether or not I'm in your life, dragging you down."

"You're not—"

"I'm sorry, baby. I should have known better."

He pushed past her.

She grabbed the back of his shirt, feeling like a psychotic stalker. "Jax, please…"

He stopped only to turn back and pull her in for a kiss. "I'm so sorry."

He broke free of her grip and skipped down the stairs as if he couldn't get out of there fast enough. Lexi had to force herself not to plead with him, but she was desperate enough.

She turned toward the balcony and gripped the metal rail. "Jax, if you really loved me, you wouldn't leave."

He stopped with the front door halfway open.

Please don't go.

He turned his head, looked up at her. "I'm leaving *because* I really love you, Lex."

TWENTY-FOUR

Six weeks to the day that Jax had walked out of her studio, Lexi sat at her drawing table, a pen in hand. She toggled it back and forth between her fingers. Dragged her lip between her teeth.

"Just write it already." Rubi sat cross-legged on Lexi's bed, surfing the Web. "I'm not staying here all night."

Everything with Jax had been a risk. That was what Jax was all about—risk. Lexi was pretty good at taking risks. Calculated risks. But this wasn't the least bit calculated.

Still undecided, Lexi penned his name on the envelope, each letter careful and deliberate.

Bentley Jaxon Chamberlin

He would find it ridiculously formal.

But Lexi wanted him to know that she knew every part of him, loved every part of him, wanted every part of him.

On the bottom of the invitation, she added a personal note. Had to fight herself from adding *I miss you. I love you.* And just signed her name.

She sighed and slid it into the envelope.

If he doesn't respond, it wasn't meant to be.

She licked the tip of the flap and pressed it closed.

If he doesn't show, something better waits for me.

She turned it over and ran her fingers over his name.

"Tick-tock, tick-tock," Rubi said, pushing to her feet and sliding into rhinestoned flip-flops. "I'm tired. I want to go slide into a bathtub."

Lexi glanced over her shoulder. "Did you find him?"

"Yep. He snagged that Bond job back and he and his crew have been playing on the Sixth Street Bridge." She walked up to her drawing table, met Lexi's gaze, and held out her hand. "Now or never."

Lexi pulled the inside of her cheek between her teeth and offered the invitation to Rubi.

When she started to close her fingers, Lexi pulled it back. "Just…don't…say anything. Just give it to him and walk away."

"Sure, hon, that's going to happen."

Rubi grabbed for the envelope. Lexi pulled it back again.

"And…if he's with a woman…*absolutely* don't give it to him."

Rubi's lids lowered in warning. "Lexi. Let go."

Lexi closed her eyes and forced herself to let go of control. Rubi snatched the invitation, kissed her cheek, and her flip-flops tick-tick-ticked down the stairs to the front door.

"Rubi," Lexi called. When her friend turned and faced Lexi, she said, "Thank you."

As soon as Rubi closed and locked the door behind her, Lexi turned to her sewing machine and the yards of butter-like crimson leather she'd bought at the London Fabric Expo.

TWENTY-FIVE

Jax swung his legs over the steel beam running beneath the Sixth Street Viaduct and seated the bend of his knees solidly over the metal.

Then let go.

He swung upside down over the concrete running alongside the trench that guided the Los Angeles River through the city.

He clapped his gloved hands. "Let's finish this."

Troy, the Renegades' rigging master, tossed him the first cable. "Start with the third hole and thread them backward."

Jax did as directed. Sweat dripped from his chest to his neck. Neck to cheeks. Then slid into his eyes.

"Goddamn." He used his forearms to wipe it away.

"Welcome to my world, bro."

"So fucking complicated..." He caught the next cable, threaded it. Wiped at sweat. "Can't just make..." He caught the last cable, threaded it. "A simple jump anymore."

Another cable came at him. A fourth cable, for which there was no use. Jax turned his head and caught the carabiner attached to the end just before it cracked his jaw.

"What the fuck?" he sputtered, hand in front of his face in case Troy decided to throw another. "Troy!"

"Oh yeah." He pulled his gaze up from the concrete below, where the rest of their team worked. "Sorry, boss. Little distraction."

"I'll distract you, dumbshit," he muttered. "You don't get *distracted* thirty feet above concrete."

"Dude, relax. Look down there. That's some good mood walking, right there. If that don't perk you up, you need medical help."

Jax reached toward his feet, grabbed the beam, and pulled his legs out. He relaxed into the safety harness and wiped more sweat from his face. Then opened his eyes to a red Ferrari parked one hundred feet below.

His heart skipped, then sped. His gaze scanned the scene, searching for Lexi. Rubi sauntered toward the men, but his gaze held on the Ferrari, willing Lexi to step out. His banked hunger broke through and started gnawing at his raw gut. What he'd give for the mere sight of her.

"Mmm-mmm," Troy said. "That is some sweet stuff."

"I'm going on belay," Jax said, taking the safety rope from Troy and switching the rigging around so he'd be secure up there alone. "I'm going down."

"Dude, we've got six more pulleys—"

Jax shot Troy a look. "I'm going down."

"Fine, fine. You're the one who's going to have to climb back up here."

Jax loosened his anchor and started toward the ground. The slide lasted only seconds but felt like it took forever. His mind darted a hundred different places, but fear took the lead. He hit the ground, unhooked the safety harness, and jogged toward Rubi.

Lexi's okay. Lexi's okay.

As he approached Rubi, she turned. As soon as he saw her smile, all the fear drained out of him. The relief was so complete, he staggered backward a few steps before he caught himself. He braced his hands on his knees and stared at the cement until his head stopped spinning.

"Dude." Wes's boots came into view. "You okay?"

Jax nodded, unable to speak.

Fuck. That had hit him out of nowhere.

He'd been repressing everything so completely—how much he missed her, how empty he felt without her, how she was better off without him—it lashed back on him now like a whip.

He finally looked up and met Rubi's frown but was still

breathing hard when he asked, "Is…Lexi…okay?"

Rubi studied him with intense blue-green eyes filled with a mix of curiosity and humor. She wore skintight blue jeans that showed the perfect shape of her highway-long legs, heels that made those legs look even longer, and a halter top that showed both her flat belly and her cleavage.

Jax's guys were tripping over themselves to take in every inch of her.

She turned to them, offered a flirtatious smile. "Can we have a minute, boys?"

The guys wandered back to their gear, muttering to each other, laughing quietly. Everyone except Wes. He crossed his arms and kept grinning like an idiot.

"You think you're special," she asked Wes, "don't you, Golden Boy?"

"I know I'm special." Wes's grin widened. "Just ask my mama."

That pulled a deep, rolling laugh from Rubi. She might mesmerize every other man on the site, but her playfulness was bugging the shit out of Jax.

"Wes." Jax pulled his friend's attention. "Get lost."

Wes turned a lazy gaze back on Rubi. "Dinner sometime, beautiful?"

Her eyes narrowed. "Last I heard, you were taken."

He lifted a shoulder. "We're on a break."

"Sorry…Wes." Rubi drew out his name in a voice that he thought would make Wes drop to his knees, but his friend just kept grinning. "I'm not a *break* kinda girl. Besides, I hear you like *sweet*. And, handsome"—she lowered her lids—"I'm not the least bit sweet."

"If Chamberlin can go from sour to sweet"—Wes drew a business card from his wallet—"I can certainly change my tastes to something on the tangy side."

"Are you two done?" Jax straightened, used the bottom of

his T-shirt to wipe the sweat from his face and rested his hands at his hips. "We've got work to do here."

"Ignore him." Wes sauntered over to Rubi. "He's grouchy when he's not getting any."

"Wes," Jax warned.

When Rubi ignored Wes's card, he slid it along the edge of her halter and tucked it beneath the fabric at the curve of her breast. "My tastes are changing as we speak. Besides, I know there's a lot more sweet beneath that tart surface than you let on. I bet you'd set my taste buds on fire."

"You bet your rock-hard ass I would," Rubi returned.

Wes started toward the trailer, yelling at the others, "Is it hot out here?"

He caught the bottle of water one of them threw, uncapped it and, walking backward, grinned at Rubi as he poured the water over his head.

The guys bust out laughing. And Rubi sputtered a surprised chuckle. "He is a character."

Jax shifted on his feet. His fear had transitioned into annoyance. "Rubi, *is Lexi okay?*"

She pulled the card from her top and slid it into the back pocket of her jeans. When she looked back at Jax, her expression had sobered. Her serious gaze seemed to penetrate him. "Lexi's a survivor."

That wasn't what he'd wanted to hear. That made it sound like she was struggling. He wanted Rubi to tell him that she was great. That him leaving her was the best thing that had ever happened in her life.

"Why are you here?"

She pulled a square white envelope from beneath the cross of her arms. "She asked me to deliver this."

From five feet away, Jax could see his full name on the envelope. He didn't like the look of that. Wedding invitations came in envelopes like that.

They'd only been apart six weeks… She couldn't have found…

But then Jax realized he and Lexi had gone from zero to sixty in about the same amount of time, and a spear of anxiety pierced his chest.

"What is it?" he asked, his voice rough.

"Find out for yourself. Lexi instructed me not to open my big mouth."

Jax took the envelope and stared at his name printed in Lexi's hand.

"And since she's the sister I never had and I love her more than anyone," Rubi said, strolling back toward the Ferrari, "I'm *not* going to tell you that Lexi deserves stability in her life. I'm *not* going to tell you that she's worthy of a guy who can merge all his sides into one unique and outstanding person the way she has."

She opened the Ferrari door, holding his gaze. Hers was serious, deep, showing a side of her Jax guessed not many people noticed beneath all her flash and beauty. Showing him the side of her that he guessed Lexi loved so much.

"I'm *not* going to tell you to ignore this invitation if that's not you," she said. "I'm just going to keep my mouth shut, like I promised. And, by the way, thanks for taking care of that shit photographer."

She turned on the sparkle, blew a kiss to Wes, who dramatically acted out getting shot in the heart and fell to the cement to the laughter of the group.

"What a hottie," she said, affection and longing softening her voice. "Too bad I don't go for those mama-lovin', sun-streaked country boys who adore sweet women."

Rubi slid into her sports car, slipped on sunglasses, and turned over the engine.

Jax didn't move as she roared from the cement canal, and thought about the photograph that had changed everything. He'd hired a private investigator who had gotten to the bottom of it within the twelve hours he'd promised Lexi. Hardly compensation for all the trouble and stress he'd caused her, but all he'd been able to do, other than getting the hell out of her life.

Wes turned from watching the car go and settled his gaze on Jax. One look and he turned toward the guys. "I think it's lunchtime." Then yelled toward the bridge. "Troy, get your ass down here. We're eating out today."

A loud whoop sounded behind Jax, followed by the shrill grind of Troy sliding down his cable. The rest of the team loaded into nearby trucks, arguing over where they'd eat.

Wes strolled up to Jax and looked down at the invitation. "Let me just tell you now, if that's for Lexi's wedding, I quit."

Jax scowled up at Wes.

"You've been hell to live with, dude." Wes gave him a pitying half grin. "I won't be able to stand you."

"You're not all joy and sunshine yourself," Jax said to Wes's back as he headed toward one of the trucks.

Wes flipped him off.

Jax waited until the guys were on the road to pull off his gloves and open the envelope. His dirty hands turned the pristine cream envelope gray and left a streak across the torn flap. He couldn't help but feel like that symbolized how opposite they were—Lexi all light and promise, Jax all grunge and shadow.

Jax took a deep breath and slid the card inside halfway out.

You are cordially invited to

The Luxe Couture Bridal Show

Jax released the air he'd been holding. The tension left his body, and he bent at the waist, resting his hands on his knees again.

He closed his eyes and swore at the relief coursing through him. Jax struggled to get his air back, then pulled the card the rest of the way out of the envelope. His hand was shaking.

The invitation gave the date in less than a week, the time, the location, and allowed him to bring a guest.

As if.

At the bottom, Lexi had handwritten a note.

If you come, come as you are.

TWENTY-SIX

"Lexi."

Lexi stopped fussing with a strand of lace that wouldn't fall right on the dress worn by the fifth model, Kylie, and looked toward Rubi's voice. She stood near one of the makeup tables in the LaCroix section backstage at the Luxe Couture Bridal Show. On one side of the space, makeup tables with mirrors and lights lined the wall. On the other stood small dressing spaces separated by black drapes, each with the model's assigned gowns and accessories and a dressing assistant standing by.

Rubi gestured to the hairpiece she was helping a stylist place in another model's hair.

Lexi squinted, assessing. "Nice, thank you."

The young woman in the chair stood and started toward her dressing area.

The models lined up along the space, all lace and sparkle, tulle and satin.

"No," Lexi said, "Carly goes before Stephanie."

The girls changed positions in the lineup. Lexi moved to the front of the line. The third model, a stunning sixteen-year-old who looked twenty-five at the moment in professional makeup, sparkles in her hair, and a ten-thousand-dollar couture wedding gown, turned toward her with a serious expression.

Lexi scanned the dress, adjusted the fall of one shoulder, pulled the lace taut over her abdomen. "Happy brides, okay?"

The girl broke into a gorgeous, nearly authentic smile. Lexi breathed out and shook her head. "Stunning."

The smile reached the girl's bright blue eyes.

She went down the line, inspecting each girl. By the time she reached Rubi putting the final touches of makeup on the last model, Lexi pressed a hand to her stomach.

"I want to puke," she murmured.

"I'm almost done here. I'll go see if I can find him."

"I don't know if I want to know whether or not he's here."

"Your choice, but I have to know." Rubi called to another makeup artist messing with the collar of the lead model's dress. "Doug, take over here. I'll be right back."

Doug rushed over and took the finishing powder and brush from Rubi's hands, then back to the front of the line, prepared to douse any shining surface.

Lexi ignored Rubi as she turned out of the room. "Focus," she reminded herself. "This is your career."

But Lexi already knew she couldn't change anything now. All the plans and props were in motion. The dresses made. The choreography decided. The models rehearsed. She'd made this decision weeks ago.

Now it was all or nothing.

Now, Lexi just had to let go, the way Jax had taught her to let go.

As the applause out front died down and the announcer started speaking again, Lexi turned on autopilot. She shut down all peripheral thought, focused on the moment, and moved to the front of the line.

She put a hand on Naomi's arm, smiled at the eighteen-year-old beauty and said, "Happy brides. Best day of your life. Cloud nine."

Naomi beamed. Her dark skin sparkled with glitter, mouth painted the same color as the girl's crimson leather gloves.

The music cued, and Lexi squeezed Naomi's arm. "Go, sweetheart."

***

Jax wasn't as uncomfortable as he'd expected, even though his best Armani suit jacket was too tight and his suit pants too loose. His stunt work had honed his body over the past few years. But beyond the discomfort of wearing a suit, he had to admit he was enjoying himself. As much as a man preparing to grovel could enjoy himself.

He'd come early to make sure he'd gotten the best seat in the huge showplace and sat front row along the middle of the runway. The designs were amazing, the women—though he knew they were just girls—stunning, the music great, the mood around him all shock and awe, the room dark but for spotlights and sparkles.

Lexi's line hadn't shown yet, and he'd already been there over an hour. He sneered to himself when the announcer introduced the line of the designer whose father had hired the photographer to stalk Lexi. The father was now dealing with a lawsuit. Jax didn't give a rat's ass whether he won or not; he was sending a message. One which had worked, if the fact that he hadn't received any more nastygrams against himself or Lexi was any indication. And a recent call to Martina Galliano confirmed she hadn't received any more communications either.

As the designer of the last line came out to acknowledge the crowd, Jax shifted in his seat and curled the program into a tube. Lexi's line was next. And last. A grand finale of sorts, which pleased Jax to ridiculous levels.

The applause died down, and the announcer climbed the few stairs to the runway. Dressed in a tux, the middle-aged man addressed the crowd.

"We have a special two-part finale for you today, ladies and gentlemen. Lexi LaCroix has been a bright spot on the industry's radar for some years now, and this is her fifth year at Luxe Couture Bridal Show. To celebrate her anniversary, Miss LaCroix has put together a brand-new design line we'll be seeing for the first time here tonight, so get your cameras...and order forms...ready."

The man paused as light laughter drifted through the crowd.

"Known for her exquisite artistry in bridal gowns, Miss LaCroix incorporates character and femininity into all her design, whether created with timeless elegance or modern flair, and has even been called by some in the business an up-and-coming Oscar de la Renta.

"As an innovator in the bridal gown industry, Miss LaCroix delights us with surprises season after season. Tonight is no different." The announcer ended with a flourishing gesture toward the runway just before taking the stairs to the floor. "Regal elegance with *passion* from Lexi LaCroix."

Dramatic, upbeat music filled the air, and Jax clapped crazily as the lights went out and the spotlight brightened on the entrance to the runway, designed as an ornate Roman archway painted in gold glitter. When the first model appeared, the applause died and the flashes began.

Jax marveled at the uniqueness of the designs, the flowing beauty of the dresses, the sparkle and shine on each and every dress. Each model, regardless of dress style, wore elbow-length crimson gloves, definitely adding flare to the designs. It might just be Jax's twisted imagination, but the gloves almost seemed like an erotic touch.

And after watching all the other designs pass by, he could see pieces of Lexi in every one of these. Her subtle richness, her unique character, her endless dedication to understated class. There might not be any doubt that he was partial, but he found Lexi's designs far and away the most stunning, the most elegant, the most distinct.

Two dozen gowns, probably more, had shown already. Gowns that had all been created by Lexi's own hands. He might not have had the right, but he was still so incredibly proud of her. And also humbled by the reality that she'd gone on to put all this together even after he'd put her through the stress of a hidden relationship and then leaving her on the spur of the moment.

Lexi was indeed a survivor.

Jax couldn't keep the smile from his face. Couldn't drag his gaze from the dresses, each more stunning than the next.

When the model at the end of the runway turned and headed back toward the arch and another model didn't appear, Jax knew they'd reached the end of the show. He crushed the program in his hands, brimming with anticipation for the sight of Lexi.

Instead of disappearing through the arch, the last model made a sharp turn back toward the runway. The music changed in tandem, signaling not the end of the show, but the beginning of the second act, which the announcer had alluded to.

The model's movement changed, her steps far more deliberate and pronounced. No longer was she smooth and cool, but sharp and intense, mirroring the music. Then another model came out behind her, and another behind her.

Models streamed onto the runway with accentuated charisma and started...

Stripping.

The audience gasped. Murmured.

Little by little, the models tore away their dresses to reveal various garments underneath. A traditional, formal gown became a chic dinner dress, then a nightclub dress. Each design fell apart into different pieces, and once Jax recovered from the shock, he realized what Lexi had done—created several dresses within one.

"Genius," he murmured.

But then even more pieces came off and bits of crimson began to show. Red bras. Red garters. Red panties. Red corsets. Red teddies. More gasps erupted around Jax, immediately followed by a burst of insane applause. Within moments, every model paraded along the runway wearing searingly sexy crimson lingerie and dragging their stunning white haute couture gowns behind them along the floor. And Jax thought the applause would bring the roof down.

Whistles, cheers, shouts poured from the audience as the models returned to the entry arch and lined up along either side of the runway. Once they were all in formation, the models turned toward the opening and joined in the applause.

Everyone in the audience stood, the cheering so loud it rattled Jax's eardrums as they waited for Lexi to appear.

TWENTY-SEVEN

Backstage, Lexi covered her mouth with both hands and started crying.

Rubi bounced on her toes beside Lexi, clapping and screaming to be heard over the applause, "Didn't I tell you? *Didn't I tell you?*" She squeezed Lexi's arm. "Good-bye Galliano! Hello LaCroix. Girl, you don't need *anyone* now. It's all about *you*."

Lexi couldn't speak. She could only shake her head. She'd dreamt of this moment. Of the ear-shattering applause, the standing ovation, the recognition, the validation. And now she was too overwhelmed to move.

Rubi grabbed her hand and pulled her out onto the runway. When she tried to let go of Lexi's hand and push her toward the audience, Lexi held tight.

"I couldn't have done this without you." Lexi pulled her into step beside her.

The ham ate it up, strolling down the runway like the elegant model she was, beaming, holding Lexi's hand. Lexi waved to the cheering audience, bowed, continued crying, unable to stop and not giving a damn.

Rubi pulled her to a stop at the middle of the runway, leaned close, and said, "First row, directly on your right."

Lexi gasped, suddenly terrified to look and see Jax standing there. She'd hoped he would come. Prayed he would come. But a big part of her didn't believe he would come.

"You do your part," Rubi said. "The girls know theirs." Rubi released Lexi's hand and stepped back, giving her the spotlight.

But now that she was here and Jax was right there, she was terrified.

Risk. Jax is all about risk. And letting go.

And both had led her here. Despite whether he still wanted Lexi as a lover or not, she knew he deserved that recognition.

She bowed to the audience again, mouthing thank-yous. Then she took a deep breath and turned right, searching for a black leather jacket. But every male in the row wore a suit. Trepidation snuck in. Maybe Rubi was wrong. Maybe she'd just seen someone who looked like Jax.

She skimmed the faces and passed over Jax's before halting and scanning back.

Yes, he was there. Dressed in a dark suit, white shirt, and crimson tie—as if choreographed. His hair was shorter, combed off his face in a sophisticated style. He looked so incredibly handsome, Lexi's head went light.

He was standing and clapping along with the rest of the audience, but Lexi's hearing seemed to have gone, because it all sounded muted now. All she could focus on was the beam of his smile, the sparkle in his eyes.

This was the moment each designer brought out those significant to the line and shared them with the audience in a show of appreciation. Designers often brought their wives, husbands, business partners, or a special model onto the runway. Lexi had always been up here alone.

Now, she managed to reach out to Jax.

When he stepped forward and took her hand, everything turned dreamlike. The applause dimmed. Her vision narrowed to include only Jax. And time seemed to float as Lexi tugged him forward. With one smooth leap, he stood on the runway with her.

She circled his waist beneath the blazer. Jax's hands cupped her face, and he looked down at her with love and tears in his eyes. His lips moved as he spoke, but Lexi couldn't hear a thing over the noise. She didn't know if he was with another woman now, didn't know if he still saw their differences as too large to bridge, only knew she needed to feel his lips on hers. Lexi pushed up on tiptoes to kiss him.

"I told you to come as you were." She forced the words louder than felt comfortable to make sure he heard them.

He leaned down, put his mouth by her ear. "I did. This is

part of who I am too. I was just resisting that uncomfortable merge."

He pulled back, and the expression in his eyes when he looked down at her again was filled with so much love, Lexi's heart flipped in her chest.

Jax pulled her face close, pressing his mouth hard against hers. Then he opened to her, and in that moment she knew he was still hers. A whole new sensation of relief and gratitude and excitement flooded her body.

Sound and sensation rush back in. The applause pierced her eardrums.

In her peripheral vision, Lexi saw two of the models approach Jax from behind. She smiled into his eyes and lifted her hands to the knot of his tie at the same moment as the models stood on either side of him and slipped his blazer off his shoulders and down his arms.

He darted a surprised look at the women, then a questioning look at Lexi.

"I love *all* of you," she said as she loosened his tie and unfastened the buttons of his shirt to the increasing roar of the crowd. "And I want them all to see my inspiration for the new line."

Then the models slipped the shirt from his shoulders. Lexi couldn't keep the smile off her face as she wrapped her arms around his neck and kissed him the way she wished she'd been able to kiss him for the last six weeks. Jax kissed her back, his mouth generous, his lips unsteady with laughter and emotion. She guessed it was the actor in him that played up to the crowd and leaned her into a deep dip onstage, kissing her until she couldn't breathe.

He finally brought her upright and pulled out of the kiss. Lexi beamed, held tight to one hand, and turned toward the roaring crowd with a sweeping gesture toward all his stunning male beauty, including his tattoo.

The crowd exploded with approval. Jax laughed, bowed

graciously, then swung an arm around Lexi's shoulders and turned her toward the archway, walking her offstage.

***

Jax's heart was hammering as they walked through the rows of lingerie-clad models, all grinning and clapping. As soon as they stepped off the runway, Jax pulled Lexi aside and kissed her like he was possessed.

She didn't flinch, didn't push him away. Even as models and announcers and others passed by, she just kept kissing him.

She finally broke away, stroking his face with warm fingers and taking him in as if she'd never seen him before. "I didn't think you'd come."

Tears streamed down her face. He lifted a hand from her waist to wipe them away. "Baby…"

He couldn't find the words. He was overwhelmed. He'd never felt so completely accepted or loved in his entire life.

"Excuse me," a voice said behind them. "Lexi, can we have a minute?"

Lexi glanced past Jax, and he turned to see Martina standing nearby with another tall woman. One of the models came over and handed Jax his clothes. Along the runway, the audience remained abuzz.

Jax's nerves returned. "I'll give you a minute while I get dressed."

"No." She squeezed his hand. "You're part of my life, and if they want me, they have to take all of me, which includes you. Stay with me."

Martina looked both contrite and excited as she introduced the head of Galliano's board of directors. Neither of them looked Jax in the eye again after a quick acknowledgment, which didn't bother him in the least. The only woman whose opinion mattered to him was Lexi's.

She patiently listened to Martina's retraction of her earlier statements and the board director gush over Lexi's designs. When the offer for the partnership came, Jax squeezed her hand.

Lexi grinned at Jax briefly, then turned to the women. "Thank you. It's a fabulous offer, and I'll seriously consider it. I'll get back to you next week sometime."

Both women's expressions fell from polite excitement to shock.

Lexi turned to Jax and slid her arm around his waist. "I'm ready to go. How about you?"

He only nodded, wrapped an arm around her shoulders, and followed her lead as she led the way deeper backstage.

Jax stopped her again before they reached the area where photographers crawled over the space.

She glanced up at him. "What?"

"Photographers…"

She grinned. "You can't be camera shy."

He laughed with the joy of feeling so complete. Then he circled her in his arms and sobered. "I should never have left you that night," he said, his voice a hoarse murmur. "I didn't know what else to do. I've missed you so much. I'm so sorry—"

She pressed her fingers to his lips. "Just tell me you'll stay."

"I'll stay." He lowered his lips to hers, whispering, "Always."

SNEAK PEEK FROM *REBEL*

Rubi Russo whipped her brand new Aston Marten into the designated parking area for the filming crew of the new Bond film. Nice first ride straight from the dealer, even though Los Angeles traffic kept her from pushing the legendary sports coupe anywhere near its top speed of two-fifty-one. She'd have to find her mid-day adrenaline surge elsewhere. And there was no better place to get juiced than among the studs of Renegades.

One special stud in particular.

The thought dragged her gaze toward the charcoal four-wheel-drive Ford F150 parked nearby, and her mind veered toward its owner. He'd become a permanent fixture in her mind—those wide shoulders, that lazy stance, his cocky grin.

A giddy, tingling lust tightened her insides. "Oh, yeah. The perfect surge."

Dried mud caked the truck's bottom half, the same way it had when she'd first seen it at the airport. Strange to think they'd only been friends for two months, more or less forced into the arrangement when their best friends started dating. Impossible to comprehend how the mere thought of seeing the man could still shoot a thrill through her blood.

She smiled down at the collection of notes she kept in the ashtray—notes he'd started leaving on the windshield of her car at different times of the day, almost every day, for the last two months. Sometimes it was a cartoon or a joke or a reference to something they'd experienced together recently. Sometimes they were a simple, "Hope I see you today" or "Good morning".

Todays had read:

PREPARE FOR AMPED PUCKER FACTOR.

Whatever that meant.

The rumble of a motorcycle engine drew her attention down the long strip of concrete known as the Sixth Street Viaduct, a manmade cement canal guiding the Los Angeles River through the heart of the city.

Machinery, cameras, props and equipment lined the flat gray length of the channel. Off to one side, crumpled cars, burned out and still smoking, huddled in a haphazard heap as if they'd recently crashed. Production staff milled among white tents dotting the site.

Rubi grabbed her iPhone and her notebook from the passenger seat and stood from the car. The midday Southern California sun bathed her skin in warmth, draining some of the morning's tension from her shoulders. It felt good to be out of the house, away from all that goddamn computer code, like a real person with real friends. She hadn't realized how plastic her life had become until she'd started hanging out with this hunky group of fellow adrenaline junkies.

She started toward the action. Toward the man in the motorcycle helmet and black neoprene bodysuit, straddling a Ducati, one of the world's fastest motorcycles—Wes Lawson, Renegades' top stunt driver.

"I'm ready for a little eye candy."

She smoothed her hands over the filmy skirt that rode too high on her freakishly long legs. Tried to tug at her halter's bottom edge exposing a bare inch of skin, but ultimately couldn't hide the diamond stud at her belly button without exaggerating her cleavage. Oh, well.

Finger-combing her hair off her forehead, she sauntered toward a group of tall, well-built men loitering near one of the cameras. She recognized the owner of Renegades, and her best friend's new love, Jax Chamberlin, gesturing as he spoke to Daniel Craig's co-star on the film, Jason Bolton, and the director. A couple of younger men Rubi knew as production assistants, hung at the edge.

She passed one of the site's security guards, who grinned and saluted. "Lookin' good, Rubi."

"Right back at you, Max." She turned to face him while

continuing to walk backward toward the set. "Celia pop yet?"

His grin was wide and bright in his dark face, a man filled with pride every time anyone mentioned his pregnant wife. Rubi could respect his happiness, but with a father like hers, couldn't begin to relate to that kind of love.

"Soon," he said. "Any day now."

"Congrats in advance. Love to Celia."

She approached the set and focused on Wes. There was no outward sign the man covered in black from helmet to boot tips was him. It could have been any of the other Renegades' stunt men who rode motorcycles, which was, of course, all of them. But what gave Wes completely away—beyond the studly build she'd memorized—was his impatience. He navigated a slow, tight pattern around the group, like a circling shark. Occasionally, he revved the engine, smothering their conversation with the bike's growl.

Rubi grinned at his antsy behavior—ever the kid who couldn't wait to reach the playground. And he maneuvered dangerously close to Jax on each pass, the action surely designed to either annoy Jax or hurry him up. Maybe both.

Every last one of the Renegades she'd met was a kid at heart. A smartass, feisty, too-sharp-for-his-own-good kid inside a hot man's body. But Wes was the most mischievous, most daring, and by far, the sexiest of them all.

The click of Rubi's heels drew the director's attention. The rest of the men followed his glance—all with the same stupefied expression. All except Jax.

"What the fuck are you wearing?" He planted his hands at his hips. "You can't come here dressed like…like…" One hand lifted, gesturing the length of her body. "Like…*that*. Guys are working here. I can't have them off in porn fantasy land while they're running stunts."

She stopped several yards away, crossed her arms and smiled indulgently. "I'll take that as a compliment, Jaxy-boy." The irritated press of his lips made her grin. He hated the nickname she'd given him. "I was in the middle of something when you called." She'd been negotiating a sale price for the Aston, and estimated the outfit had saved her at least five grand. "And I'm taking your girl out to lunch today, remember? If you'd given me a little more notice I could have nunnified myself for the boys."

The Ducati revved and Wes shot the bike between the group and Rubi. She pulled up short with a gasp. Heat from the bike whooshed over her body.

The helmet hid his mouth, but those deep gray-blue eyes crinkled at the corners with his smile.

"Don't listen to him." His deep voice was muffled behind the gear. "You look perfect. And you're just in time. We're going to run the real thing."

That giddy electricity in her belly intensified. She lifted her sunglasses to the top of her head and worked up her easy, sexy grin. "Wes, if you run over Jax's toes, he's going to take away that pretty toy between your legs."

He laughed, his head falling back. The sound was so rich, so damn happy it trilled through Rubi, leaving her body a sizzling mess of carbonation. Then he released the Ducati's handles, letting the bike idle while he pulled off his helmet.

His hair fell all over the place as it came free. Light gold on top, wheat-colored underneath, it gleamed in the sunshine. Static electricity from the helmet's padding grabbed a few strands and pulled them into the air.

Rubi reached up to finger them back into place. Only when the soft, warm, sweat-dampened strands slipped between her fingers did she realize the misstep. A wicked craving kicked deep in her body. Delicious, languid desire tightened her throat.

And, shit, she'd floated over that damn no-touching line again—a line he had a way of making her forget all about.

REBEL
Coming December 2013

Dear Reader,

Thanks for reading *Reckless*, book 1 in the Renegades series! I hope you enjoyed Jax and Lexi's story. This was a very fun, sexy book to write, and I look forward to writing more books in this sexy series. Books two and three in the Renegades series will release late 2013 and early 2014. So stay tuned for more stories from the sexy Renegades.

If you enjoyed *Reckless*, I would appreciate it if you would help others enjoy this book, too.

Recommend it. Please help other readers find this book by recommending it to friends, readers' groups and discussion boards.

Review it. Please tell other readers what you liked or didn't like about this book by reviewing it at one of the major retailers, review sites or your blog.

Until next time,
Skye

ABOUT THE AUTHOR

New York Times and *USA Today* bestselling author Joan Swan writes red-hot contemporary romance under the pseudonym Skye Jordan, also a *New York Times* and *USA Today* bestseller. She lives in magnificent wine country on the central coast of California with her husband and two daughters.

Visit Joan Swan at:
Web: www.JoanSwan.com
Or Skye Jordan at:
Web: www.SkyeJordanAuthor.com

MORE BOOKS BY JOAN SWAN AKA SKYE JORDAN

Phoenix Rising Series
(Romantic Suspense with paranormal elements)
FEVER (Book 1)
BLAZE (Book 2)
RUSH (Book 3)
SHATTER (Book 4)

Covert Affairs Series
(Romantic Suspense)
INTIMATE ENEMIES (Book 1)
FIRST TEMPTATION (Novella 1.5)

More Renegades from Skye Jordan late 2013

Made in the USA
Lexington, KY
08 April 2015